MEINE RACHE
MY REVENGE

A novel of International Intrigue
By Pete DeHart

This is a work of fiction and imagination. References to historical names and places exhibit that imagination. The creative use of objective imageries may not accurately reflect reality. Characters, situations, dialogue, descriptions, and interactions within the story are fictional.

Copyright © 2013 Pete DeHart
All rights reserved.
ISBN 10: 1481800434
ISBN 13: 9781481800433

MEINE RACHE
MY REVENGE

CONTENTS

Chapter One: Introductions 1

Chapter Two: War, Flight, and Respite 19

Chapter Three: High Ground and Protection 37

Chapter Four: Building and Expanding 55

Chapter Five: Vanguards 71

Chapter Six: *Die Verschwörer* (The Conspirators) 91

Chapter Seven: Return to Africa 107

Chapter Eight: Diedrich's Discovery 127

Chapter Nine: Transportation 147

Chapter Ten: Fragile Cargo 167

Chapter Eleven: *Die Herausforderungen* (The Challenges) 187

Chapter Twelve: Reflections 201

Chapter Thirteen: *Victoria Ultimo Sumptu* (Victory at all Costs) 215

Epilogue 235

"Revenge is a kind of wild justice....Certainly, in taking revenge, a man is but even with his enemy; but passing it over, he is superior....This is certain, that a man that studieth revenge keeps his own wounds green, which otherwise would heal and do well....Vindictive persons live the life of witches; who, as they are mischievous, so end they infortunate."

- Francis Bacon (1561-1626)

CHAPTER ONE
Introductions

News Wire

DAR ES SALAAM (Reuters)—(July 24, 1986) Discovery of a wrecked corporate plane on the lower slopes of Mount Kilimanjaro closed a multinational three-day search for two DVS Technologies executives. Reportedly, the executives were traveling from Kinshasa to an exploratory site in Tanzania when the crash occurred. Both men survived the crash and the extreme nighttime cold in a remote part of the national park. A spokesperson for the Tanzanian Emergency Rescue Team (TERT), which assists stranded climbers in the national park, reported airlifting the two executives to a major Dar es Salaam hospital for treatment of their injuries. Rescuers explained that both appear to be suffering severe dehydration and blood loss sustained during their ordeal on the mountain. Medical personnel released no further details about the condition of the executives. The twin-engine, Dutch-made aircraft, capable of landing on a variety of surfaces, including grass and unimproved runways, generally carries a single pilot and up to eight or nine passengers. On the plane with the two DVS executives, were the pilot and two crewmembers, who did not survive the crash. Searchers also recovered their bodies.

A representative for DVS released the following statement: "We're saddened by the accident involving employees of DVS Technologies as they traveled to a potentially new exploration site in Tanzania. We extend our sympathies to the families of those who did not survive the accident. At the same time, we offer the resources of the DVS group of companies in assisting the government of Tanzania in caring for Hanns Krieg (Founder and CEO) and Diedrich Erhard (President of DVS Laboratorios) while they recuperate in that country. As soon as practicable, we will return Mr. Krieg and Dr. Erhard to Argentina. Additionally, we dispatched from our headquarter offices in Kinshasa an airplane to return the bodies of the three crewmembers killed in the crash."

In his Kinshasa office, Joseph Mbandaka folded and laid the newspaper on his desk. The minister of Commerce and Trade in Zaire smiled knowingly as he thought about how he came to be involved with DVS Technologies and its two German executives. Their stories seemed so distant from how they came to be in Zaire.

1944 Germany

For a period during mid-1944, the German war effort against Russia appeared to a few leaders in Berlin as a lost endeavor. Despite earlier successes, Germany's Operation Barbarossa, which began on June 22, 1941, could not hold against the continual onslaught of the Russia armies in Eastern Europe. The Allied landing at Normandy was imminent but in the meantime, the Allied forces pushed aggressively against German resources on the Western Front. German confidences in the führer's war machine often wavered but Hitler's control seemed strong in the face of disputes and defeats. Italy's surrender to the Allies in September 1943 opened a wide crack in the wall of confidence and more than a few German leaders questioned the führer's decisions; some cleverly began to secret family wealth and plundered treasure out of Germany, just in case the war turned against the Reich. When on June 6, 1944 the Allied forces invaded the Normandy beaches, it signaled the ultimate collapse of the Third Reich.

Shortly after the Normandy invasion, the most extraordinary of the many Hitler assassination attempts occurred. On a hot summer day in July 1944, during a scheduled briefing of war leaders, Claus von Stauffenberg placed a bomb under a conference table at the Wolf's Lair in Rastenburg, East Prussia. Operation Valkyrie, *Unternehmen Walküre*, failed but the bombing left Hitler with minor injuries and an increased malevolent distrust of virtually everyone around him. Just a few hours later, loyal Nazi leaders arrested and shot von Stauffenberg and three co-conspirators.

Others aware of the conspiracy watched its failure from a distance and concluded that with the Allied invasion's success, now was the time to finish the outward movement of their treasure to safe havens away from the ravages of war. The coming end of the war in Europe beckoned these self-styled refugees to follow their wealth to far distant areas, such as South America. They fled and took with them their hatred of all who brought down their dreams of world domination by a privileged few.

Some disaffected nationalists found safe havens in out-of-the-way, little-discussed locations such as small cities high in the Andes Mountains. The city of Mendoza, on the mountains' eastern side, between Argentina and Chile, was welcoming. The area reminded the German exiles of the Bavarian Alps and their arrival drew little attention from the local or national officials, especially when some of the secreted wealth found its way into greedy hands.

As they settled in their new location, they formed a tightly knit league they called *der Verschwörer*, or DVS, "the conspirators." They had little in common with one another except an intense hatred of America and all things connected with its people. Privately, they vowed to avenge their beleaguered and crushed national sovereignties.

With time, the DVS collective invested in developing companies, which prospected for minerals and scarce resources in the least sophisticated and developed areas of the world. There seemed to be an easy, unrestrained activity as DVS officials exploited all but the best informed, regardless of where they went. More importantly, the collective provided respectability and masked their intent on avenging their supposed wrongs.

Not for many years, following the war, would the DVS chance upon a weapon to bring about a hoped-for, crushing defeat of their enemies. The consequences they sought were as cruel and so complete as to absorb resources, tie up personnel, and nearly collapse governments. Then, and only then, would the world look to the DVS for solution; then these misled adventurers would assume their rightful leadership of the world governments.

Plauen, near the Prussian/Czech Border

As Hanns Krieg looked out the window of his home in the small Saxony village of Plauen in east-central Germany, he saw the commotion of the day's activities in the town square. Hanns felt an exciting surge in his youthful fourteen-year-old body as he thought about the new adventure. Today's meeting would decide so much for him. He knew Kurt Gruber as the charismatic and energizing founder of the new *Großdeutsche Jugendbewegung*, Greater German Youth Movement, or GDJB, and he was sure that the young men of Germany would accomplish great things in re-establishing the glory of the former Reich.

Hanns hurried down a cobblestone path leading to the town square where he joined in with an already growing group of young men. Some of them he knew from the village, but there were many from other parts of Saxony he did not know. He felt a friendly, intensely growing excitement with the founder of the GDJB but when a new man spoke to the group, the hair on his arms stood on end with electricity never before felt. After the speeches that morning, he agreed with his friends that the new fellow called Adolf would bring real changes to the country. Along with nearly all of the young men in his village, Hanns was anxious to be part of those changes. He wanted to be part of the new youth league announced that morning.

As the meeting ended, Kurt Gruber caught the eye of the young Hanns and motioned to him to join them near the fountain. Kurt and the new man were in deep conversation when Hanns finally made his way through the smaller groups of young men as they each discussed the things they heard about a new socialist party and the role planned for the young men of Germany.

"Hanns, come here and meet a friend of mine!" Kurt was as energetic as ever, and smiling, as he reached out for the boy to join them.

"Adolph, here is the young man I told you about. Is he not a fine example of Germany's exceptional youth, and only at fourteen years old?"

"I'll be fifteen in a few months, Herr Gruber."

"Right you are! How are your mother and father, Hanns? Do they still keep you up with their incessant talk about the *Kaiser*? I do not remember ever meeting two people more loyal to the *Kaiser*. Is your father doing well in his business?"

"Things do not change too fast around here," replied Hanns.

Hanns was still unsure of the new man and stood rather rigidly as the small group seemed caught up in discussing his family. Then Kurt said, "Hanns, how foolish of me. I've not introduced you to our guest. This is Herr Adolph Hitler, and he's very interested in our youth league. He feels the future belongs to the youth of Germany."

"It is a pleasure to meet you, Hanns," said the new man, emphasizing the verb as he spoke, and turning his full attention on the young man. His deeply set eyes seemed to pierce Hanns and capture his very thoughts. Perhaps, a little too much sincerity, if that was possible. Hanns felt a little uncomfortable.

"Thank you, Herr Hitler; I enjoyed your thoughts today."

"We have much to accomplish to bring about a new order. The old practices must be swept away as a giant wave washes the seashore." As the new man spoke, he wigwagged with broad movements of his arms. He seemed to be looking into a place far beyond the current Saxony village of Plauen. "I need young men like you, Hanns, to be part of the new order and to help us achieve the *lebensraum* we must have for it. May I count on you, personally?"

Never had anyone spoken to Hanns with such sincerity about a new world and Germany's place in that world. Of course, he would be part of it. There seemed to be nothing else quite as important to him now.

The walk home was thoughtful. Why did Herr Gruber ask about his father? Everyone in the surrounding area knew that the Krieg family was one of the oldest families in the Free State of Saxony and frequently extended their substantial wealth to various causes, even after Germany assumed control of the area under the Weimar Republic. Still, did the new Germany intend something different for the future?

Herr Hitler seemed focused on completely overthrowing the old Republic and forming a new social order based on the workers in Germany. As Hanns walked past several of the houses in Plauen, he thought of the many advantages his family enjoyed because of their heritage, and their wealth. He remembered visits with his family to relatives in the Dresden and the exclusive school he planned to attend in the fall.

As he walked, he began to talk to himself aloud, wondering how a new social order would change things. He did not notice that others were watching and listening to him until his friend Willi said, "Hanns, these questions are best discussed behind closed doors."

"Oh, hello, Willi. You're right, of course. But I can't stop thinking about—"

"I know, but just think of the excitement of a new youth league and Herr Gruber's plans," interrupted Willi.

"Well, I think there'll be a lot to do before any of the visions of Herr Hitler ever come to our part of the world. He speaks as if he is in an ideal world where everything comes easy to those who pledge themselves to the cause. I'm just not sure. Besides, I still have my education to think about."

"Well I'm joining the GDJB and you should too," challenged Willi. "It's our duty to see that the future belongs to the German people and that we've enough room to expand and live as we were intended to live."

"You sound like Herr Hitler and Herr Gruber. I'll talk to you later," said Hanns, as he left Willi standing in the road and headed up the long pathway that led to his house on the hill.

Royal Saxon Polytechnic

The largest university in Saxony, in the years just prior to the Second World War, was the University of Technology in Dresden; founded in 1828, it was also one of the oldest in Germany. The young men of the Krieg family all graduated from the university and each made tremendous contributions in their respective fields. Hanns wanted to follow his grandfather's example in engineering but found enrolment with the Faculty of Mathematics and Sciences more inviting. It seemed that Hanns just had a knack for the physical sciences and especially liked working with minerals.

The faculty members made him feel exceptional, mostly because of his ability to grasp highly detailed concepts, and because of his exceptionally outgoing social attitude toward all the students. He seemed to like tutoring other students. He was an outstanding student in both chemistry and physics, but his real passion came outside campus life, as he made close friends with other young men in the GDJB. It did not take Hanns long to settle into the flow of university life in the big city. There seemed to be electricity in the air every time the group met and discussed the new social order spoken of by Adolph Hitler.

During these formative years for Hanns, another person observed his activities. Shortly, Kurt Gruber began to pick Hanns for special assignments in the youth league and came to depend on the impressive skills of organizing and communicating that Hanns demonstrated. To many people in Dresden, it seemed an obvious choice when Herr Gruber picked Hanns Krieg to be the Dresden leader of *Hitler-Jugend*, or the Hitler Youth League, the new name for GDJB.

By 1930, all Germany recognized the Hitler Youth League as an officially sanctioned arm of the Nazi party. Kurt Gruber successfully developed the cadre of young men throughout Germany to follow the motto of the league, *Jugend dient dem Führer*, Youth in service to the führer, and to be an effective training of young men capable of entering the military services. The youth league molded bodies, minds, and souls into thinking and behaving in a unified manner. Late in 1931, Adolph Hitler picked Herr Gruber to be in several leadership positions in the national party. As the *gauleiter*, or political leader, of the municipal activities in Saxony, he conferred with Hanns Krieg frequently as they sought to bring all the young men into the service of the führer.

One young man Hanns met during this period in Dresden was another student at the university with interests quite different from those of Hanns. Every time the two talked, it ended up that one or the other needed to win the discussion about which branch of science offered the greater challenge. Hanns was sure that his field was more challenging, while his friend, Diedrich Erhard, argued convincingly that the biological sciences were far more interesting. In spite of the differences, the young men enjoyed each other and spent much of their free time in one another's company, even when that time involved the activities with the youth league.

Their favorite coffeehouse in Dresden was *die Kakao-Bohne*, the Cocoa Bean, which was almost a daily stop for them. Here they frequently met others who shared similar feelings about the events in the world. It was their habit to meet every day at the same time and share the same table in the far back of the coffeehouse. Hanns and Diedrich enjoyed *kaffee* at their table in *das Bohnechen*, the nickname they gave their little hangout.

Sundays were especially busy days for Hanns because the youth league took up the entire day. Rather than walking together, Hanns and Diedrich usually met on that day at the coffeehouse, arriving separately. Because Hanns had so many duties as youth leader, Diedrich found it easier to wait at their table for him. Besides, since so many friends seemed to gather at the coffeehouse Sunday evenings, Diedrich never waited long before becoming deeply engaged in a serious discussion. There were many opinions about the events happening in Germany.

It was later than usual when Hanns finished his work at the sport field. He wondered if he missed Diedrich for their evening chat over *kaffee*. He hurried along the now darkening streets; he hoped

Diedrich would still be at their table because of the news. As he opened the door to the coffeehouse, he looked for Diedrich but could not see him as he entered. Clutches of people were already busily talking about the day's activities. Small clouds of cigarette smoke seemed to halo each group. He headed knowingly toward his favorite table, stopping briefly here and there to chat with some friends.

Diedrich looked deep in thought as Hanns approached the small round table covered in a greasy, deep blue-colored tablecloth. The table was barely large enough for one, but a special closeness grew into the center of the table when two crowded around it.

"Diedrich, I missed you at the league today. What happened?" Hanns's voice sounded friendly and without accusation.

"*Ja, ich weiß es, Hanns*, yes, I know, Hanns—I've many things to tell you. Please, hurry and sit down. I ordered you some coffee," and with a quick turn of his hand he motioned to the cups already on the table. "I hope it's not cold."

"Well," said Hanns after he squeezed up to and almost around the tiny table, "so do I have exciting news. You tell me your news first." The coffee was still a little warm.

"You know we talk about the future in Germany and what we think will happen, once the war starts," he leaned his head in and somewhat whispered the last phrase.

"Yes, Diedrich, that's what I wanted to tell you—I enlisted in *der wehrmacht*! I leave just after graduation in the spring. I thought you were planning to do the same?"

"That's my dilemma, I know the military is what we're supposed to do, but I want to go to another university and study medicine. The University of Poznan accepted my application in virology studies and I would really like to go there."

Hanns interjected, "You can't go there! That's in Poland and we need all young men who have able bodies and minds to stay in Germany!"

"You always have the party line, Hanns."

"*Die wahrheit ist die wahrheit*, the truth is the truth!"

"I just don't understand," said Hanns, still shocked at his friend. "Tell me what you'll gain from going off to another university rather than helping Germany prepare for its future."

"The school here in Dresden has been a lot of fun, but I want to finish my doctorate in a new and exciting field. With all the turmoil in the country, I thought it better to go outside, to Poland. I understand the faculty at the university teaches nearly everything known about the new science. Besides, Herr Hitler gave assurances that his plans didn't include invading Poland to gain *lebensraum*. It'll be safe."

"Please reconsider. I'll ask Herr Gruber if he can help get you an officer's rank when you join, just as he did for me," Hanns pleaded.

"*Nein danke, Hanns*. I already decided to go. I guess you'll have to win the war without me," Diedrich joked half-seriously. "We graduate soon, and I plan to leave for Poland the next week."

"Well, then, let's have a night of it! How about we begin an early celebration at the *biergarten*?" offered an eager Hanns.

University of Poznan via Berlin

As Diedrich planned his trip to Poland, he discovered that all trains to Poznan from Dresden required connections in Berlin. He was happy to have the five or six hours on trains to see some of the changes in the countryside that he had only heard about.

Diedrich did not mind spending most of the day traveling to the university, but because he had not visited Berlin for many years, he thought about staying the night in the big city. His family trust paid the first-class cabin seat, and costs of a night in Berlin posed no difficulty. Just as all respected the family of Hanns in Saxony, nearly all the influential families in Bavaria knew the Erhard family as being financially secure and *respektiert*. Neither of the young men wanted for money to spend.

The train from Dresden pulled into the Berlin *Hauptbahnhof*, central station, and Diedrich grabbed his portmanteau, and moved toward the door of the train car. His decision to stay a night seemed easy enough; besides, 1933 in Berlin was alive with vibrant energy.

Stepping quickly into the station, Diedrich stopped at a coffee shop to read a newspaper and decide what to do with his time in the capital city.

"You look like a student," an older man said to him as Diedrich sipped his coffee.

Diedrich looked up to see a man in gray-green traveling jacket standing at the next table. The man appeared to be slightly older than he was, maybe thirty or thirty-five years old, his pince-nez hanging from a gold chain attached to a vest. Over one arm, he carried a gray-colored overcoat and his hat showed his preference to a style frequently seen in the Bavarian Alps. His satchel lay loosely next to the leg of the table, but Diedrich could see that it carried more than its allotment of paper.

"Yes, I'm on my way to the Poznan University of Medical Sciences," replied Diedrich as he turned to face the stranger.

"Odd, I thought all young men your age wanted to enlist," replied the man. The question hung in the air, perhaps accompanied with a little reproach, thought Diedrich. Diedrich knew that choosing university over the military was not common for young men his age; even he, a proud member of the Erhard family of Dresden, needed his father to intercede with the officials in Berlin to allow him to study in Poland.

"And I will, when the time comes, but right now I want to study virology. It's something, like a new science, taught at the medical school in Poznan. Papers from universities in Delft and in Berlin talk about their research in the field, but I understand the professors in Poznan are the best in all of Europe," answered Diedrich, not sure that the stranger would understand what he said or feel the passion he felt for the new science.

"You surprise me, *Herr*—?" the question once again hung in the air for Diedrich's answer.

"Diedrich Erhard from Dresden."

"Is your father Herr Erhard who's the minister of Finance in Dresden?"

"Yes, do you know him?"

"Well, *das Ministerium* forwarded a letter from Herr Erhard last month about his son wanting to study in Poland. I didn't realize that I would meet that son in the train station in Berlin," the stranger began to take on a different appearance, a little less critical of the younger man, perhaps.

"So, you know of my desire to study in the laboratories in Poznan," said Diedrich.

"Maybe I should introduce myself. My name is *Herr Doktor Blome*, and I am in charge of the virology laboratories at the university. Unless I'm mistaken, you're on your way to see me."

Diedrich was a little surprised to find his professor under these circumstances and did not know quite how to respond. All Germany knew of *Doktor Kurt Blome*'s work with cancer and here he stood in front of Diedrich drinking coffee.

"Herr Erhard, if we're going to be working together, may I call you Diedrich?" asked the doctor.

"*Natürlich,*" he replied, even more surprised by the warming nature of the well-known research scientist.

"Diedrich, I stopped for a quick coffee on my way to a small gathering with some important people in the new Germany. Would you like to join me?"

The two hired a taxi that drove them to an officious-looking building in central Berlin. As they entered the building's social hall, Doctor Blome quickly took his leave with a promise to return. Diedrich surveyed the gathering; there was no one he recognized. There were many uniformed men talking in smaller groups, each group seemed to engage one another as they spoke; something energized the whole, if that were possible. Diedrich wandered over to a refreshment table for a cup of coffee and a small biscuit, a hunger he had forgotten since meeting the doctor returned.

"You're new. You must be one of Herr Blome's new students?" a voice caught his ear over the noise of the gathering.

"Yes, I was just on my way to the university when I met the doctor in the train station," replied Diedrich as he turned to the voice. He saw a distinguished looking man, maybe about the same age as the Doctor Blome, standing before him. The man carried superiority as if it were a barrier to the world and stood erect with pride. His wine glass, held so daintily by its foot, seemed to float just above his hand.

"I see," said the man. "Then you don't know any of the people here?" motioning to the group with his free hand. "I guess that's just as well, for now. Perhaps the doctor will introduce you to others, when he feels comfortable."

An odd thing to say thought Diedrich.

With a gentle head nod, the man turned his shoulder and whisked himself to another group leaving Diedrich standing alone, wondering about what just transpired.

"I see you made yourself known to the führer's young doctor," the familiar voice of Doctor Blome chimed in from another direction. "He's a little difficult, maybe he has to be careful being so close to our führer all of the time," sounding a little less reassuring than what Diedrich would have enjoyed hearing.

"No, I didn't get to talk with him at all," said Diedrich.

"There'll be time enough for that. Come let me introduce you to a few of the people you will want to know in the future." With these words, Diedrich and Doctor Blome headed toward one of the smaller groups of men busy in conversation.

It appeared that the doctor followed a plan during the next hour. He carefully visited several of the smaller groups where he introduced Diedrich as the son of Herr Erhard, the Finance minister in Dresden, and his new assistant at the university. Just as Diedrich began to feel a little more at ease, and almost as if he turned a switch, the doctor finished introducing Diedrich and asked the young student to find his way back to the station or wherever he planned to stay for the night. He would meet him at the university after Diedrich arrived in Poznan.

The dismissal seemed abrupt to Diedrich but so were the mannerisms of the current German *menschen elegante*; besides, he was enjoying meeting some of the people who were leading the new movement in Germany. Nevertheless, he planned to be alone in the city for the night in any event and knew of a student hostel near the train station.

Poznan University of Medical Sciences

Many Germans resented changed borders of their country resulting from the Treaty of Versailles. Particularly onerous to the new German Reich was that the Weimar Republic turned over much of the eastern provinces to a newly formed Polish Republic. In the province of Poznan, or Posen in German, was the capital city of the same name. Despite the mounting German disputes regarding the basic ownership and control of this area, Diedrich sought his doctorate at the medical sciences university in Poznan.

In the years leading up to the Second World War, passions over lost territory in Poland grew more intense with each fiery speech from Herr Hitler, and at the large rallies where he spoke, the intensity became palatable.

Such rhetoric did not seem to worry Diedrich; he reasoned that in spite of not joining the military, attending to his schooling might shield him for some time. Conceivably, the high-ranking Erhard family status might even buffer him while he was in Poland. Additionally, working directly with the well-known Doctor Blome proved to be more of a shield than he realized initially.

His thoughts of the evening's adventures in Berlin occupied him as he traveled to Poland. There were no quick answers to some of his questions but as he learned in Dresden, some questions are best unanswered in the present political state the engulfed Germany. Upon arriving in Poznan, Diedrich easily found the university, which stood within walking distance of the train station. In his excitement, he took no time to find his apartment but went directly to the university to complete registration. In spite of reading about the school, as he walked onto the campus, he seemed absorbed by the ambiance and grandeur of the buildings. He remembered that the medical school, founded in 1919, initially specialized in studies of pharmaceuticals. However, at this moment, he reflected on the changes in the medical world that helped to introduce a "new" science that brought him to this place. All else forgotten, he went immediately to Doctor Blome's office.

"I see you made it quite safely, Diedrich," the doctor welcomed.

"Thank you, yes. No problems at all," Diedrich was not quite sure how much information needed to be volunteered about the long delay at the border and the military checks that now seemed to be set up almost at every corner in Poland.

"Good. We've much work to do here. First, let me explain that I contacted your professors in Dresden and they gave you exceptionally high marks. Second, I selected you to be my assistant in this laboratory. You begin tomorrow morning. Do you have any questions?" Diedrich stood silent at the announcement. He had not expected to start in the doctor's personal laboratory.

"Thank you, *Herr Doktor*," he replied weakly.

"Good, be here tomorrow morning by seven and I'll show you what I expect. You may have the rest of the afternoon to get yourself settled in your apartment," the doctor generously extended.

Diedrich turned and left the laboratory office as by this time the doctor already busied himself with another project. "This is going to be interesting," Diedrich silently muttered to himself.

Weeks turned into months as working under the tutelage of the learned doctor proved interesting, indeed! Diedrich moved quickly through the basics of his "new science," as he liked to call his work, and soon began to publish papers in scientific journals. He presented several of his papers, along with Doctor Blome, at medical meetings in Berlin and other places. Soon, his name became associated with other key scientists as an expert in virology. In particular, he enjoyed studying the effects of viruses within cells and surfaces of the blood vessels. Doctor Blome showed increasing interest in one particular study he pursued, his work with the effects of viruses on blood coagulation.

September 1, 1939

Despite agreements and assurances to the contrary, German troops and planes launched their *blitzkrieg* on Poland just as the sun started to rise over Warsaw the first day of September 1939. Civilians and troops came under a terror that soon engulfed not just Poland but the entire world, as Hitler and his war machine set in motion their plans to subjugate and control any who disagreed with their form of cultural society.

German troops moved into Poznan, setting up a provisional government that closed the university and dispersed administrators, professors, and students. Not until 1941, when it became a *Grenzlanduniversität*, or Borderland University, set up under guidance of Nazi ideologues, that it re-admitted students to the newly named *Reichsuniversität Posen*.

Diedrich seemed to expect, however, that Doctor Blome's laboratory would remain open and active. *Doktor Erhard*, through his research and unquestioning support of the directions coming from Berlin, advanced sometime earlier becoming an integral part of the Reich's cancer and virus research headed by Blome. Leaders of the *wehrmacht*, or armed forces, Science Section, including Himmler and Goering, frequently visited the laboratory to encourage research in the military use of carcinogenic substances and viruses. Diedrich, or *Herr Doktor Erhard* in the laboratory, soon received the nickname, *der Wissenschafter*, the Scientist. Noticeably, his years in Poland treated him well and he enjoyed the attention paid him.

The invasion of Poland brought with it other consequences and tipped the scales negatively for many Germans. Some found quick escape to other countries, fleeing the certain outcomes of catastrophic war and leaving many of their possessions with friends or family. Other people, not so convinced of destructive outcomes of the Hitler regime on the Germany they loved, remained with a determination to make the best of what would occur. A few transferred family wealth and treasures, as much as was fungible, to Swiss banks and private accounts in foreign countries. The senior Herr Erhard, minister of Finance in Dresden, chose the Swiss bank option for his family.

Much of the substantial Erhard family wealth moved quietly into Switzerland throughout the last months of 1939 and into January 1940. The Polish invasion convinced Herr Erhard that his family's wealth was safer in the historical haven of neutrality, Switzerland. His prescient move proved timely, as he died less than two years later, leaving instruction for the younger Erhard to serve as steward with complete signature authority for the ten million Reich marks secreted in three Berne banks. In addition, Diedrich was to keep confidential all information about the money and to tell no one of its existence. He found neither instruction difficult and adhered to them without exception. Although he worked closely with several Nazi leaders, the family wealth remained safely and secretly ensconced, as planned by his father.

CHAPTER TWO
War, Flight, and Respite

Wehrmachtoberst Krieg

After seizing power in Germany, the Nazi party divided the country into thirty-two administrative sections, each headed by a *gauleiter*, an administrative political position. Hitler selected personally each *gauleiter* and each reported solely to him. Kurt Gruber enjoyed his role as the administrative head of the *Sachsengau*, or Saxony region, and continued with similar leadership successes that established him in the eyes of *dem Führer*.

He took pride in knowing that he helped establish, in the city of Plauen, the first unit of the Nazi party outside Bavaria. His political guidance remained consistent, and in the best German fashion of the time, with crushing strength felt by all. Nearly everyone experienced the heel of his boot. If there were fickle expressions to his mannerisms, they were in his selections of and associations with a small cadre of leaders. In a strange quirk, Gruber demonstrated a permissive friendliness with these men. Together they reveled in many nights of piggishness, drinking and singing until morning. They enjoyed many excesses that came from seizing power, delighted in exercising authority over others, and grabbed for their own whatever pleased them. No one seemed to escape the lechery. Nevertheless, a few local minor officials liked a perfunctory inclusion they received infrequently from *Herr Gauleiter Gruber*.

One of the closer confidants and a personal advisor to Gruber was Hanns Krieg, who benefited from his devoted association cultivated through their years together in the youth league. In the Gruber administration, he served as *Stabsoffizier*, a staff officer.

On the other hand, he enjoyed his military role as a *Wehrmachtoberst*, or colonel in the armed forces, and as the head of *das Hausverteidigungskräfte*, the Home Defense Forces in Saxony, which later became the *volkssturm*. During the early summer of 1945, this group organized as a paramilitary force, determined to defend the Harz Mountain region but were of little consequence when the Allied forces simply bypassed the region on their way to Berlin. Nevertheless, in his role as colonel in the armed forces, people frequently feared *Herr Oberst Krieg* more than Gruber, as he supervised the territory without leniency. The Saxony region was quiet and sufficiently distanced from Berlin to allow greater latitude in authority of the local Nazi leadership.

Perhaps, somewhat curiously, Hanns received another responsibility; someone in the Reich leadership noticed his expertise and knowledge of mineral sciences and suggested that Berlin allow him to serve the Reich, using his knowledge, in a little known administrative position. At a bureaucratic level, certainly well below the führer's purview, officials felt that cataloguing the Reich's precious minerals would be critical to controlling their use. As a result, they established the Mineral Resources Section, reporting to a murky branch of government—the National Bureau of Treasury Resources.

Of all his positions, Hanns found the greatest contentment working with this less-than-significant section. As a young boy and throughout his university studies, Hanns enjoyed the Harz Mountains, which encompassed a large swath of lower Saxony countryside within its rugged terrain, including one of Germany's highest peaks, the Brocken. The discovery of silver and other precious metals in the Harz led to extensive mining, and it seemed natural that metallurgy was as a second nature to him. Because of his experiences in these mountains, he sometimes envisioned himself as the young Goethe who frequently visited the area and wrote of his geological discoveries around the Brocken. These writings of Goethe actually stimulated the younger Hanns Krieg, metallurgist, as he sometimes thought of himself. However, at present he used his title of *mitleiter*, associate leader, to travel extensively and when possible, to travel outside Europe to examine how other countries utilized their mineral resources.

When traveling, he always carried an air of militarism despite not wearing his uniform. People who met him felt immediately the strength of his presence and the command of each situation he assumed. Many feared and begrudgingly respected him.

It was on one of these junkets, to Argentina, that he met the army general Juan Perón. The occasion was a reception for other visiting Axis officials where Hanns fit easily into the knot of invited guests. Perón regaled the visiting bureaucrats with flowery descriptions of how he would ensure their continuing achievements, *los logros* as he called them, if they were to export scientific knowledge to Argentina. Although unnecessary, the army general, and soon-to-be dictator, seemed to feel his offer needed further justification by extending it to include any scientist desiring to immigrate to Argentina would receive safe passage. Apparently, the Vatican also developed safe routes through Switzerland, which guaranteed anonymity for those seeking travel documents.

He described how sympathetic he and Eva, his wife, were with the cause of the people's party. More specifically, he endorsed the socialist agenda of the Third Reich. Many of the *burócrata*, a word Perón favored privately when he referred to these unelected officials, seemed caught up in the moment but only catalogued the promises for later use; however, Hanns took the messages of exporting scientific knowledge to Berlin, where his messages received little interest.

In spite of Berlin's negative reactions to exporting metallurgical science, Hanns continued researching the possibilities of international business and established several commercial contacts. He thought, "The world is at war now, but soon the Reich will succeed. After the war, we will need new markets for our technology. At the very least, mineral resources of the conquered land in the east will bring much needed revenues for Germany."

He had many similar thoughts about a time after the war and anticipated cessation of the fighting. At these times, he wished he could return to Dresden, to sit at his table in *das Bohnechen*, enjoy a cup of dark coffee, and talk about his plans with Diedrich. His growing responsibilities pressed hard on his mind and allowed little time for such *träumerei*, or daydreaming, but in quieter moments, he wondered what Diedrich was doing, or if he lived.

Der Wissenschafter

During this time in Germany, it was preferable for doctoral candidates in medicine or natural sciences to submit, as a cumulative research work, several essays or research papers published previously in prestigious scientific journals rather than a single monograph or dissertation. Additionally, the candidate must stand for oral examination by a group of doctors and experts in the field of study. This oral *examen rigorosum und disputation* could be exceptionally difficult, as discovered by Diedrich Erhard.

Diedrich's successes in the laboratory drew acclaim throughout the Reich. His papers on the effects of viruses on blood coagulation found publication in the best of German scientific journals. Nevertheless, one area of his published research drew most acclaim: how an obscure, yet to be described virus, created chaos with the endothelium within blood vessels. His work excited nearly all of Nazi Scientific Section; no one had described the disruption of blood flow in similar fashion, as had the young scientist in Doctor Blome's laboratory. Diedrich was fast becoming a sensation with many in the Nazi party.

In the late spring of 1938, he stood for his oral examination at the Medical Sciences building at the University of Poznan; it surprised him to see the entire lecture theater filled with lab-coated fellow scientists, properly dressed physicians, and military-uniformed party leaders from Berlin. A few most notable attendees that he recognized were Josef Mengele, Hermann Voss, an anatomy professor at the university, Erich Schumann, the powerful head of the Science Section, and Karl Brandt, the young physician he met years earlier at the reception in Berlin. The attendance of Doctor Brandt, the personal physician to Adolf Hitler, surprised and confused Diedrich because he had not expected that his work carried any weight with the führer.

As he took his place in the center of the examination hall, Diedrich surveyed the audience and thought for a moment that he saw the führer, but his eyes deceived him. Moreover, the large number of influential people attending caused him to think, "What have I done to deserve so much attention?" These people came rather than in respect of Erhard's importance but his mentor, who was highly influential within the party leadership, extended personal invitations to some of his closer colleagues.

When questioned by the audience, he found that his viral research had taken the Scientific Section by surprise.

"Such a novel approach," he overheard someone comment.

"When will you begin human trials?" was another question from the audience. He took no offense to the suggestion of using prisoners as potential subjects in these trials.

Then Doctor Blome asked, "I see using the results of your work in our vaccines research very promising, don't you agree?" This comment/question gave him confidence that his future in the Reich was secure.

Following an official award ceremony, Diedrich Erhard became *Herr Doktor Erhard* and began to work more closely than in the past with the elements of Blome's cancer research; however, it was almost immediately apparent to him that the real intent of his research switched toward multiple forms of bacteriological warfare. Cancer research was only a ruse. In spite of the change in directions, he found fertile possibilities for his research, and his very noticeable enthusiasm won him the nickname of "the Scientist," *der Wissenschafter*.

When the combined armed forces of the Third Reich invaded Poland in September 1939, they immediately closed the university.

Nevertheless, *der Wissenschafter*, Kurt Blome, and their laboratories remained open. Continuing the research seemed critical to the Reich, even more so when the medical school reopened a little more than a year later as the *Reichsuniversität Posen* fully aligned with Nazi ideology.

December 24, 1943

Many traditional Christmas decorations had been in place early in December in Dresden for the usual month-long German holiday. While considerably dampened due to fear of air raids, a few garlands brightened streets, occasionally shop owners tried valiantly to interject festive overtones into display windows, and in spite of the war, the German city feted throughout December. Even the faint tones of favorite Christmas carols, or *weihnachtslieder*, occasionally floated in the cold air as the citizens of Dresden hurried through the streets. The *Nationalsozialistische Deutsche Arbeiterpartei*, the NSDAP, failed in attempts to remove these traditions completely from the people.

As of this date in 1943, no Allied bombings had reached Dresden, although many other cities suffered extensive damage from sustained bombings by the British.

Herr Gauleiter Gruber, recently promoted in the party leadership to *Standartenführer* in the *Sturmabteilung*, or Storm Troopers, enjoyed the Christmas festivities. His staff ensured that he had countless parties and receptions to visit as the highest-ranking Nazi in Dresden. At many of these celebrations, Hanns Krieg also attended with Kurt Gruber. The pair frequently appeared in public together.

The morning of December 24, Gruber and Krieg met privately in the Gruber's office. They discussed normal appointments and complained about routine activities affecting the Saxony region. Without much ado, Gruber turned to look out his window, as Hanns thought, to survey the newly fallen snow covering the streets of Dresden.

As he stood facing the window, he said in a rather low tone, "Hanns, I'm very tired today."

"You've kept quite a schedule during *weihnachten*!"

"I mean more than just all of the parties. I'm concerned at how slowly the war progresses; so many cities are receiving heavy bombing from the British. As you know, they bombed Berlin last month and I think they will hit us very soon."

"But our *luftwaffe* has been very successful over Dresden! I don't think they dare attack us," voiced Hanns, half-believing what he said.

"I hope you're right," offered Herr Gruber in less-than-reassuring tones. "But tonight we party. Where do we go first?" His voiced sounded more like a leader of the Storm Troopers as he turned from considering scenes out the window, now he smiled and was ready for an evening of joviality.

Hanns led the way to one reception and then to a second. He noted nothing out of the ordinary in behavior of the officer until he heard more than a usual slurring of words as *Herr Gauleiter Gruber* began a toast. Then, the Nazi officer started to slump toward the floor and before Hanns reached his side, he died of a massive cerebral stroke.

A New Commander

Early in the morning of the next day, the first day of Christmas, local authorities, members of the *Sachsengau* leadership, and several military officers met with *Herr Oberst Krieg* in Gruber's office. The overnight chaos among some of the leaders reached a boiling point as the meeting began, strident voices extended to shouts, and anxious men talked over one another, each trying to make his point. Uncertainty created by the Nazi practice of not naming replacement senior officers for positions, such as the *gauleiter*, while preventing coup attempts by an heir-apparent also left voids in the basic command continuum. The führer had no problem with furthering this ambiguousness in his leadership cadre because he enjoyed making changes, as it pleased him.

As the highly decorated and uniformed Krieg rose from his seat and stood erect, he measured the room, which now reached a fever-pitched full throatiness of the small minded, as he perceived them to be. Several men saw him standing and reacted by stopping their conversations in mid-sentence. He cleared his throat and silence fell quickly in the group.

"Until I hear from the führer, there will be no further discussion as to who is in charge as *gauleiter*. I am assuming complete control of the *Reichsgau* and you all report to me directly," Krieg's voiced carried with it authority and an unvarnished threat. Everyone realized that he indeed now assumed control of the *gau* and that any attempt to counter his decision would result in immediate harsh judgment. Indeed, Hanns Krieg filled the void left by the death of Kurt Gruber.

The new commander made certain changed assignments that he felt would assure continued operations in the Dresden office, at least until he heard from the führer. Then he announced, "Beginning today, the usual curfew hour for all people on the streets will change to sunset. I want this strictly enforced; we can't have any uncertainty of the direction the *gau* takes. I assume there will be no questions."

The meeting continued for another three hours with all in attendance understanding the strict directions and changes to expect until Berlin dispatched or appointed a new *gauleiter*. Herr Krieg showed no vacillation in his feared reputation that all learned earlier to expect from him.

Hanns Krieg sat in his new office after dismissing the people who occupied it for the last three hours. As he leaned back in the chair, he contemplated the many changes about to occur when his thoughts froze in place as his eyes focused on a ringing phone—the direct line to the führer.

He recognized the voice on the other end of the line and stood at attention behind his newly assumed desk.

The conversation lasted only a minute or two but in that time, he received orders to be in Berlin tomorrow to meet with the führer. As he hung up the phone, he arranged for a car and driver to depart early the following morning for his meeting at *Reichskanzlei*, or the

Reich Chancellery. The meeting would change his life dramatically and give authority to the assumptive *gauleiter* role he appropriated the day before.

Following the meeting, the new *gauleiter* for the Saxony region understood more completely the required reporting he was to make directly to the führer. He retained his colonel rank in the *wehrmacht*, but he was to promote a new *volkssturm* commander for the region. If he so desired, he could keep his meaningless *mitleiter* position with the National Bureau of Treasury Resources—it appeared the führer did not regard the bureau as of much value to the Reich.

Thinking about his meeting at Wilhelmstrasse Seventy-Seven on the return trip to Dresden, the new *gauleiter* fantasized over what he could make of his now-official appointed importance.

"Tighter control of people moving between cities," he thought, "would give me an advantage by keeping unwanted people from migrating, or worse, joining together in opposition against the Reich."

"Seize, in the name of the Reich, additional bank funds, personal jewels and assets hidden in homes, even gold artifacts from museums; these the local bureau of Treasury Resources will protect from possible loss. Some of the less significant things can stay where we find them, others need to be in a general treasury, under guard," with this last thought, he smiled knowingly to himself. His experience moving funds around between banks for the now-dead Gruber gave him confidence that some of the money appropriated easily moved into private accounts, and without questions. In fact, he remembered the last reception he attended in Argentina where the army general's wife wore jewelry she said came from someone in Germany. There appeared to be fluidity in other people's money, in the name of the Reich.

"Yes," he thought, "this will be a very pleasant time."

He leaned his head back on the headrest as the driver sped toward Dresden and the beginning of a new episode in the life of Hanns Krieg.

Luftwaffeoberst Erhard

With the increased presence of *Gauleiter* Hanns Krieg in Berlin, he warranted briefings concerning things that previously only those with greater political or military responsibility received, specifically things including the secret work of the Posen laboratories and of his friend Diedrich. Somewhat surprised, Hanns thought it admirable that many leaders at the highest levels in the Reich acknowledged Diedrich's work. Later, he should ask him to come to Dresden for a visit but he asked quietly to himself, "When?"

It appeared that both men entrenched in their responsibilities, felt they had little time for renewing old friendships. Therefore, it was not unlike Diedrich, hearing of Hanns's new position in the Party leadership, to delay a quick trip to Dresden because of a special research project recently given to him.

Diedrich received his appointment in the *luftwaffe* as perfunctory, only befitting an important scientist, and to require little personal attention. Other members of the Science Section maintained similar ranks in the *luftwaffe* and offered little toward fulfilling their military duties. As he rationalized, he never favored the military or being an active member of it; furthermore, he rejected an offer from Hanns to help him gain an officer rank while the two were still in the university at Dresden. Nevertheless, *Herr Doktor Blome* certainly placed an unusual importance on his new standing, particularly as it applied to the laboratory.

Sometime during the latter half of 1943, Diedrich noticed an undeniable change in the energy of Doctor Blome in the laboratory and its results. Research projects focused more toward transmission of bacteria and the effects they then created in humans. Additionally, a specific department in the laboratory worked exclusively on methods to weaponize the transmission of these agents. Although appointed Blome's assistant, Erhard felt he was not aware of all that transpired in the Posen laboratories.

Diedrich's work supervised other scientists in the laboratory and included field visits to prisons in Poland where he tested many of the results from the laboratory. He was a familiar face with the guards and allowed highly simplified access to the prisoners. At the Auschwitz prison near Krakow, he received an especially open reception from two of the scientists who attended his *examen rigorosum und disputation*. Both Doctors Schumann and Mengele appeared impressed with his credentials and he found their openness to his work encouraging.

At one meeting, Mengele asked, "*Herr Doktor*, there are other countries waiting for the information we develop here in the Reich. What do you know of Argentina and Juan Perón?"

"Really nothing," replied Diedrich.

"The Argentines are interested in our work, they know of our forward-looking accomplishments with science and extended an invitation to the Reich to export its technology. What do you think of the offer?"

Diedrich was somewhat unsure how to respond, as he thought silently, "Is the famous doctor testing me, or does he really expect my opinion?"

"I suspect that we are right on the edge of breakthroughs in our knowledge regarding bacteria and how they are transmitted to humans. We need to continue our research before others examine it for fault," Diedrich thought his answer safe.

"Perhaps you're correct. I'm visiting Buenos Aires next month. I will scrutinize the seriousness of their offers then," Mengele replied, thoughtfully, as he turned away from Diedrich, who realized their conversation ended.

As he reached the door, he heard instructions that stopped him mid-stride: "*Herr Doktor*, when I return I expect a full report from you and Doctor Blome regarding methods for the successful use of *saringas*. We need to consider it for use here in the prison and elsewhere in the war effort."

He then added emphatically, "There are no excuses for failure with this project!"

Diedrich turned to ask but saw that the doctor stayed motionless, looking at a report, and that he remained with his back turned.

Oberst Erhard continued on his way through the door, making his way out of the prison gates, pausing only shortly to read the words etched in the metal, *Arbeit Macht Frei*, or "Work Makes Freedom," and a strange thought entered his mind, "Whose freedom are we working for, and who is doing the work?" He shook off these odd feelings and hurried on his way back to Posen.

Diedrich knew of a cyanide-releasing pesticide produced by two German companies, Degesch and IG Farbin, which they called *Zyklon A* and *B*. He knew that Mengele and others authorized the use of the dry formula, *Zyklon B*, for extermination of prisoners but he had not heard of tests with the new agent *saringas*. He wanted to know if Doctor Blome had a secret project to research another agent. The assignment from Mengele was clear enough: the doctor expected a complete report upon his return from Argentina.

When he arrived back at the laboratory, from his trip to Krakow, Diedrich's first meeting with Doctor Blome confirmed the existence of another charge for *Herr Doktor Blome* and his Posen laboratories.

"Diedrich," began Blome, "Berlin instructed us to examine a new compound developed by a group of researchers at a center near Köln. Some of the scientists in the group feel that their *gas* is more effective as a nerve agent than is *Zyklon B*; however—," Blome paused for extra emphasis, "there's disagreement among the scientists and Mengele wants results from actual work with prisoners. He charged us to complete the assignment before he returns from a trip to South America."

"I thought the prisons find using the present gas quite efficient and easy to use," replied Diedrich. "Why," he was careful not to sound challenging when he continued, asking his superior at the laboratories, "is there a need for another?"

"We need results and data to complete the report, which I suspect Berlin will use to make their decision," opined Blome while skirting Diedrich direct question. "You will make a trip to Köln to gather more data from the researchers at the IG Farbin center; as you know, that center is across the river from *der Kölner Dom*. I will telephone the head to the center to receive you. However, it's likely that he'll instruct a junior researcher to work with you—not a problem—start there, and confirm your work before you return." The instructions sounded clear to Diedrich, but he sensed an underlying nervous anxiety in Blome's manner of speaking.

"Our problem so far is that we don't seem to have a delivery system with the new *gas* that's non-toxic to handle and quickly administered." As the doctor spoke, Diedrich sensed where a problem might exist but he needed much more information.

"I'll use a *luftwaffe* plane and leave immediately," Diedrich confirmed.

"Again, *Herr Doktor Erhard*," he understood the warning given for a second time, "I'm sure you're aware that no failure is possible?" Doctor Blome gave increased emphasis on the negative sounding words in his stern reminder so that Diedrich comprehended his instructions completely.

Wolf's Lair, Rastenburg, East Prussia

Hanns found his position exhilarating as chief of the political party in Saxony. He received many accolades reserved for the very elite, and he soon developed behaviorisms that were more arrogant. He found getting hold of the money and treasure, as he planned, presented few problems. He perceived quickly that other *gauleiter* did the same in their regions. His ideas did not appear premature to the general actions for the group. No one noticed as he syphoned a small percentage for his personal use, nor was there concern expressed with his infrequent trips to Berne. The banks in Berne asked no questions when he deposited cash, gold, and jewelry.

He remembered an earlier thought, convinced he was correct then, and commented to himself, "This is a pleasant time. Everything seems to be going my way."

Occasionally, Hanns received orders to attend war briefings with the führer, so it did not seem out of the ordinary that the führer ordered him to Rastenburg in July 1944.

The attempted assassination and bombing at the briefing left Hitler unsettled. The bombing intensified the growing vulnerability the führer felt to the outside world: it was a world set up by his immediate staff, those people who established a false bubble around him that the bombing shattered. While the führer received only minor cuts from the blast, his extreme distrust of virtually everyone intensified.

Even Hanns felt threatened by the assassination attempt and reasoned, "If von Stauffenberg, a trusted associate, could get so close to the führer with a bomb, is there anyone in Germany that I should trust?"

As a flaw common with most self-absorbed people, his concern for his own safety drove his unreasonable actions, even to the point of deciding to flee any possibility of personal danger in the war zone.

During the next few weeks, he worked out escape plans; not just to flee should the Allies succeed in their push to Berlin and the Reich collapses but in anticipation of that possibility. He had sufficient millions of Reichsmarks secreted in Berne; however, reason suggested that he transfer as much of that wealth as possible to a safer place—Argentina and Perón's proffered protection now seemed a natural solution to him. However, his getaway plans remained utterly and completely intimate. No one could he trust with a slightest hint of his ideas to leave Germany.

As *mitleiter*, he retained some inconspicuousness that he could use in his escape. If he made a reasonable excuse to travel to Africa and to one of the Moroccan ports, perhaps the port of Casablanca, a ship to Argentina would provide cover for his escape.

His plan involved moving from Berne his stashed gold and jewelry, concealing them in shipping cases among mining equipment; and, perhaps, fictitiously directing them to a counterpart administrator in the Argentine Treasury Resources. The rest of his wealth: the artwork, and some cash, he would leave in the banks—to access later. If he could keep the cartons in his control during the shipping, he would prefer it.

By the end of September, he prepared for another trip to Berne to supervise packing the seagoing shipping cases so that there was no chance of discovering the valuables he stashed among the equipment. He planned to travel with the cases so that when they arrived in Buenos Aires, he personally could supervise the offloading and storage of the cases. It would involve some risk crossing the Atlantic but if sailed under a neutral ship, maybe a Swedish shipping company, he assumed there would be minimal risk of loss.

Prior to his final Berne trip, he easily fabricated reports from the Rommel's Desert Corps, which described substantial gold and other mineral treasures discovered in an obscure city in the interior of Morocco. He also ensured that the reports cycled through his office and in his summary reports to Berlin, suggested a member of the Mineral Resource Section investigate the findings and validate their value to the Reich. In addition, he proposed that he assume the lead of an investigative team.

It did not surprise Hanns that the führer, disproportionately involved with supervising daily battles after the invasion at Normandy, paid no attention to a quick trip to Africa by one of his *gauleiter*. Furthermore, with his *wehrmachtoberst* rank, he easily persuaded the *luftwaffe* to provide transport to Casablanca for him and ten shipping cases of metallurgical research equipment.

A Swedish ship, scheduled for Argentina, sailed out of the Casablanca port two days after a *luftwaffe* plane touched down carrying a *wehrmacht* colonel and several cases of equipment. Reports of a large cache of Arabian gold in the desert had many people in the city buzzing. Rumors included a *wehrmacht* colonel taking an investigative team into the desert to recover the gold. But then again, as with most rumors in Casablanca during the war, they were vague and no one really saw the colonel's team leaving the city or returning from the desert.

Aboard the Swedish ship, the crew noticed that the metallurgic scientist onboard stayed mostly in his cabin. Occasionally, he went to the storage hold of the ship to ensure his equipment remained safe. Nothing out of the ordinary, thought the crew, for a German scientist.

Keine Ausreden (No Excuses)

Diedrich's meeting with scientists in Köln provided needed scientific data concerning the chemical components of *saringas*, which the researchers claimed discovering about five years earlier, but they did not answer questions concerning safe handling of the *gas* by German soldiers in the Reich's prisons. Diedrich remained concerned with the volatility of the gas during shipment and storage.

Throughout the next few weeks, *Herr Doktor Erhard* appeared anxious to coworkers. He required of them special handling and storage when working with the new gas; in spite of his precautions, a minor explosion of unknown origin set the laboratory in flames. Seven of the ten half-liter canisters of *saringas* stored in a safe cabinet swelled in the heat of the fire causing them to burst. The escaping gas killed four laboratory workers before the free gas could be contained. Diedrich was away from Posen at the time of the explosion and was uninjured. That is, he was uninjured in the explosion but his absence did not protect him from the onslaught of blame and personal insult, which came his way as project leader.

No one knew what caused the accident in the laboratory, but Blome suggested sabotage. He added his conviction in the report sent to Berlin that conspirators worked in the university laboratories. When special Nazi investigators arrived, they examined the remains of the laboratory carefully then quickly placed the blame on the sole surviving scientist of the blast. The investigators, acting under authority from Berlin, dispatched the scientist to a local prison.

As Erhard and Blome conferred later, Blome had no option but to remove the younger scientist from the project.

"Diedrich, I told you that there were no excuses for failure on this project. You disappointed the führer with this accident." Diedrich understood how blame moved down the ranks when serious setbacks occurred.

When *Herr Doktor Blome* spoke, Diedrich's mind wandered, pondering what happened to conspirators against the Reich. He thought, "How long before they blame me for the explosion?" However, he did not expect to hear the next words from Blome.

"I'm removing you from the special *saringas* project and assigning you to another where you can be more attentive to your duties!" Blome seemed to enjoy punishing his assistant of nearly ten years and inflicting a changed assignment on him.

The explosion drew unwanted attention and criticism to the work of Blome. Mengele, he heard rumored, told the führer that the blast was clearly "a failure of leadership." Rather than understanding that accidents frequently may occur when dealing with experimental agents, the doctor appeared to enjoy his new castigatory stance toward Diedrich.

"Never mind," thought Diedrich, his mind already working on a new project of personal importance. Reassigning him in the laboratory simply brought him to the final decision: he needed to leave Germany. Realizing that he narrowly escaped this time, he now became serious about finalizing his plans.

Fortuitously, and with extreme confidentiality, his father arranged for forged diplomatic papers and travel documents to await possible family use at one of the banks in Berne. Before his death, he called Diedrich home and shared possible escape plans with his son. Diedrich needed to arrange a trip to Berne to retrieve the papers, sufficient traveling money, and authorize transfer of the family wealth to a correspondence bank somewhere in the world before escaping the war.

A science conference in Zürich provided *Herr Doktor Erhard* with a possible opening that Blome permitted. During the short, sixty-minute train trip to Berne from the conference city, Diedrich reviewed the consequences of his flight. His entire life, the one he worked so hard to create, now rose completely altered before his eyes. What lay ahead was unchartered and very disquieting to the nearly thirty-year-old scientist who conceived many of the "tools" that resulted in so much suffering to people in German prisons.

No questions arose in Berne while he retrieved his father's travel documents and sufficient money for traveling. He converted the

Reich marks for Swiss francs, thinking the currency would draw less attention when he used it. He decided to have as much as possible of the remaining money transferred to a Swiss branch bank in Santiago, Chile. Even in Switzerland, the restrictions of money leaving the country needed some explanation, as the Third Reich curtailed doing so. Nevertheless, he transferred several millions of marks, converted to Swiss francs, in his name and to a correspondence bank, misrepresented as research funding for the Reich.

The return trip to Zürich passed quickly but he had some time to reflect. He selected Chile because he knew that Germans received a benign courtesy if they immigrated to that country. His father foresaw the possibility that now was a reality and prepared acceptable documents, which no one would question. With his colonel rank in the *luftwaffe*, he could make air connections through one of the airfields in Africa and then on to South America. It would be a long trip, with many stops, but he steeled himself for a fresh start elsewhere in the world.

Again, as he did when leaving Dresden for medical school, Diedrich Erhard and his well-used portmanteau, stepped into an uncertain future. He boarded the first of many planes on his journey leaving Zürich airfield and into obscurity.

CHAPTER THREE
High Ground and Protection

Hochland und Schutz

Both Hanns Krieg, metallurgic scientist, and Doctor Diedrich Erhard, biochemist, arrived in South America within a month of each other during November and December of 1944; Hanns arrived by ship at the port of Buenos Aires, Argentina, and Diedrich at a Chilean airfield in Santiago. Neither prepared themselves adequately for the arduous trips they endured; however, the Swedish-flagged ship proved a wise decision for Hanns when a pack of German U-boats sank three or four of the ships in the convoy in which they traveled. His ship sailed through without attack.

Diedrich fared poorly in the *luftwaffe* planes, which constantly fought back at Allied attacks until he reached Casablanca. He was ill suited for the air turbulence during the attacks and felt convinced that his decision to fly to Chile might be unwise. Nevertheless, he obtained a seat on a *Deutsche Luft Hansa* commercial flight using the papers prepared by his father. He was grateful that his father secured diplomatic status for the travel documents; otherwise, leaving Casablanca might have been impossible, even for a German scientist traveling surreptitiously as a member of a Swiss delegation, on assignment to South America.

Buenos Aires, Argentina (Latitude 34° 35' S, Longitude 58° 22' W)

Despite his attention to the geographical location on a world globe as he sought out the site for a new life, nothing he contemplated could have been more distinctive to Hanns Krieg than his first impressions after stepping off the ship at the port of Buenos Aires, Argentina. Absent were the bureaucratic fanfare and flourish which accompanied his earlier trip to the country. Now Hanns Krieg, a German metallurgic scientist, drew only a small amount of attention from the government workers and travelers arriving in the immigrations hall. Present were the hot, southern hemisphere climate, the crowded conditions of people foreign to him, and a loneliness he felt for the first time in many years.

He purposefully avoided his learned habitual stiff military stance; rather, he slouched slightly and said as little as possible. Spanish was an uncomfortable language for the aristocratic German from the Free State of Saxony. It annoyed him that he could not control his surroundings, not even to understanding what people said to him.

While at sea, he disposed of his uniform, keeping the medals and ribbons awarded him by the führer; the tightly wrapped and weighted package containing his military uniform sank quickly when he dropped it over the side of the ship. However, he paid little attention to his distinctively cut three-piece suit from a Berlin tailor that set him apart from other travelers. The loden green wool suit and summer heat looked like an odd combination in Latin America. Despite trying to alter his image, the clothes Hanns wore marked him as a foreigner in the new country, especially a German foreigner of higher social standing.

The different nature of heat in Argentina annoyed him. In the southern hemisphere, it was mid-summer and the heat was uncomfortable for the German leaving the winter cold of Europe and of a somewhat stormy ocean crossing.

It disordered his thinking slightly, as Hanns tried to follow his meticulous plans for arrival, that some of the people moving around him appeared suspicious of him.

He tried not to show his mounting frustration as the line inched very slowly beside an elongated counter-like cabinet toward immigration agents. He thought, "They really seem to enjoy reviewing papers in great detail. In Germany, we would teach them some efficiency." Under the circumstances, it was fortunate that the agents did not hear his thoughts but merely continued with the greatest of assumed authority, keeping the line purposefully slow moving.

"*Documentos, señor, por favor.*"

Hanns, supposing the agent requested his traveling papers, handed them to the agent without a second thought. The immigrations and customs agent, seeing the German documents, asked in English, "Why do you come here?"

"For my health," replied Hanns also speaking slowly and in English.

"Tell me, *señor*, how long will you be in our country?"

Hanns expected the question and explained that he had no firm itinerary but would see how his health improved before returning to Germany. Hanns skirted the edges of truth but just slightly. Indeed, he was in Argentina for his health and to be sure, he did not know if or when he would leave.

"*Señor*, I see from your documents that you have *diez, perdóneme*, ten shipping cases of mining equipment to declare? Tell me, *por favor*, what you are planning to do with so much mining equipment?" The agent narrowed his officious-appearing inspection of the documents as he asked the question.

Hanns felt insecure with his answer, started speaking in German, and then switched to English as he tried to explain his plans.

"*Agent, ich plane, eine Erforschung zu machen.* Sorry, my English is poor and I don't speak any Spanish," Hanns spoke in English without asking or excusing his abrupt change to that language. "I plan an expedition for mining with the National Bureau of Mines. If there is a problem, you may check with Señor Lopez." He hoped that a bluff might get him through this agent without having to open the cases. Besides, he had met a person named Hector Lopez with the Bureau when he visited a year earlier. He had no idea if Lopez still worked in the Bureau.

Rather than vacuity on the agent's face, the agent now considered Hanns with an interest and scrutiny greater than he had before. He now seemed to focus his questioning directly toward the response offered by Hanns. "You say, *Señor Lopez*? Does he work here in Buenos Aires? Tell me, *señor*, what does this Lopez do?"

"Yes, yes," Hanns gathered his composure with each breath, "at the National Bureau of Mines. I think it's the *Officinal Nacional de Minería* in Spanish, or something similar." Hanns tried some Spanish to help give him control of the situation. He thought that he used the correct name of the Bureau.

"*Oficina Nacional de Minas* is what you mean, *señor*. I know a Hector Lopez who works at the *Oficina*. Would you like me to call him for you to tell him you are here?"

"No, thank you, I'll get settled and call on him tomorrow," Hanns thought better of having any official contacts until he found out what happened after his disappearance from his political position and silent departure from Germany. He was sure that the führer would have him shot or hanged, if he could. It was better to remain as characterless as possible for some time.

"As you wish, everything is in order. *Buena suerte, señor.*"

As he departed the din of the arrival and immigrations hall, he had some difficulty obtaining a porter who spoke a little English so that he could retrieve his shipping cases and place them in a secure storage. His experience just in entering the country, raised serious doubts that his plan to stay permanently in Argentina might not have been as good as he imagined.

"I must learn Spanish and soon," he thought as he mentally checked off agenda items, which he prepared for his stay and rehearsed frequently. "Well, at least my money in the cases is secure for now," he muttered haplessly to himself.

Earlier when planning his escape, he decided to use as a base for his operations, one of the smaller hotels on the *Avenida de las Flores* near the city center, a hotel that he noticed on his previous trip. There was no difficulty at the hotel in booking a room for an indefinite stay; the Argentine economy was sluggish and few people were staying at hotels. The hotel, pleased to have him, asked few questions.

Hanns Krieg, metallurgic scientist, ex-Nazi, and now an escapee from Germany lay on the bed without undressing. He was exhausted and feeling a little out of place. His careful world of control and power was a memory, but not one he wished to forget. He enjoyed the adulation of others that his former office and rank afforded him. His last thought as he drifted off into a somewhat restless sleep, "Should I have left *das Vaterland*?"

Santiago, Chile (Latitude 33° 28'S, Longitude 70° 45' W)

The hectic *luftwaffe* flights left *Herr Oberst Erhard* unsettled and dispirited upon arriving in Morocco. Using his military rank, he arranged for a room at a convenient hotel until he obtained a departing flight. Discarding his *luftwaffe* colonel's uniform seemed easy enough, after removing all identifying marks that might direct the military police searching for him as a deserter.

In the commotion of 1944 Casablanca, the colonel seemed to fade away as a somewhat younger appearing Swiss consulate member arrived. No one gave the impression of questioning how the consulate member arrived in the country or why he stayed with the colonel. Neither man checked out of the hotel nor left a forwarding address. As with so many people in the city, they simply and quietly disappeared.

Confusion and turmoil at the airport took turns surging and subsiding, almost independently of what happened with ticketing. Diedrich felt lucky to procure a ticket aboard a commercial flight when he saw so many people trying to buy any passage out of Morocco. As a result, it steadied his nerves that as a Swiss consulate member, he received preferential treatment.

The long hours of flight over the ocean seemed to drone on interminably; he watched the propellers out the porthole by his seat and in his mind, he returned to when he was a student at the university in Dresden. He had so enjoyed those seemingly unrestricted moments of his life. As he watched, he heard the engines turning to a rhythmic hypnotic beat, he faded in and out of consciousness, and then into the first real sleep he had in three days of traveling.

He awoke to the purser preparing the cabin for landing in Rio de Janeiro and a four-hour layover before the climb over the Andes Mountains to Chile. He looked out the porthole to survey the cerulean-blue waters of Guanabara Bay, the recently finished Corcovado statute with outstretched arms, and Sugarloaf Mountain atop the promontory jutting outwardly toward the ocean; all these were recognizable landmarks to a scientist who took pride in his meticulous preparation.

Stepping into the terminal, Diedrich discovered that he understood some of the people speaking Portuguese. He felt competent with the Spanish learned in Posen and it pleased him that even in Brazil he could communicate reasonably well.

The grueling flight over the extreme altitudes of the Andes Mountains would consume much of the fuel the plane could carry. Diedrich's minimal attention to his past *luftwaffe* duties did not prepare him to observe more of the flight preparation only that responsible personnel attended to some of the plane's external parts.

During the flight, he looked at the rugged peaks and deep valleys as the plane climbed in a slightly northwest direction over the Brazilian side of the Andes, across the high Altiplano region of Bolivia, and then southwest as the plane descended over the more extensive and sprawling Chilean plains. He noticed the color change in flora from the deep jungles of the Amazon rainforests, to the expansive grasses of the high plateaus, and then to the sloping plantations of the Pacific coastal region. He stretched out slightly in his seat and thought of the new places he planned to call home.

The plane approached from the northeast, passing the Tupungato Volcano whose 6,570-meter height rose impressively and unmistakably to the left of the plane. The Mapocho River now clearly visible cut a wide path through the middle of the city of Santiago. The German aircraft carrying Diedrich Erhard, a purposefully nondescript biological scientist, escapee from the war in Europe, and seeker of a new home, landed in Chile without a display by anyone on the ground.

Diedrich Erhard, the young Swiss consulate member deplaned, passed expeditiously through immigrations and customs quietly using his false diplomatic papers, and melted into the crowded streets of Santiago. He carried only a well-worn portmanteau with a few clothes and papers but a trunk full of the psychological damage resulting from a war still raging in Europe.

Because he adequately spoke Spanish, he easily initiated more of the plan for his personal and positional disappearances. He trusted that the Nazis would conclude that *Luftwaffeoberst Erhard* died in Africa, a victim of an untoward attack by an anti-German fringe group. Now, any connection to the diplomatic papers and passage he used to arrive at this point must vanish.

Using a Swiss identity, providentially included in the papers his father provided, he obtained a provisional position at the *Universidad de Chile* in Santiago with the faculty of Chemical Sciences and Pharmacy. Diedrich Erhard, the assumed consulate member simply ceased to exist; *Profesor Erhard*, adjunct professor of chemical sciences, emerged.

Throughout the remainder of the school year and into the next year, students, and faculty enjoyed the good humor of the Swiss professor. He entertained and delighted nearly everyone in his lectures and laboratory assignments.

The most astute of the chemical sciences faculty noticed his uncanny sense of biological chemistry and wondered where he developed the knowledge that he brought with him. Because the war interrupted the communications with Europe, the university accepted as accurate his *curriculum vitae* without further verification. He offered no answers to satisfy the curious but simply continued hoping not to draw attention to his work. Notwithstanding his efforts, soon it became obvious that *Profesor Erhard* surpassed the expertise of all on the faculty in applicative biological chemistry. It seemed apparent that the university would appoint him to full professorship at the beginning of the 1947 academic year.

Diedrich, not desiring the attention such an appointment might bring him and still concerned for his safety because of his role at the

Posen laboratories, moved south to *Pontificia Universidad Católica de Valparaíso*. In this southern port city, he hoped to avoid further attention or probing questions about his background. The university in Santiago provided adequate references for his appointment as a simple instructor in the science department.

As was his penchant since being a student at the university in Dresden, Diedrich frequently enjoyed the coffeehouses, or *cafeterías*, in Chile. He was particularly fond of a daily *café chico*, a small cup of strong, black coffee. Once or twice, he sampled *maté* tea, a favorite with many of the people, but he did not find it tasty or as satisfying as his daily potion of strong black Chilean coffee.

Valparaíso and the neighboring city, Viña del Mar, were distinctive even to Diedrich's inclinations. He found the multicolored painting of the houses invigorating when he remembered the darker greens and grays preferred in Germany. The hues injected a freshness, which seemed to invigorate the society of people living in these cities. In public gathering places, people sang, danced, and quoted poetry. Diedrich felt at ease in these surroundings and with the people who squeezed every ounce out of their moments in life. His favorite place to meet friends at the end of a day was the *Un Pequeño Café* on a side street just off the Concepción Hill funicular. The cable car reminded him of his home in Bavaria. Frequently, he watched its movements and contemplated some less troubled times of his past.

The political climate in Chile, as with other places in the world, was not yet stable from the world at war and the party in control restricted any political opposition, especially the Communists. Diedrich sympathized only to a slight degree with the Communist philosophies but admired how ardently some supporters expressed their ideals, freely criticized the government, and voiced unrest in the country.

Perhaps the Latin rhythms of life, which seemed to permeate the coastal regions of Chile, stirred different feelings in him. Soon he made close friendships with several artists associated with the Communists in Chile. Pablo was one of the more vocal and well-known poets that Diedrich met. When they talked, Pablo frequently expressed his displeasure with the government in Santiago.

"You understand our problems," observed Pablo one evening at *Un Pequeño Café*.

"I understand only to a certain point. I think you know that I don't agree with many of the things you talk about, but I find the government suppression quite unfair," replied Diedrich.

"It is possible that we will have to leave Chile. There is a new man in charge in Argentina who is partial to our views and I've heard he may support our cause." Pablo's eyes revealed concern and hope simultaneously.

"I hope you can stay here, but I understand if you must go."

"If we go, why not come with us? Your knowledge could help us in our work and you can see another part of South America!" Pablo's suggestion and invitation did not seem to fit into the plans Diedrich had for himself. However, a short time later, when the government outlawed Communism and issued an arrest warrant for his poet friend, Diedrich was by his side when they fled the country.

A small group accompanied Pablo and Diedrich as they made an escape through the *Paso Lilpela* mountain pass that separated a more southerly part of Chile and Argentina near *Lago Maihue*, or Maihue Lake. For Diedrich, the urbane scientist trained in one of the more progressive medical schools in Europe, traveling horseback and camping through the forested Andes Mountains was more than an inconvenience. The group of escapees stayed alert for searching *Carabineros* guards. Fortuitously, they avoided the guarded passes, saw no *Carabineros*, and no one diverted the path of the escapees who arrived three weeks later in Buenos Aires.

Las Tierras Altas (The High Ground)

The political freedom, which existed in Argentina beginning in the late nineteenth century and into the twentieth century, attracted many European immigrants. Consequently, two of the most prominent of immigrant nations, Britain and Germany, developed close trade associations with Argentina. Even though these relationships advanced over several years of successful trade, during the Second World War, Argentina declared state neutrality. This nonalignment to warring powers attracted many more refugees, and at one point, Germans comprised nearly thirty percent of all the immigration. Nevertheless, taking advantage of the freedoms permitted by the Argentine government, many Germans living in the country openly expressed their sympathies for the Axis powers during the war.

Hanns found one such immigrant group that was especially vocal; they called their association *das Gesellschaft der Deutsch Freunden*, or the Society of German Friends. While many of the immigrants to Argentina did not separate themselves from general society, the Society of German Friends supported a daily newspaper published exclusively in German, developed German-only hospitals, and encouraged German families to send their children to German-speaking schools.

When in 1946, Argentina elected president, Army General Juan Perón, the country provided safe passage and unbothered living for any former Nazi leader seeking to escape prosecution for their crimes during the war. Some of the escaping Germans assumed new identities in Argentina; others simply continued using their real names. Hanns Krieg found the former personal aggrandizement in which he basked, missing from his life as he mingled in this passé—ethos in Buenos Aires, and yearned to change his standing in the émigré culture around him. With his normal assumptive characteristic behavior, he soon controlled several leadership positions in the Society, and seemed to flourish as a former *gauleiter* and *Wehrmachtoberst*. Other Society members appeared willing to defer to his leadership; as in Dresden, when he assumed control of the *Reichsgau*, no one openly challenged him.

* * *

Initially, Perón was a populist leader and sought means to increase the economic foundation of the country so that he might establish many of his socialist plans. He knew of the Society of German Friends in Argentina and realized that within the group, there were men who possessed the means to aid his plans for economic expansion; therefore, *El Presidente Perón* invited Hanns Krieg and several other prominent members of the Society to join him for coffee in his palatial offices, the *Casa Rosada*.

In the president's offices overlooking *Plaza de Mayo*, Hanns remembered his offices in Dresden and thought how he missed their stateliness. He missed looking out of his offices onto the streets, busy with daily activity. Things in his current life just did not fill his insatiable desire to control and direct the affairs of other people.

"They were comfortable!" he smiled as he remembered the offices and emphasized the last word.

"I should be in an office like this, not this South American army general," thought the former Nazi political leader in a moment of self-puffery.

He looked around the room assessing the Germans sitting in various chairs holding their coffee cups and saucers; Hanns Krieg concluded that these people no longer excited him, nor did he enjoy their company. As he contemplated his place in the odd arrangement in which he found his life, he heard Perón speaking.

"*Caballeros, señores*, thank you for coming to our country. I hope you enjoy your new home! We have much to do to bring this part of the world into a place that possesses as much of the wealth to which most of you are accustomed." Perón, sounding now very much like a Germanophile, knew how to address the group of former plutocrats.

For the majority of an hour, the president described much of where he hoped to lead the country and where he hoped the Germans would play a collaborative role. As he concluded and a time for questions allowed, he observed that with no dissention, he had their support.

The president and Hanns remained briefly in conversation as the reception ended and the group of German Society members departed the president's office.

"*Señor Krieg*, I have a proposition for you." Perón extended his hand for Krieg's and held on to it longer than with a normal handshake.

"We have a great need to expand our mining industries and to more fully utilize our mineral resources in Argentina. I understand that you have an expertise in mineral sciences?" The president's questions interested Hanns; perhaps, Perón meant to flatter the German exile as he addressed him personally. Regardless of his purpose, Hanns, somewhat thrown off balance by the direct reference to his passion and study while at Dresden's Royal Saxon Polytechnic, considered the Argentine more intently.

"I believe you and I spoke of these opportunities when you visited several years ago with a scientific mission sent from Berlin?" As the president spoke, Hanns remembered the conversation but it surprised him that Perón remembered. Hanns also recalled the lack of interest shown by officials in Berlin when he returned with the offers of collaboration.

"Indeed, Mr. President, I remember our conversation, as brief as it was. Much has transpired in the meantime," Hanns responded warmly.

"High in the mountains to the west, near the city of Mendoza, there is much undeveloped land, open for exploration for minerals of many kinds. If you are interested, we might be able to provide the necessary licenses for you to organize a company, prospect, and develop what you find. Are you interested?"

The president's offer hung like ripe fruit ready to pick.

Hanns Krieg asked, "What will I need to return to the state?"

"I think we can work together as equal partners." Juan Perón smiled broadly; he saw that his offer stirred a deep-seated interest in the German.

Caught completely off-guard, Hanns thought a moment or two before responding.

"Mr. President, your offer is very generous. Thank you. If I'm to develop the company fully, I believe that it is more than I could reasonably expect to pay. However, may I suggest that I retain at least a controlling interest in the new company?"

"Agreed. We'll begin the licensing of your new company as soon as possible. Welcome to the Argentine economy, *Señor Krieg*. I'm sure we'll enjoy a long and productive partnership."

"Of that I'm convinced!" Hanns smiled warmly and departed the Presidential offices; thus, he concluded one of many meetings he would have in future years at the *Casa Rosada*.

Hanns had a little inkling of the place where the president told him he wanted to open the area for development. When he discovered that Mendoza was high on the eastern slopes of the Andes Mountains and along one of the few roads connecting Argentina and Chile, his enthusiasm for the project slumped.

As he came to learn, Mendoza was two hours by plane or thirteen hours by car from Buenos Aires. Few of the refinements that Hanns enjoyed in Buenos Aires were in the small mountain city. Nevertheless, people took pride in their mountain, Aconcagua, which clearly seen from the city, is the highest mountain peak in the western hemisphere.

At the airport, when Hanns stepped out of the plane he looked toward the towering Andes and a strange feeling stirred in him.

"Those mountains look much like the Harz but much higher, of course," thought Hanns.

"Maybe, just maybe—" his thoughts trailed off as he considered the vast possibilities of the wild and yet undeveloped country that stretched out before him. Perón's offer began to look more viable to the German from Plauen who once considered himself similar to the wandering Goethe, tramping through the foothills of the Brocken in the Harz Mountains.

Llegada de Diedrich (Diedrich's Arrival)

Argentina's economic renaissance seemed to catch fire during 1948. That year, a Gran Prix ran through the streets and avenues of the city; its course ran along the world's widest street, the *9 de Julio*, with its twelve lanes of traffic and grassy park like center strip, included part of the thirty-five kilometer-long *Avenida Rivadavia*, and ended at the *Plaza de Mayo*. Never mind that the Italian Gigi

Villoresi won the race, citizens of Buenos Aires thrilled to the excitement of the race in their city.

In March, President Perón signed agreements with the British and the French ambassadors nationalizing the railway system, the largest in Latin America. The president's plans for a growing, prosperous Argentina matured with each month. The Argentine tenaciousness for *libre determinación*, or self-determination, intensified with ownership of the rails. As explained to Hanns, Perón envisioned a widening economic base for the country and mining in the Andes was an integral part.

It was about this time when Diedrich, along with the group of political escapees from Chile, crossed the mountains to find respite in Buenos Aires. They arrived in the southern part of the city, near the San Telmo neighborhood and found a lively activity in the streets and taverns.

"What is this kind of dance?" Diedrich asked Pablo. "I've never seen anything like it!"

"It's called the *tango*, my friend. Quite pleasant, don't you agree?"

"I think I'll enjoy Buenos Aires," Diedrich admitted to his friend.

"Yes, this is a place where you can relax and enjoy life!"

"The music has a different beat and the words to the songs—" Diedrich listened to the soft tango rhythms that seemed to permeate the air.

"Let's sit for a few moments," offered Diedrich as he sat at a table in one of the street side cafes to savor the flavor of the new music.

"You know," began one of the Chileans in the group, "much of the music that we hear in these neighborhoods is very popular because it reminds people of pleasant moments of the past in these smaller communities."

Indeed, the music, filled with rhythmic undercurrents, seemed to have a life of its own. As he listened, Diedrich remembered Dresden, his favorite German city, and that as a university student, he spent many hours with friends in small coffeehouses. While the sights, smells, and sounds differed from Germany, Diedrich felt as he belonged in the community of San Telmo, one of the many environs of post-war Buenos Aires. Here in this completely new country, where everything around him differed so widely from Germany, Diedrich felt as if he belonged.

Nevertheless, as he enjoyed the magical rhythms of the tango, he also felt something missing. Just as many displaced expatriates feel alone among myriads of people in their new country, Diedrich was German and he longed to associate with others who experienced similar twinges of *heimweh*, as it were, homesickness for *das Vaterland*.

During the coming months, Diedrich discovered, while thumbing through a German newspaper published in Buenos Aires, that the Society of German Friends met weekly and sought new members. The announcement pushed him to attend one of the meetings, which interested him, and he made friends easily with the group of displaced Germans.

At one meeting, he wondered aloud to a small group enjoying a beer about a friend he knew in Dresden, *Herr Hanns Krieg*, and had anyone heard of him since the war? Now everyone in the group turned his attention to the questioner. It was as if all had the same questions: "Did he know Krieg? What was his part of the *Sachsengau* during the war?" While Diedrich felt no fear or alarm concerning his role in the war, he infrequently volunteered any information. This time was no exception.

"Hanns and I were at the Royal Saxon Polytechnic as students. We enjoyed many evenings at *die Kakao-Bohne*, but I don't suppose any of you know of the small café?"

"Yes, I went there often as a young student, but I don't remember you being there," offered an overweight, slightly balding man, shifting hands to hold his beer stein in his left hand, and taking his reading glasses from his nose to study Diedrich a little more closely.

"Hanns and I studied at the school well before the war; then Hanns stayed in Dresden and I went to Posen to study medicine."

With this last bit of information by Diedrich, the group grew somewhat quieter and took quick glances at each other.

"Did you work with *Herr Doktor Blome*?"

Diedrich wondered what he had not heard in the intervening years and then asked, "Tell me of the good doctor. I lost track of him some time before the end of the war."

One of the older men in the group explained the role Blome played in the trials at Nuremburg and that the doctor testified for the Allies against the other physicians in the Reich. The military tribunal acquitted Blome, but the French convicted and sentenced him to twenty years. Diedrich was not quite certain but he thought he detected deep anger and resentment in the man as he spoke, but at whom he directed that resentment he could not be sure.

The group fell silent again. One of the men in the group broke the awkward silence.

"Diedrich, you were looking for an old friend, Hanns Krieg, right? He's working with the government in mining. He left here some time ago, perhaps several years, and now lives in Mendoza. We don't hear too much from him—occasionally—but he's well known in the government."

If there remained questions about Hanns and if the group wanted further details about Diedrich's past, all simply disappeared as the group melted short distances away from him. The tight knot of jovial drinking and clinking beer steins loosened ever so slightly. Individually, they did not speak of their roles in the war, nor did they ask more questions about Diedrich's role. There appeared an invisible cloud of unspoken answers, thoughts without words, and implied knowledge not discussed. That which was interesting now was no longer. If Diedrich wanted more information about Hanns Krieg, he needed to go to Mendoza.

* * *

The flight to Mendoza was uneventful for Diedrich, but the beauty of the Andes foothills to the west of the airport was breathtaking. As he thought of his expedition with the escaping Chileans that took him through an area farther south, he commented quietly, "That was extraordinary and beautiful but this portion of the Argentine countryside is indescribably stunning!"

The joint venture between Hanns Krieg and the Argentine government proved highly successful. It appeared to Diedrich that nearly everyone in Mendoza knew of the German-led mining and exploration company. Diedrich easily found the offices.

"*Señor Krieg*," the secretary spoke to the company president, "there is a friend to see you. He says that you know him from Dresden."

CHAPTER FOUR
Building and Expanding

The Visitor

Hanns wondered half aloud, half silently, who from Dresden would visit him in his distant Argentine office; certainly few, maybe no one, in Germany knew of his joint venture with the government and his company that now grew faster than any company in the country did. His successes outstripped his ability to build and to add companies. It looked as if he needed to begin rethinking his arrangement with Perón, perhaps purchasing the entire company from the Argentine government and finding someone to help build the organization.

"Yes," he thought, "I've built a significant company. But who would be interested—and come all the way from Germany?"

"Maybe they're not interested in the company," he concluded to himself and slid his desk drawer open. Hanns learned sometime earlier to keep a loaded pistol in his desk, and he always carried one since becoming an officer in the *wehrmacht*. He felt a special need to have the comfort of a pistol since leaving Germany undercover. "Personal protection," he reminded himself.

Some less desired considerations of his past, which emerged unsought from deeper recesses of his mind, changed in mid-thought by the entrance of a smiling broad-faced man. The mustached man of not quite forty years looked as if he were Chilean but there was something a little unique. His basic coloring was slightly dark-complexioned and he wore a clean, woolen suit that did not distinguish; for all that was outward, the man appeared a Chilean intellectual. Hanns had seen many of them in the streets of Mendoza because the city was the first substantial rest stop on the long road over the mountains from Chile. Nevertheless, Hanns saw something in the man that stood before him that touched memories. Then without further considering the man, he recognized his friend Diedrich Erhard.

"Diedrich, is it really you?"

"Somewhat older, perhaps a little fatter, but it's definitely me!"

Both men met midstride in front of the desk, embraced warmly, and then stepped back to survey one another.

"Come, sit, let's talk," Hanns was the first to speak after the brief meeting in the center of the room. "Tell me all that's happened to you in the last eight, or is it ten years since we last spoke in Berlin."

"I think we met in forty-four. I was with a science mission when we briefed some of the *gauleiter, und dem Führer* just appointed you the *Sachsengauleiter*."

"You're right. Those were heady days. I remember them with great fondness, but I've not thought on them recently; there's so much work to do here in Argentina," Hanns's mood swung from maudlin toward optimistic within the same sentence.

"But Diedrich, let's spend some time talking about these things at a place less formal. Do you still enjoy good coffee served strong and black?"

"There is at least one decent thing about South America, they have excellent coffee," replied Diedrich. "I've had some pretty good coffee in the last few years, some that may have been almost as good as Dresden!"

"Then let's go into town. I know of a café that reminds me of *das Bohnechen* in Dresden. You'll love the coffee they serve, and we can speak German with no worry about anyone listening or understanding. If you're hungry, we'll have some lunch."

Both men eagerly left the office, and the driver waiting for *el Jefe*, knew where to go when Hanns said simply, "*Jorgé, café*."

In one of Argentina's less significant cities at the time, Mendoza, there lived less than seventy thousand people, who collectively retained a quaintness in their manner of living that attracted Hanns, and which he enjoyed showing off to Diedrich. As they traveled through the somewhat narrow streets, Hanns explained that in the city, advertisements for the many restaurants and taverns described each as being either "in the city with or without mountain view" or "in the mountains." Hanns had as one of his favorite, *El Restaurante Alemán*, a smallish restaurant near the center of the city that resembled a German *biergarten* and it was here that his driver, Jorgé, took them.

Once inside, Hanns had a favorite table, near the back of the restaurant to which the *maître d'* showed them. When seated at the table, Hanns and Diedrich looked through a large window with an excellent panorama view of the Andes to the west. Often, this landscape relaxed and calmed Hanns as he contemplated the issues facing his growing mining and exploration enterprise. Each man ordered a small cup of hot, black, and very strong Argentine coffee before beginning to talk about his experiences.

"Tell me what happened to you at Posen," began Hanns. "I heard of the explosion and fire but not many of the details of the Reich's discipline. What happened to you?"

"Things fell apart for me when *Herr Doktor Mengele* and *Herr Doktor Blome* expected too much of the *saringas* project," Diedrich, as if to disparage the names and titles of the doctors, emphasized them when speaking. "They anticipated a simple answer to a very complex chemical entity. Handling the gas was very difficult, very dangerous. By the time I left, there was no answer to how we could use the gas in the prisons without poisoning the guards."

"All very interesting, but what happened to you? How did you come to be in Argentina?" Hanns pressed Diedrich for more of his personal experiences but recognized reticence in his friend. "I suspect you had quite an escape route planned," Hanns said, trying to soften the inquiry.

Diedrich shared a few of the experiences he had escaping from Germany, including how much he enjoyed teaching in Santiago and Valparaíso, and then described his travels with the quixotic poets of Chile. He told Hanns about the Swiss documents and money his father secreted in Berne and how both saved his life several times. His family coloring, which gave him very dark hair and a slightly olive-toned complexion, helped him to blend in with many of the people in Chile, avoiding too much attention.

Diedrich explained why he transferred to a smaller university when in Santiago after the university wanted to appoint him to a professorship. While he would have dearly enjoyed the appointment, he felt that it might bring unintended awareness to his background. He felt safer that no one knew of his past. To the world, he was a Swiss biochemist living and teaching in Chile.

"But, how did you come to learn such beautiful Spanish?" Hanns interjected; since arriving in Argentina, Hanns learned only enough of the language to make handling business operations more efficient but felt inadequate otherwise

"Fortunately, I had an excellent instructor, a *señorita*, in Posen who helped me learn the language." Diedrich smiled as he remembered the enchanting times he spent with his "language teacher" at the university in Posen. "And, the last few years in Chile refined my vocabulary and pronunciation. I don't think they can tell I'm German now!"

"Did you hear about Blome and his testimony against the Reich?" Hanns returned the conversation to a more pressing topic, for him at least: his *großes interesse* in the outcome of the war and the defeat of the Reich. "I understand the French got him after the trial and gave him twenty years."

"The first I heard of the doctor and his testimony was in Buenos Aires a few days ago," replied Diedrich. "I can't tell you any more about him than you know but it sounded to me as if the Allied Military Tribunal favored him for turning against the Reich. Maybe they used threats, torture, promises of leniency, or money. I just don't know what happened, but it didn't sound like the Blome I knew for nearly twenty years. He was not likely to turn on the Reich unless pressured in some way."

"Blome disciplined you after the fire, didn't he?" Hanns now tried another pathway to get at the information he wanted about what happened in Posen to *Herr Doktor Erhard*, the well-known *der Wissenschafter*.

"The fault for the accident rested with me, although it was a technician's error that caused the fire. After Blome demoted me, my station in the laboratories gradually faded away; and, when I heard what happened at the prison to the surviving technician, I thought it best to take advantage of my father's good vision, so I used an escape route out of Germany that he prepared before he died. I think I left no tracks but—" Diedrich trailed off as Hanns took up the thought.

"I think you were right in leaving," admitted Hanns. "And if I hadn't done the same, I probably would hang just as von Stauffenberg and his gang did. Not for anything I did wrong, just that there were so many conspirators and staying on the right side of the führer became a fulltime chore."

A silence fell between the two men, as if each were recollecting something long forgotten or intentionally set aside.

"You heard that I was at Rastenburg when von Stauffenberg set off the bomb that nearly killed the führer?" Hanns asked his friend, who seemed genuinely concerned that he nearly did not survive the blast.

"I heard about the assassination attempt but I didn't know you were involved," replied Diedrich, relaxing now that the conversation moved away from his past and into an area more neutral between the two ex-Nazis. "What really happened? I heard only the propaganda but didn't know what actually occurred. You weren't hurt; I can see that, right? But tell me how it all transpired."

Hanns explained some of the details as only a person who was in the briefing room could relate. During the warm summer day in July when the assassination attempt happened, he was on the far side of the room, away of the bomb satchel, and a few paces back from the table when the bomb exploded. He did not receive any injuries as a direct result of the blast but the explosion threw him many meters out through a window behind him and onto the gravel outside the building.

"I'm certainly glad that I still wore my uniform jacket when I hit the ground," Hanns said, "but I couldn't hear for several days because of the noise. Good thing it was so warm that day; all the windows stood open, otherwise we might not have fared so well," concluded Hanns, as he finished his harrowing story of the bombing.

"You think von Stauffenberg was the main culprit in the conspiracy?" examined Diedrich, showing interest in his friend's harrowing experience.

"Of course; but he was not alone. I think he collaborated with many Reich officers. It seemed that there was growing disunity and disloyalties in their ranks because, I think, we can safely say that they gave up after the invasion of the Allies at Normandy. They were simply out to save their own necks."

"What caused such breakdown in discipline? Why did they give up?" Diedrich asked. "Why did we have so much difficulty in forty-four and forty-five when for such a long time things went along so smoothly with the plans of the Reich?"

"This will be a longer conversation than just coffee. Let's have some lunch," said Hanns as he motioned for the waiter. "Diedrich, have you enjoyed the *asado*, the Argentine barbecue, since coming to this part of the world?"

Lunch and Conspiracy

"Let's start with a small plate of *empanadas*," suggested Hanns. "I prefer the ones filled with meat and cheese but there are many varieties here in Argentina. I think people enjoy these small pastries at nearly every meal, at least, at every party. For our meal, I think I prefer the *carne asado* with beef but we can have any of several kinds of grilled meat. But if you'll take my suggestion, let's stay with the beef, what do you think?"

"Hanns, I'm starved so anything we order is going to be fine."

Diedrich started to relax somewhat with his surroundings.

"There's a tea most of the people from here drink; it's called *maté*. Have you tried it?" Hanns thought he might suggest something new for his friend but discovered that Diedrich did not like the traditional drink.

The conversation, renewing memories about and experiences from Germany, started again, when Diedrich asked, "You asked me why I escaped from Posen after the accident, and I'm not sure that I really thought I would ever take such an action. I'm not a quitter, and if I remember correctly, neither are you. So, Hanns, I'm curious to know why you left your post in Dresden. It just doesn't sound like you."

The question hung in the air without condemnation for a few moments before Hanns answered. His answer sounded a little odd to Diedrich but in full context of the experiences of both men sharing a similar passion, maybe the former *wehrmacht* officer and Nazi political leader filled in some gaps in rationale for the biological warfare scientist from Posen.

"First, let me explain that had I stayed in Dresden, the Allies would have put me in prison at the conclusion of the war. Even now, I'm somewhat cautious of everyone I don't know. In spite of the relative freedom I enjoy in Argentina, there are Nazi-hunters, as they called themselves, searching for trails of those they want to take back to Germany or elsewhere for trial. I'm always on guard.

"However, my greatest fear during the war was that as the Allies approached a city, they engaged in a psychological war of propaganda on the citizens. It was futile to try leading them in any resistance because the propaganda put so much fear in the hearts of the German people. It seemed to me that the Allies defeated the heart and soul of Germany in a cruel manner. I can never forgive them nor forget their methods."

Diedrich commiserated by telling Hanns of something he remembered reading while in the Dresden University, something that an English poet, Samuel Butler wrote.

"Did you ever read what an old Brit named Butler said about a similar situation," asked Diedrich.

"Diedrich, you know I studied only what I needed, nothing more," Hanns laughed, a little dismissively, but still he showed interest in his friend.

"Well then, my friend Hanns, listen to this sage about the situation you find yourself in. Butler said, and I think I remember it correctly, 'For those that fly may fight again, which he can never do that's slain.'"

With these words, Diedrich seemed to create an especially heavy and thoughtful few minutes at the table. Hanns sat silently, his cigarette smoke curled above the table, taking no particular direction but in it, Hanns appeared to look for something that he recognized. As he removed his round-lensed glasses that set his appearance apart as an intellectual, Diedrich wondered if his comments were insulting or painful for his friend. Finally, he broke the awkward silence.

"Hanns," Diedrich asked thoughtfully, "are you all right?"

"You've struck on a thought," replied Hanns, "as you always did when we talked in *das Bohnechen*. We have a chance to correct some of the wrongs the Allies imposed on our country and the rights we should now enjoy with the *lebensraum* we never got to possess!"

"I don't think *we* can do anything like that," observed Diedrich. His emphasis on the plural showed Hanns that he did not understand nor comprehend the extent of the ex-Nazi leader's mental picture of a personal retribution on the world.

The platter of *empanadas* arrived and the two men, each caught in his personal thoughts, simply pecked at the food and the table remained in silence. Neither expressed his thoughts, discussed the food in front of them, nor approached eating with much vigor. While the first round of meat, carefully skewered on a large spit, arrived at the table and the gaucho-attired waiter carved it skillfully onto their plates, Diedrich looked at his friend for guidance and resumption of their conversation. He waited somewhat impatiently, and Hanns sensed his uneasiness.

"You think I'm talking nonsense, don't you, Diedrich?" Hanns finally started after he carefully tasted the meat to confirm his expectation of the usual palate-pleasing flavor of the *asado*.

"*Ich verstehe nicht was du meinst*, I'm completely in the dark, *Herr Gauleiter Krieg*!" Now Diedrich smiled at his friend.

For the next couple of hours, Diedrich and Hanns thought aloud about what they could do to bring some degree of suffering on the governments and people that were part of the Allied "suppression" of the Third Reich. They came to no final answers to the questions as the discussion rose in tenor, although not in a volume to be overheard, and intensity. Diedrich sensed a reawakening in fervor as Hanns spoke of retribution and vengeance for the crushing defeat of the führer. Hanns reminded Diedrich of the personal oath he made to the führer, not just to the honor of the Reich.

"Diedrich, I made a solemn oath that I still honor and repeat to myself frequently. Let me tell you what it said."

He began to recite his pledge, only without standing at attention, as required in Germany:

I swear by God, this sacred oath, that I will render unconditional obedience to Adolf Hitler, the führer of the German Reich and people, Supreme Commander of the Armed Forces, and will be ready as a brave soldier to risk my life at any time for this oath.

Hanns reminded Diedrich of the sacred and solemn nature of the oath. Then he concluded, "This oath was to the führer personally and I still feel tied to him through this oath. I hope you understand what I feel!"

"Hanns, you were *wehrmacht*, but I was *luftwaffe*! I pledged myself to the honor of the Reich and to the führer exactly as you did," Diedrich said to remind Hanns of his military service, despite having done little with it while he remained in Germany.

Both men felt relieved of a burden that nagged, which they needed to express openly to someone, if nothing more than to ease the itching pangs of conscience for having fled Germany before the conflict concluded. Neither would admit their pusillanimity openly, but deep inside, they knew that they forsook their oath to the führer in order to save their own lives. Now, having expressed and reaffirmed their allegiance to the Reich, if only to each other, they relaxed into a rhythm of less apprehensive talking.

In this atmosphere, Hanns described situations that he fancied and saw in his future. He described a new *weltanschauung*, or worldview, as he saw it. His friend listened, first with admiration for a soldier willing to pursue, figuratively and literally, revenge on an enemy; then, enthused with creative energy as Hanns assembled ideas to make his *weltanschauung* workable.

As the men spoke, they fed off one another seeking revenge: idea met with idea, concept challenged concept. In conclusion, they agreed to develop something, perhaps a weapon, so cruel and so complete as to absorb resources, tie up personnel, and collapse the governments of their enemies, the enemies of the Third Reich, and of their führer.

To complete their agreement, they vowed to take as long as might be required to achieve their goal but realized that success would require money and they needed a money generator. They became conspirators for the future and in the present; together they were *die verschwörer*, as they described themselves, the conspirators to right the wrongs they felt unjustly meted out on their country, their manner of living, and their collective futures.

The Company

"Diedrich, we're sitting on a goldmine of wealth in mineral development here in Argentina. Think about what we can do here in the mountains in this obscure countryside. Let's talk about what's possible, agreed?"

"Hanns, what kind of company do you envision," asked Diedrich, now fully enveloped with the ideas he thought he understood but was not quite sure. "You have so much more experience in organizing and managing people than I ever had. I suspect you plan operating here in Argentina, but aren't we very isolated here?"

As the two men walked out of the restaurant and into the waiting car, they continued talking about possible outcomes, potential organizations, and anticipated results. However, assuming Diedrich had no place to stay for the night, Hanns invited him to his expansive estate situated just at the base of the Andes Mountains.

"As you see, Diedrich, life can be very good for you here in Argentina, if you know the right people and are willing to see that they receive a little for their efforts. I've enjoyed a lot of benefits and protection here locally because I make sure the men in charge have a little extra cash in their pockets at the end of the month. Nobody makes much money here in the highlands, especially those who work for the government, so my *mordida*, as they call it around here, helps some men to have a little more. Some use it for their families but most of them simply drink it away—who knows what people do with their money." Hanns sounded dismissive and disdainful of the local officials.

Hanns and Diedrich so reveled in old memories about the war and talking about their plans for revenge that the overnight convenience stay for Diedrich extended into several weeks and then months—neither saw any reason for Diedrich to find another residence when Hanns had sufficient room for the two of them.

Using the mining and exploration company developed by Hanns and the Argentine government as a footing, a new organization emerged with its operating goal to purchase other companies within similar industries. For a time, the original company ran parallel with the "investment adventures" of the two Germans but it was apparent that changed ownership of the original joint operation needed consideration.

As in the past, Hanns found that the right sum of money to make the needed changes in corporate registrations and ownership eased the pains expressed by the resident of *Casa Rosada*. It was not legally possible for the government to divest itself completely of the company, but Hanns achieved sufficient distance from government micro-controlling operations that the platonic relationship proved an advantage. Additionally, it proved helpful to use the government association in negotiating purchase prices for sought-after companies; although, Hanns and Diedrich ensured that the organizations purchased fell under control of a separate global holding company designed for that purpose and were technically not included in the government-private partnered company charter.

Hanns and Diedrich found a name for the holding company to be an easy enlargement of their personal eccentricities and temperaments toward the world. As they agreed together earlier, they were *der verschwörer*, the conspirators; so they named the holding company simply *DVS Technologies*.

Hanns was particularly happy with the inclusion of the German without its obvious use. "*Fein, subtil*," he told Diedrich in German, referring to the very subtle play on words and grabbing just simple letters to form the logo.

Hanns agreed with Diedrich about his addition to the logo, "I like your idea of 'Technologies' added to the name," he said. "It clearly expands our outlook in the customer's eyes."

Neither realized the meaning of an English word resulting from the phonetics of speaking the three letters, D-V-S, in a normal conversation rhythm. Had they recognized their oversight, it is unlikely that they would have changed, so enamored were they with their originality.

Within the first three years after organizing the holding company, Hanns and Diedrich made no changes in the corporate name and few changes in the methods they employed. As the company grew, the two men used extensive international recruiting practices that favored Spanish speakers and Germans. With an ever-expanding financial reserve and operational budget, they bought and sold companies, initially in South and Central America where they further capitalized on their base of operations in Mendoza. Their greatest successes resulted from their ability to take advantage of businesses and business owners that lacked sufficient expertise and sophistication to compete within their own industry or with the single-minded German executives.

DVS Technologies quickly became one of Argentina's largest growth companies during a ten-year period beginning in 1953. Company executives transitioned smoothly between administrations and regimes controlling the government in Buenos Aires; the company appeared to run without constraints fiscally, administratively, or diplomatically, regardless of the region or country in which they sought business. Issues that reflected past activities by the ex-Nazis never arose, perhaps due to the permissive legal atmosphere in which the headquarter company existed, or perhaps because they never discussed their past with anyone. To the world, they presented a single-minded face of staunch German and Swiss executives working within the nearly unrestricted energies resulting from the rapidly expanding Argentine economic climate.

The two executives acquired vast expanses of property in the Andes mountain highlands for their personal fortunes and for the company. Diedrich built a significantly smaller estate than had Hanns but equally as comfortable. Both men prospered financially and as they did, domestic and foreign corporations sought their advice; numerous boards of directors invited them to join and counsel with their members.

These external corporate contacts often provided DVS Technologies with rich resources for potential business expansion, which Hanns scrutinized with exceeding thoroughness. Hanns developed and utilized teams, each headed by an expert in the field of analysis, to assess every department of a company under scrutiny: accounting, legal, manufacturing, raw material sourcing, logistics, distribution, personnel, and marketing. After each team dug deeply into the workings of their specialized area, the entire group met to discuss the general "feel" of the company, to debrief one another in their specific areas, and to decide whether the company was a viable candidate for acquisition. The model for such thorough analysis allowed each team member to challenge any other team member in his or her findings, which facilitated an extensive scope in the examination of the studied company.

The DVS Technologies business development teams remained active primarily in the western hemisphere, assessing the value of offers to purchase companies, expanding their business models, and bringing the "reprocessed" companies through the procedure, usually with a more viable operation. In the wake of this "reprocessing" of a company, people employed in the organization often became expendable, evaluated in the same fashion as other operational functions, and retained only if other options failed.

Perhaps due to their experiences in Germany and Poland during the Second World War, neither Hanns nor Diedrich saw any conflict in jettisoning individuals for the sake of a common good; generally, the greatest benefit was for DVS Technologies and their executives. Missing in these two men were elements of human compassion that so many people in the world rely upon in their interactions with others in the community where they live and work. Conceivably, the loss was due to a palatable desire they harbored, deep-seated in their psyche, to exact a cruel revenge on the world. As part of their *weltanschauung*, they sought to inflict their revenge on the nations that fought against Germany.

A Laboratory in DVS

Late in 1963, during a non-DVS corporate officers' meeting in Santiago, board member Diedrich listened to reports of a foundering company and discovered that the owners wanted to divest their holdings in the company. Further, the troubled company was a biochemical laboratory, specializing in blood testing procedures and devices. The following day, after returning to Mendoza, he discussed his findings with Hanns privately and suggested that a laboratory company specializing in blood analyses might offer financial incentives for DVS Technologies.

"Hanns, this company is Chilean-owned but situated so that we could buy their entire holdings with very little real cash," Diedrich suggested. "The valuations are very low because they have done nothing with the company—it's virtually a bust. I suspect we might offer something attached to DVS general stock or even an earn-out agreement. The owners are anxious to get out of the business."

"Then why should we want to get into it?" asked Hanns.

Earlier, Diedrich primed himself to answer just this question; when it arose, he realized that now was not the time for a thorough discussion with Hanns. Rather, he suggested that the two go to *El Restaurante Alemán* for a late lunch and a discussion of what Diedrich saw in the company. Diedrich, like Hanns, found that he gained clarity in his decision-making from the strength and comfort seen in the mountain vistas at the restaurant. He thought quietly to himself as they traveled the streets of Mendoza toward their favorite restaurant, "Now we start our quest for the revenge long postponed."

"Diedrich," began Hanns when the two situated themselves comfortably at their favorite table, "what is it about this laboratory company that attracts you and makes you think it will be a fit for DVS?"

"Perhaps you remember my research work at Posen before the war; I wanted to learn all that was possible about a new science, as I called it at the time?"

"You were certainly headstrong in those days," replied Hanns.

"Since gaining my doctorate and working in the laboratories with Blome, I discovered numerous nuances to that new science that I didn't share with anyone. Periodically, I took some of my findings to a drug form, which I tested in the prisons. The results were usually marginal but I continued the work as long as I remained at Blome's Posen laboratories."

Hanns continued listening to his business partner and friend but did not perceive a connection to the proposed acquisition of a biochemical laboratory company in Santiago.

"Mengele interrupted my work with his crazy *saringas* project," continued Diedrich, "so I never got to finish my work on properties of viral agents affecting blood coagulation. I know it sounds a little far-fetched, but I think I found a way to interrupt the normal coagulating processes with an external virus-like agent. I would have had it if Mengele and Blome had left me alone."

"Admittedly," countered Hanns, "I know nothing about those things!"

"Let me explain it this way. Suppose you had a virus, which could interrupt the blood systems in a person, and that could spread much the same way as a common cold. Such an agent could prove to be an effective weapon against an enemy. But the important thing in using it, you need complete control to prevent the virus from multiplying and changing its structure at will."

"I guess I still don't see the use," Hanns remained a little less convinced than he was before about investing in a new company.

"*Hören Sie mir, Hanns, dies darf sein unsere perfekte Rache zu!*" Diedrich asked Hanns to listen more intently. Carefully now, Hanns listened to Diedrich explain that this laboratory might be the opportunity to find a perfect agent helping them gain their revenge.

"With this laboratory and company, we might expand business in a new direction while giving me the means to work quietly on my *blutgerinnungsunterbrecher*, or blood coagulation interrupter, until I perfect it," Hanns saw a former passion he had not seen for many years in his old college friend.

"It sounds very complicated, Diedrich. Do you think we can pull it off?"

"I'm sure of it, but it will take time and money," Diedrich's confidence seemed to stoke a fire in his executive business partner.

"Well, then, let's drink to the new laboratories of *der verschwörer*," Hanns smiled at his friend. "What do you think we should call our new venture?"

"I thought in keeping with the Argentine nature of our company and the Chilean structure of the new company—maybe we should call it *DVS Laboratorios*. I don't think we need anything Germanic, if we continue to work in South America."

"*Natürlich, d' accord!*"

Both men agreed to the purchase, to a name for the new venture, and the start to a new direction for *der Wissenschafter* who longed for a laboratory to call his own.

CHAPTER FIVE
Vanguards

The Laboratory

Hanns remained uncertain concerning the viability of expanding his business into an unknown and untested area, despite his agreeing with Diedrich. In fact, Hanns still considered the business "his" and that Diedrich, while an important contributor, came second in all his calculations regarding the outcome of the business. In order to gain time to examine the options, Hanns suggested, "Let's send a team to look at the company, determine what is its condition, and then we'll have good information on the direction to take."

Diedrich advocated that he head up the due diligence team going to Santiago, which was perfectly logical because of his technical education and experience. Hanns thought it a splendid suggestion.

The two Germans prided themselves on their aptitude, their impeccable logic, and flawless timing, even to the point of implying that they led the industry in analyzing potential companies. In reality, the sharp business practices and *vollkommene arische logik*, or perfect and comprehensive Aryan logic, on which they prided themselves, edged closely on the unethical and often uncaring exploits of audaciousness. It could be argued that the same practices and logic employed by Hanns and Diedrich resulted in the defeat of the Third Reich and the structural downfall of the German Republic following the Second World War.

Few people dared challenge DVS Technologies group of companies, due to its financial strength and political influence, and not necessarily because it was an excellent business model on which to emulate or to build a fledgling organization.

Hanns, the chief executive officer, managed the company in a similar manner as he conducted himself when he was the *Sachsengauleiter* in Dresden. Any lapse in employee judgment or performance within the DVS Technologies group resulted in immediate termination of employment, no questions asked, nor excuses accepted. Whatever shameful lack of courage Hanns Krieg exhibited in the face of eminent personal danger in Germany, his brazenness toward complete industrial control and his perceived rights of ownership of virtually everything he encountered was antithetical to his spineless behavior in fleeing Germany.

Diedrich supported the business practices of his friend and associate; however, he expressed concern that because the company and laboratory in Santiago performed below standards set by the DVS Technologies for acquisition, Hanns would reject the proposal. Hanns was ruthless in dealing with business and people.

On one occasion, as a due diligence team wrapped up their work on a smaller mining and exploration company in central Mexico, Hanns decided, essentially without consent from Diedrich, to acquire the company, which employed one hundred people and benefited from a reputable ten-year history in the field. Rather than fulfilling verbal assurances toward continuation of operations after acquisition, Hanns completely disassembled the organization, dismissed the executives and all employees, auctioned existing capitalized equipment, and retained fungible mineral rights and property. When queried, Hanns simply replied that it was better to eliminate competition for another DVS Technologies company operating in the region.

In Santiago, the due diligence team wrapped up their initial examination of the company, initially proposed by Diedrich, which included assessing particulars such as market potential, personnel performance, effectiveness of facilities, and financial health, but could not resolve how to evaluate the laboratory property. The Chilean company's somewhat narrowly focused business plan was outside the scope of the DVS Technologies group of companies, which primarily concentrated on mining and exploration projects.

Owners of the targeted company maintained the laboratory with significant and ongoing investment in technological equipment that represented high sophistication in blood analysis; in addition, the laboratory engaged in some pure research, principally focused on blood coagulation and other general hematologic subjects. It was an unambiguous conclusion of the due diligence team members that investments made by the owners of the company exceeded present potential market returns on income generated. Nevertheless, Diedrich demonstrated an unusual excitement toward purchase of the company for which he would not disclose the reasons to the team members. He reserved that discussion until he returned to Mendoza and could consult together with Hanns concerning the secretive purposes they had for acquiring the company and its sophisticated laboratory.

"Hanns, I think we've found it," began Diedrich in a private meeting at DVS headquarter offices. "With this laboratory I can continue work on the *blutgerinnungsunterbrecher* virus we discussed."

"You sound excited, Diedrich. Do you think it might work?"

"I was close to perfecting the agent while at Posen, but that was a long time ago. Who knows what will occur now. Science has advanced well beyond our abilities of 1943!"

"Do you want to move back to Santiago?" asked Hanns.

"I don't see any other way to facilitate a reorganization of the laboratory. Fortunately, the telephones work very well between here and there. Even though I've been away for a few years, I think my knowledge of Chile and the people will help us recruit the necessary technicians."

Hanns did not like the idea of having his friend transfer away from the company headquarters in Argentina but recognized that the present opportunity was an appropriate moment to act. After carefully considering his apprehensions, he agreed to the purchase of the Chilean company.

Together they decided the name of the new company would be as suggested earlier, *DVS Laboratorios* and that Diedrich would become the president of the operations. As they obtained the necessary licenses, funding, and planning for Diedrich to assume control of the new company, both exhibited an usual excitement that others in the company noticed and wondered what stirred such enthusiasm in a small acquisition; past deals generally concluded without a great deal of commotion, rather as a matter of fact.

Among employees of the company in Mendoza, rumors spread about why one of the principals in the organization planned moving to assume control of a new company. Nevertheless, no one sensed the true reasons behind the acquisition and transfer of Doctor Diedrich Erhard to Santiago.

En Santiago Otra Vez (Santiago Again)

Work organizing the DVS Laboratorios consumed so much of each day that Diedrich had precious little time for his former artistic friends and their political activities. Nevertheless, Diedrich did visit a few of his favorite *cafeterías* in Santiago and scheduled occasional visits to his favorite city, Valparaíso, always stopping at *Un Pequeño Café*. The city's multicolored, often whimsical designs, painted on walls and houses seemed to invigorate his energies. As he strolled through narrow alleyways, climbed the gently ascending stairs up hills, and walked some of the wider cobblestone or bricked pathways, he paused frequently to admire his surroundings. Diedrich enjoyed riding one of the several *ascensors*, or cogwheel tramcars, to the top of the hills. He especially enjoyed walking alone along the *Paseo Veintiuno de Mayo*, an esplanade that curved the top of a hill near the naval school that once served as a fort and overlooked the beautiful bay.

Valparaíso Bay continued to bustle with a lively sea trade, despite declining significantly from earlier pre-Panamá Canal shipping routes when it was the first seaport arrived at after rounding

Cape Horn at the southern tip of South America. When time permitted, Diedrich sat on one of the benches on the *Paseo* and watched the ships in the port. On these occasions, he reflected on what he planned to accomplish in his life and where he was in his struggles. The darkish, blue-green waters, churned by the continuous movement of the ships, as if in an apparition, tempted him to daydream and even to imagine he was in Dresden, or among the waving sea of trees in the Bavarian mountains.

He discovered that nearly all of the self-exiled poets he met earlier returned to Chile and resumed some of their former anti-government, communistic activities. While he remained apolitical outwardly, he kept information to himself that he did not support their communistic views or the current Chilean congress controlled by the Christian Democratic political party. He thought it paradoxical that less than half of the voting Chileans supported the party. The rest of the country backed one of the many splinter groups, including the once outlawed Chilean Communist Party, which his poet friends supported wholeheartedly.

In spite of its lack of popularity, the Christian Democratic Party received substantial financial backing from the American government and from American businesses operating in Chile. They were quite vocal in their opposition to a presidential candidate, Salvador Allende. Diedrich assumed that their outside support helped defeat Allende in the 1964 elections.

It surprised Diedrich when his laboratory manager asked him about his political preferences: "Doctor Erhard, what do you think of the current political situation in Santiago? Do you think the Christian Democrats represent the people?" she questioned.

"I've not given it much thought, Doctor Muñoz."

"I've heard it rumored that the Central Intelligence Agency from the US manipulated the recent elections. I heard that they brought in large amounts of money for candidates favorable to the US," the manager continued, a little concerned that her new boss and the influential president of an important company had not formed an opinion about the main political situation in the country.

"Well, as you know, Doctor, I'm a Swiss citizen and I take a neutral view of all these political things," replied Diedrich, trying to deflect further conversation on the subject. Diedrich, in this situation, claimed to be Swiss, a lie but one he continued with while living in Chile. He felt the American government's intrusion in Chilean politics unfair and it seemed to intensify further Diedrich's substantial and growing antagonism for all things supported by the United States.

"As you can imagine," he continued, "I'm resolved not to concern myself in politics but to organize this laboratory and company to be the very best in Chile. Indeed, I need your help working to achieve our goal; don't you agree?"

"As you wish; but there might come a time when you will have to express an opinion as to where you stand," cautioned *la Doctor Anita Muñoz González*.

Doctor Muñoz worked with the company since it opened about eleven or twelve years earlier as a pathology laboratory for hospitals and blood banks in Santiago. She was a competent laboratory hematologist, well respected in the Santiago medical associations. Similar to *Herr Doktor Erhard* of the *Reichsuniversität Posen* in Germany, she also had many papers published and frequently attended medical conferences throughout the South and Central Americas.

Nevertheless, Diedrich resolved not to concern himself, for the present, in local or regional politics. Rather, he focused his efforts toward investing in the best resources available in Chile that further improved the laboratory. For the immediate future, he envisioned establishing two laboratories, one laboratory that the public would see, and one that would work exclusively on projects he proscribed but on which the company excluded public reports.

He and Hanns resolved to maintain weekly telephone conferences and frequent meetings at the headquarters in Mendoza. Hanns was certain that his friend, Diedrich, would follow instructions and his carefully placed suggestions.

During one of their first telephone calls, Hanns asked, "Well, what's your thinking about the company now that you've had some time there?"

"I think we can categorize the company's work easily because as we found out in the due diligence, the laboratory works in two very distinct fields. The first is as a clinical pathology laboratory specializing in hematological analyses. The second is as a manufacturing facility for reagents sold to hospitals and blood banks that they use for their own analyses. The export trade is minimal but we might expand it. However, there's a small, unprofitable device line that we can eliminate, without bottom-line losses in revenue—in fact, we may actually increase our profits by dropping the devices."

"Can you build a laboratory of your own," Hanns asked and wondered if they could accomplish the research spoken of earlier.

"I see the laboratory facilities easily split into two divisions, and we can keep the work in the second *privado*, *privat*, private from all the outside reports," Diedrich added emphasis by repeating his description of the secretive portion first in Spanish and then in German.

"Although, I'll need some qualified technicians to work in the private section," Diedrich added, as if adding a second thought.

Hanns questioned if Diedrich could find in Santiago, or even in other parts of Chile, responsible people to work on the secretive projects that Diedrich planned. He found assurance in his friend's comments, "I think we'll have to be careful, but I can stage the work in such a way as to make it appear pure research in the section."

Diedrich's confidence pleased Hanns, mainly because he did not have to include management of the new facilities in his business agenda, he felt comfortable leaving it in Diedrich's hands. As they concluded the telephone conference, he turned his attention to other pressing business waiting on his desk. With a preoccupied thought, he commented, "Back to real business," and picked a report on the top of the stack of fresh documents.

Africa

The primary business markets pursued by Hanns were in South and Central America, but growth opportunities extended well beyond Latin America. Executives at DVS Technologies frequently discussed these mining and exploration business opportunities in other parts of the globe. In addition, they repeatedly determined that the single largest prospect for new business expansion lay in the African continent. However, for an Argentine company to compete in that distant location would require substantial African personal contacts, African governmental leases, and seemingly bottomless financial coffers.

Another, seemingly never-ending, difficulty for any international company that wished to operate in many African countries was the instability of the governments. European countries, with extant African colonies, such as Belgium, Portugal, and the United Kingdom divested themselves of their colonies during the decade around 1965. The void in governmental structures caused by "de-colonization" gave way to political unrest and economic volatility in most of the former colonies.

As Hanns sat at his desk, he contemplated an offer from the British exploration firm Llandudno Offshore Mining, Ltd. proposing mining claims in the British colony of Southern Rhodesia and several other sites in Africa. The offer presented a dilemma. Initially, he thought about the political situation in 1965 Rhodesia, which was precarious. The government, controlled by whites, declared unilateral independence from Britain but the United Nations refused to recognize the new nation; sanctions followed. Under these conditions, it did not appear wise to open new trade relations within the fledgling independent-minded country. If the United Nations interfered with foreign companies trading or conducting business with the new country, his business venture might fail.

He asked members of his executive board for their opinions. "Gentlemen, what is the likelihood of Britain continuing sanctions against the new Rhodesia?"

All agreed the high probability of continuing sanctions by Britain and by most of the members of the United Nations. Few of the executives expressed anything positive about opening a joint business venture with a firm in Britain when it was likely the Brits would block companies trading with the new country.

"It appears that Llandudno Offshore is liquidating its holdings in Rhodesia before they lose them to nationalization by the government and collapse of operations in South Africa," voiced one of the executives.

Two or three of the younger executives who, before the present time, waited for an opportunity to expand operations in Africa, delivered to the group interesting data about the minerals available in the southern parts of Africa.

"It's quite possible that eighty percent of the world's production of rhodium comes from South Africa, or about twenty to twenty-five metric tonnes," offered one of the younger members of the executive board. "With that in mind, I find it hard to walk away from the possibility of a market potential that could exceed ten billion US dollars."

"Historically, the price of rhodium has been about double that of gold," added another. "With the difficulties in the area, the price could easily go higher."

"Maybe finding an opening for us in the market, despite political conditions—" expressed a third without finishing his sentence.

Hanns thought as the executive paused, "To use the British company contacts as an introduction to influential people in Africa is a capital idea. We can always negotiate separately with the people in any African country."

Nevertheless, Hanns also thought silently, "After all, why should I share any of the results of our efforts with the British, or anyone else, for that matter? If I can get the right people in Africa, I can simply cut the British out of the deal!"

However, deep within, Hanns questioned whether opening discussions with a British company would create the possibility of them discovering his Nazi background. He seemed to carry the weight of his former life as a constant reminder and it bothered him. During times like these, he became somewhat morose and thought more intently of revenging the German defeat on those who forced him to flee his homeland. Not infrequently when he became moody about his past, he phoned Diedrich and the two of them commiserated, planned, and plotted ways to achieve their collective *weltanschauung*. This was not one of those times.

"*Señor Krieg*," started one of the executives, "while the industry has some respect for the work of Llandudno Offshore Mining concerning rhodium and chromium, there's another mineral to consider. Well over two-thirds of the world's chromite ores come out of South Africa; Rhodesian mines provide a fair amount of this ore. We've seen an explosion in the worldwide use of chromium in recent years but DVS is not part of it. Similar to rhodium, we're looking at billions of US dollar potential with this ore. If we have an opportunity through the British, maybe we should examine how we might manage a backdoor approach to the political arena."

Then the young executive added, "What about ferrochrome and nickel ores? They all come from Rhodesian mines; can't we get into some of that business in spite of the international nonsense about which country controls what piece of ground?" The executive appeared a little agitated with how the current situations might limit the expansion of DVS operations.

He continued, "I suspect the interruption of chromium and rhodium to the Americans will cause them to bypass the sanctions. They seem to always find ways to go around everyone else when it's in their best interests."

Another executive added. "If the Americans find a way to circumvent the UN sanctions, there will be openings for us to supply them their refined ore! I advise we enter the market as soon as we can."

The discussion continued for another hour concerning the African question.

Finally, Hanns suggested that the group table the topic for a time later and adjourned the meeting. He appreciated their comments and advice; however, they were not cognizant that Hanns indeed had ideas about expanding the company and Africa was a prime target for that expansion.

Central Africa and Zaire

The second largest country in Africa in 1965, by geographic area, was the newly renamed *République du Zaïre*, the Republic of Zaire. As occurred in other countries, when the European colonizer granted independence to the former Belgian Congo in June of 1960, a new republic formed accompanied by political unrest beginning almost immediately.

From a materialistic potential, the central regions of Africa interested Hanns more than did the southern parts. This optimism sprung from his personal contacts in the industry, from whom he learned of massive deposits of copper and cobalt ores that remained relatively untapped in the region. These deposits represented many times the potential return of those with rhodium, chromium, or chromite ores.

Historically, Belgian and British companies devastated the region and the population in obtaining rubber production needed in Europe. The mining claims in the area primarily focused on exploitation of the rich deposits of gold and diamonds.

As an exception to the interests of the Europeans in rubber, gold, and diamonds, the massive and relatively untapped copper ore deposits, fascinated American mining and exploration businesses. Perhaps swayed by self-interest, the US financially supported Belgian paratroopers and African forces in "safeguarding" the copper and diamond mines in the south of the new country, Zaire, from rebel occupation. As part of these military actions, the forces captured and executed the leader of the opposition political party thereby further solidifying the role of what appeared to be the new head of state, Joseph Mobutu.

The actions of foreigners seeking wealth in the country at the expense of the inhabitants left few Zairians anxious to open business relations with foreign companies.

Hanns Krieg often openly sympathized with the Zairians and their feelings about foreign intervention in their country. However, he did not express his concern from which his hatred of the US stemmed: that the single largest contributor to his country's defeat in the Second World War was continuing to infiltrate many other countries for its own incentives.

Hanns recognized some of the complexities of the emerging country in the Republic of Zaire and felt that he needed a reputable broker to establish contact with the leaders of the new government.

Using an acquaintance in the Argentine government's Bureau of Mining Affairs, located in Buenos Aires, Hanns established contact with a young leader in the political party trying to dominate Zaire and most likely to succeed forming a majority government for the area. The contact, Joseph Mbandaka, was an officer in the *Armée Nationale Congolaise* and functioned well with the heads of the army and within the fledgling government. He was particularly interested in protecting the vital natural resources of the Republic of Zaire and spent his infinite energies in developing global contacts to accomplish his national objectives. When Hanns's intermediary offered Mbandaka contact with one of the largest mining and exploration companies in Argentina, he immediately scrutinized the offer to see where the Argentines could help his new country. Thus far, no South American industries expressed any interest in the Republic of Zaire.

Nearing the same time as Hanns extended his interested industrial hand to the newly formed Zairian government, other countries were interested in the politics of the region and in stabilizing the Republic of Zaire in order to prevent Communism from launching its anti-democratic activities. The head of the *Armée Nationale Congolaise*, Mobutu, offered assurances of his western inclinations and received financial backing from the US and Belgian governments. With the foreign support, he consolidated control of the several factional military groups into the army, forced a successful military coup, and established some stability for the country by declaring himself head of state.

Hanns conducted several telephone conferences with Joseph Mbandaka but remained uncertain of the economic stability and potential of entering Africa to exploit the copper and cobalt deposits. He needed more than vocal reassurances and decided to travel to Léopoldville, the capital city of the new the Republic of Zaire, taking with him several of his top DVS executives.

Léopoldville (Kinshasa), the Republic of Zaire

Having changed his citizenship to Argentine and traveling exclusively with that country's passport and documents, Hanns Krieg was now free to visit virtually any country without threat of interference. Despite this relative ease and the lack of restrictions on his travel, Hanns preferred to use a corporate plane for all of his Latin American business travel. Even at the outset of his mining and exploration business, he traveled aboard chartered aircraft, reserved exclusively for his use and that of his executives. After the company achieved substantial revenues from its work, Hanns purchased several planes for travel rather than the continued chartering of flights. Of the several planes owned by DVS Technologies, the one he preferred in the mid-1960s was an aircraft built by Reims Aviation in France. Although not capable of trans-oceanic flight, the aircraft was suitable for Hanns in his South American business trips.

For the trip to Africa, Hanns and his executives traveled the commercial *Aerolíneas Argentina* via the capital city of Senegal, Dakar. The flight annoyed Hanns, which he described to his fellow travelers from DVS as, "interminably long and tedious." From Dakar, the group traveled another 4,200 kilometers to Léopoldville via the South African Airways.

When the group arrived in the capital city of the Republic of Zaire, Hanns thought to himself, "If we ever begin successful operations in Africa, we'll need to establish an office in a convenient city, one with an international airport. We'll need a locale where I can have my plane waiting and where I might avoid these insensitive commercial flights."

The limousine that whisked them from the airport to the government offices had a driver who spoke only French to them, which further annoyed Krieg for no apparent reason because he spoke the language effortlessly.

Hanns relaxed a little as Joseph Mbandaka graciously received the South American executives in his office. As a formality for the arriving guests, an assistant served the executives clear glasses of hot tea and small French-styled pastries as they settled into the rather cramped quarters of the director of Internal Resources Bureau for the newly formed Zairian republic. Hanns noted the clear glasses and their rattan base covers, the rattan woven in such a fanciful manner as to give the appearance that the glass and the rattan were a single unique identity.

Once formal introductions of members in each group took place, Mbandaka began, "You've traveled a long way, haven't you? What do you think of our city? I'm afraid that you picked a rather hot time of the year to come but the weather is always too warm for most people coming to Zaire for the first time."

"I'm glad we had a few conversations via the telephone, Director," replied Hanns.

Hanns was impatient by nature and wanted to begin the business discussions immediately; however, he realized the importance of allowing sufficient settling-in time that was often essential in dealing with African negotiators. Initial polite conversation frequently was equally as important as were details of the pending discussions. The more complex the issues, the longer the African negotiator spent preparing the scene for understanding the people with details of the ensuing discussions.

There were no translators, the conversation carried on between the two groups was in English; although, Joseph Mbandaka was much more comfortable in French and the Argentine group more comfortable in Spanish. Only the Argentines knew that Krieg was German, despite that fact, and since his arrival in Argentina, he was comfortably fluent in several languages.

When it appeared proper, Hanns offered additional complements to their host and to Zaire, bridging the business discussion skillfully. "I believe we've come to a beautiful part of the world, and I'm interested in discussing how we can work together," concluded Hanns.

"So right, *Mister Krieg*, so right," replied Joseph Mbandaka. He had an unusual manner in pronouncing some English words, such as "mister" and when combined with the Germanic last name, the sound trilled slightly as Mbandaka addressed Hanns.

Recognizing that timing and the tenor changed in the discussion, Mbandaka continued, "I understand that you're interested in our copper and our cobalt, but what is it about our diamonds and our gold that you don't like?" He seemed to delight in a not-so-gentle taunt at the expense of the Argentines' motives.

The DVS executive team dealt with this question as they prepared for the trip, so their answers were not forced, nor did the answers seem contrived.

"It's very likely that some gold will be retrieved along with the copper, and we can handle that ore without much annoyance. In fact, the gold may even help offset some of the expenses of mining the copper. But diamonds create too much attention, are very labor-intensive to mine, and fall outside our interests," replied the executive assigned to handle the question.

"Yes, we've seen the great anxiety exercised by the Americans and the Belgians in trying to get our diamonds," Mbandaka seemed thoughtful as he commented. "Maybe it's a good thing that you're not interested in them. We've enough trouble with other Africans stealing from the minefields. But, such is life in the *République du Zaïre*!"

The comment convinced Hanns that his strategy in not seeking diamonds was wise; additionally, the director appeared relieved to hear again that the Argentines were interested in copper and cobalt rather than diamonds and gold.

"You're aware of the massive outflow of wealth taken by the Belgian *Exploitation Minière de Kataganga et Exploration*?" Mbandaka wanted to be sure that the people sitting with him in his office realized the sensitivities of the Zairians toward foreign exploitation of the African resources. "They've had their way with us long enough; soon it will come to an end!"

The Belgian copper and cobalt mining operations that began in the Belgian Congo about sixty years earlier were some of the most profitable in the world, at least for the Belgians, and it was this geo-economic fact that Mbandaka wanted the visitors to understand.

He reiterated, "*Monsieur Krieg*, may I remind you that the *région de ceinture couleur cuivre*, or the copper belt region as you call it, is nearly a hundred kilometers wide and three hundred kilometers long. In the past, many foreigners came here to obtain wealth and left the Zairian people poorer. We're not ready to begin the same type of contract work with a company from Argentina. There's a new direction for *République du Zaïre!*"

The political overtones of the comments did not escape Hanns. He seemed acutely aware of the volatility of the government and was skeptical, initially, that DVS could successfully engage in contract mining operations without substantial investment. Nevertheless, during their preparations, the executive team determined that the rewards outweighed the potential risks. Hanns felt the company might be in a position to enter the market with a relatively moderate financial drain on its resources, especially if the Zairians agreed to finance some of the initial costs.

"Yes, Director Mbandaka, we're aware of the blatant abuses you've suffered at the hands of the Europeans," assured Hanns. "With our proposal, you'll receive more return for the extraction of the minerals. We've worked successfully for many years with the Chileans in their copper mining and they seem to be quite pleased with how our company respects the land, and the people. As you know," Hanns was cautious not to patronize the director nor demean his knowledge of world copper reserves, "many estimate the copper reserves in Chile to be the single largest in the world. We estimate that your reserves are very close, perhaps equal to those in Chile."

The discussions continued for a number of hours in a similar fashion. Throughout, each side of the negotiating table traded tidbits and factoids about the global mining industry. What Hanns and his group could not understand, however, was that the new leader of the country planned seizing the mining industry and running it as a state-controlled operation. In addition, Hanns could not know that Joseph Mbandaka helped formulate these plans and understood the ramifications of taking over the major foreign mining company in Zaire. With each step in his negotiations, Mbandaka pointed the visitors toward an agreement that provided substantial financial support for new *République du Zaïre*. In return, DVS Technologies entered a long-term mining and exploration agreement to explore and prospect yet undefined deposits of copper and cobalt.

* * *

At the request of the director of the Internal Resources Bureau, the DVS executives visited the copper belt region and the existing copper smelter in the southern sections of the country. They used Élisabethville as a headquarters for the two weeks they explored. After several days in the south, Hanns left his team and returned to meet privately with Joseph Mbandaka and the president.

As with other countries where DVS Technologies joined the government for exploration or mining ventures, Hanns met and discussed the agreement with Joseph Mobutu, the self-declared president of the *République du Zaïre*. Hanns was supremely confident in his political prowess and never failed to charm each leader with whom he met. However, from this meeting with Mobutu, Hanns failed to gain the advantage he so much enjoyed gaining over other people. The president was cagey, unpredictable in his responses, yet polite to the extreme. Despite his youthfulness, Mobutu was strong-willed and reminded Hanns of many *wehrmacht* officers during the war. Something about his mannerisms caused concern in Hanns; he was not certain that he could trust him.

The perfunctory details proceeded as expected. A simple handshake confirmed the previously agreed-to working relationships between the Argentine company and the Zairian government, when money was to change hands, and what foreigners should enter the country in order to complete the agreement. Nevertheless, something remained unsaid but surely felt between the president of the new country and the ex-Nazi executive from South America.

Difficult to define but unmistakable nonetheless, a distrust felt but unexpressed percolated between the two. It was as if Hanns was uncertain if Mobutu would honor his agreements detailed in paper and sealed with a handshake, while the president remained unconvinced of the South American's plans to prospect and develop new minefields exclusively for the republic. Which side was honorable now that they left a mutual fraternity in the same moment of time?

Hanns returned to Mendoza without waiting for a report from the other team members. He purposely traveled alone so that he had time to contemplate his future in Africa. Successes in South America prepared him to expect setbacks in every operation; nevertheless, the edge on the new operation left him unsettled and he needed time to think. Perhaps Diedrich might join him and together they might discuss the concepts, shortfalls, and expectations of working in Africa.

He was certain about one thing, "No more commercial flights to Africa. I need a plane for the trip and a plane in the country. I think we should fly directly into the Léopoldville Airport and operate out of that city, with a decent plane of my own."

Changes

A few months after returning to Mendoza, Hanns read a news article about changes made by the government of the *République du Zaïre*. Then he realized the significance of the feelings he experienced and some of the non-answers he received while talking with the president of Zaire.

In the interim since their agreement in Léopoldville, DVS Technologies transferred some of the required money and personnel to Zaire. Company personnel, buoyed greatly by the potential of the new market, restructured their workloads and departments to reflect the needs of the *Proyecto de Cobre Africano*, or African Copper Project, a nickname given to the work. Many convinced other employees that this project would exceed the successes of the *Proyecto de Cobre Chileno*, or Chilean Copper Project, of the past.

Hanns calculated the time differences and then asked his secretary to place a phone call to President Joseph Mobutu in the Republic of Zaire.

"Good to hear from you again, *Monsieur Krieg*," trilled the voice on the phone. Hanns bristled at the sound of the Zairian trilling his name. Hanns could not detect but he suspected that Mobutu's first language, Dutch, the one he learned as a youngster living the house of in a Belgian judge, heavily influenced the sound of his English. However, in his Nazi-engrained bigotry, he decided, "It must be something from his native tribal language that causes that awful sound."

Then President Mobutu's voice brought him back to the reason for his call, "What can I do for you today?"

"Mr. President," began Hanns, "I read of some of the changes you've made. Is the reporting correct that you nationalized the Belgian *Exploitation Minière de Katanga et Exploration*?"

"Yes, we think we shall call it *Général Operations de Carrières et de Mines* or just *Demines* for short. What do you think of the new name?"

"Does this change the nature of our agreement?" Hanns queried, completely disregarding the president's question.

"Well, let's talk about that when you complete your new offices in Kinshasa," a reply that left Hanns more than dissatisfied. "But for now, I don't think you have anything to worry about."

Hanns wondered aloud where Kinshasa was and the president replied that the people wanted several names changed to reflect their national heritage. He explained that Léopoldville was Kinshasa and that Élisabethville was now Lumbashi.

"The people plan other name changes, for the future!" emphasized the president, who also explained that he "would send a list when he had time."

"Oh yes, *Monsieur Krieg*, there's more: soon I'll eliminate the European out of my own name and assume a name of my heritage. My proper name will be *Mobutu Sese Seko Nkuku Ngbendu wa Za Banga*," announced the president. Despite speaking over the telephone, Hanns thought the vocal intonation betrayed the puffery of the man.

"What do you think, *Monsieur Krieg*?"

"Very nice, I'm sure," replied Hanns, more than annoyed at the deviation in the conversation.

"Mr. President—" began Hanns.

"You know what my new name means?"

Without waiting for a reply, Mobutu answered the question. "My new name means 'the all-powerful warrior who, because of his endurance and inflexible will to win, goes from conquest to conquest, leaving fire in his wake.' Don't you think that will be appropriate?"

"Yes, yes, very appropriate, perhaps a little long," Hanns tried to control his mounting frustration.

"Mr. President, you're taking on, no, more accurately, you're nationalizing the major mining company in your country from the Belgians. That will not make the Europeans pleased. Will you need help from us managing it and seeing that operations stay current?"

"Absolutely, *Monsieur Krieg*; didn't we agree? But, if you wish, let's say we can talk about that on your next trip," and just as quickly, the cordiality of the conversation faded and the line went dead on the other end of the call.

The next call Hanns placed was to Diedrich in Chile; Hanns wanted to calm his nerves and talk with an old friend who always seemed to cheer him up when difficulties surmounted the high walls of this unique German character.

CHAPTER SIX
Die Verschwörer (The Conspirators)

Doctor Erhard sat in his Santiago office, reviewing laboratory reports for accuracy; each series of tests measured precise amounts of plasma, protein, cells, or chemical content. Daily, the laboratory established baseline values to ensure accuracy of test values, in addition to assuring the laboratory personnel that they could expect reproducibility of the test performances. As the ultimate responsible scientific officer of the company, Diedrich relied on his laboratory manager and technicians to perform necessary confirming tests, using accepted standards, to validate the reliability of the laboratory results. Nevertheless, frequently he reviewed all results of their work to see that the standards used met criteria relied on by the local blood banks and hospitals. He insisted on preciseness in all equipment, devices, and human functioning applied in the laboratory.

The ringing telephone on his desk interrupted his thoughtful review.

"*Hola, digame.*"

"Diedrich, is that you," Hanns asked at the other end of the telephone line. His friend's voice still contained the faint and pleasant Germanic clipped sounds he enjoyed hearing, although the familiar voice, now changed slightly, modified from years of conversing in *ausländische sprachen*, or non-German languages, spoke Spanish fluently and without accent for many unaccustomed to his pattern of speech.

"*Hanns, begrüßen du zurück von Afrika!*" Diedrich changed smoothly from Spanish he used to answer the telephone to German when he realized who was calling. "Welcome back from Africa. How was your trip?"

Hanns recounted some of the adventures he and the DVS executives experienced in getting around Africa and of his meetings with Mbandaka and Mobutu. Diedrich noted irritation in his friend's voice as he described some of the results of the trip.

"You sound a little irritated, Hanns," asked his friend in Santiago.

"When is your next trip to Mendoza?" asked Hanns, completely dismissing an answer to Diedrich's query.

"Things here move rather slowly, even in our research section of the laboratory." Hanns understood the reference to the special section of the laboratory without more details. "I think I can leave about anytime."

"Let's meet to review my trip, the research section of the laboratory, and what we can do in the next few months to take advantage of things we've started," suggested Hanns. "I'll see you soon."

El Restaurante Alemán

At their favorite restaurant for over ten years, the German exiles sat watching the sun slide behind the Andean peaks to the west, leaving a crimson path in its wake.

"Still a beautiful sight, those mountains," commented Hanns. "I enjoy sitting here probably more than any other place I've been since leaving Germany."

"I agree," replied Diedrich, "and the place is so quiet around us. They know how to respect our privacy here at the restaurant."

The two remained quiet for some time before Hanns began his amalgamation of thoughts for the future of DVS Technologies in Africa. It was clear once he started that Diedrich was to listen while the former *gauleiter* expounded.

"There's too much unrest in Zaire," began Hanns, "for us to approach the market in a normal fashion. The risks for loss outside our control are extraordinary. Nevertheless, I think we can easily use the political unrest and confusion for our own benefit. One doorway might close but we can find another open just as certainly!"

"Well, we've had some close calls in other speculations and seemed to come out of it all right," suggested Diedrich, smiling a little as he thought of the missteps taken by DVS Technologies in Brazil, and the government pressure in Mexico. Maybe Hanns was a little less sensitive to the risks in those ventures, but Diedrich felt that the company never really achieved much from the mines after the governments took over virtually all of the operations in both areas.

Diedrich verbalized an obvious thought, emphasizing the negative, "A break-even position on investments *does not* rest well with our other investors."

Hanns explained that, "The new president of the country in the former Belgian Congo, President Mobutu of the *République du Zaïre*, is far too egocentric for dependable business relations. If trust is measurable between parties in an agreement, then I set the measure extremely low, as I view our working agreement with the Congolese. I'm certain that the money we transferred to the country, if not lost already, soon will be. We need someone in that office, with an eye for recognizing and preventing losses through corruption, to watch out for our interests."

"Which office and where is it?" Diedrich thought he knew but wanted to be certain that Hanns still had his mind set on Kinshasa.

"I've thought about keeping our temporary offices in Kinshasa but Lumbashi offers some advantages because it's quite a distance to the south and not directly under the scrutiny of the government in the capital city. There are a lot of white Africans and Europeans still living in Lumbashi and it seems to be where a lot of turmoil bubbles, almost out of the streets."

"That sounds rather poetic, my friend," observed Diedrich. "What is a white African?"

"Earlier, mostly in the last hundred years, Europeans took ownership of much of the land area and resources in the Congo. Belgium, for example, made the Congo a colony and exploited the region until granting it independence in 1960. Since then, the former 'ruling parties' begrudgingly acceded to the majority of the people in the Congo from whom their progenitors took the property, the blacks. The remaining and subsequent multi-generational white families consider themselves Africans rather than Europeans. They are Africans but they are also white; hence the term, 'white Africans.'"

"There's a deep unrest and near total dislike between the two groups of Africans, the blacks and the whites; it seems to hang in the air, it's so prevalent," concluded Hanns.

"A few inter-racial families exist. They often side with the whites in any dispute. However, in virtually every situation, the governing families are all white. Hence, the historical animosities and unrest developed among the black majority who felt it was their place to govern their country," added Hanns. "The black majority appears in charge in nearly every new nation under development in Africa. The ruling white class is totally passé."

The two executives conversed over their *asado* for another hour with Hanns describing his basic ideas for entering the mining markets through "the front door" with the knowledge, perhaps even the financial assistance, of the Zairian government. At the same time, they would be entering "a back door" using rebels and some officials of selected countries that are at odds with the *République du Zaïre*, in not so safe and covert operations.

"Some of the tribes to the east and south are still fighting with the regime in Kinshasa," explained Hanns. "If we could fund them and manipulate them, to some extent, we might control the vast, outlying regions of the mining fields. These areas are too expansive for the national army to control and as I mentioned, corruption is rampant. Foreign mining companies are taking what they want at the expense of the Zairians and they hire their own protection forces. In addition, we've the black and white issues that we can use for our own purposes. That might make an excellent ruse for our operations. We might be able to have our own army, for the right price."

Diedrich noticed that his friend warmed to the concept of having his own, personal army in Africa. "Always a *wehrmacht* officer," Diedrich joked, netting a smile out of his friend.

"The next question," continued Hanns, "is getting the refined ore and semi-processed metal out of the country. There are brokers dealing in the secondary markets for these minerals."

"Did you still plan to stay with copper and cobalt," interjected Diedrich, "or have you changed your mind to branch out into other things, like gold and diamonds?"

"No, we should stay with copper and cobalt because we know how to handle them. In addition, we can use our work with the government as a cover for some of the other operations. I think some of the processed gold, which comes, as collateral in the refining, will pay for our cover at the various stages along the path. I can think of government oversight payments, rewarding smelter workers who slice just a small amount of the workings toward our needs, ensuring rebel protection rather than interference, paying truckers who take many risks and others who are all going to need some kind of payment. The collateral gold from the refining processes will satisfy a lot of greedy hands."

Hanns completed his thought by adding, "There's a copper and cobalt smelter in the city of Lumbashi about 1,600 kilometers from Kinshasa, at the southern end of the new republic. The Kafue River divides Zaire from Northern Rhodesia; another British colony that I think will declare its independence. I heard that they might call the new country Zambia.

"The river passes near the city and the smelter, which provides a good and adequate source of cheap water for the smelter. The river's a quiet piece of water that wanders through parts of Northern Rhodesia to the Zambezi River. I don't know how to organize it yet but if we gain control of the smelter operations, I'm certain that we can use the river to transport some of the refined metal out of Mobutu's jurisdiction and into the hands of the willing secondary or black market brokers. We might have to go north, upriver, rather than south; we'll have to see what is possible with river transport."

"So far, so good," commented Diedrich "but how do we sell the semi-refined metal?"

As Hanns spoke for the next hour, it appeared to Diedrich that Hanns already had a well-devised and in-depth plan of the operation, which he described at length.

Hanns concluded with, "We'll need armed guards, maybe even an army, to protect our work every step of the way. If we don't use the river, we'll get trucks from the neighboring countries, strike a deal with them, sell them the metal, pay them off with gold from the smelter, and let them sell the product as their own. We don't have to take the product to a far-flung market; we'll create a market for the partially processed metals in the countries fighting with Mobutu and the *République du Zaïre*."

Their after-dinner *coñac* arrived about the same time that Hanns finished describing his African project. Diedrich smiled and offered, "Well, my friend, you've been busy these last few months! Two questions remain for me: First, how much of an investment do we need in order to make this secondary market work? And second, who are we going to find to run the operation in Zaire?"

"Let's talk about these questions tomorrow." The smiling Hanns seemed pleased with himself and the operation he laid out for Diedrich that evening; notwithstanding, he was aware that there remained many uncertainties and problems that he could not anticipate.

Tomorrow

The unexpected scene of the CEO Hanns Krieg and laboratory president Doctor Diedrich Erhard from Santiago wrapped tightly in conversation seemed oddly out of place as the executive assistant for *el Presidente de DVS Technologies* opened the offices early the next morning.

Señora Nicolita Jaipa was an efficient middle-aged Argentine who worked for DVS Technologies from its first months in Mendoza. She enjoyed her association with the German founder of the company, although her work demanded longer hours than did the employment of other executive assistants whom she knew. Her husband of about twenty-five years died nearly five years earlier and since his death, her energies seemed narrowed toward creating a life of her job, frequently arriving at the executive offices well before most employees and at the same time as the early morning guard change.

Fluent in four languages, as was Hanns Krieg, she appreciated the adage he often quoted when he was less tense, *"Kaiser Karl das fünfte, seinem Gericht erzählte, 'Eine andere Sprache zu besitzen, soll eine andere Seele besitzen.'"*

The game they played was when he spoke in German; she often translated what he said in English or Spanish. The English translation of the adage was, "Charles the Fifth, told his royal court, 'To possess another language is to possess another soul.'"

She enjoyed speaking different languages with him and greeted him in her own way each day and in a different language each morning, so it did not surprise him when she greeted him this morning in English.

"Well," she began with a start, "you two appear to have been here all night!"

"*Buenos dias, Señora Jaipa*, no we've just begun but we have a lot of things to discuss. Please bring us *café* and be sure we're not interrupted this morning. *Gracias*," greeted Hanns in Spanish, mentally noting the English greeting of the person who kept much of his day-to-day activities properly focused.

As the morning session continued, Hanns and Diedrich worked out the method for getting their covert operations working in Zaire but failed to define a person to whom they could trust the operations' management. In the end, they decided to leave for Kinshasa within the month to find a few key people on whom they could rely, to set up the criteria for the quasi-fraudulent, even treacherous operations, and to finalize their African office in Zaire.

Diedrich started to wrap up the morning's discussions, "Hanns, as I see it, we need to fly to Zaire and meet with that fellow Mbandaka on whom you've relied in the past. Perhaps he can get us started with a few dependable people to manage the office."

"Unfortunately," observed Hanns, "he's in the side pocket of Mobutu and I don't think we can afford to put much stock in the fellow. Mobutu's moving to control as many private companies as he can get his hands on. I think the man's fast becoming a dictator but that's fine with us because we can use his power against him. Remember, whenever someone seizes vast land or resources from others and controls these as treasures for his own use, there will be people willing to find sinkholes into which the confiscator will step. Always, there are people whom, for a price, will cut a little off the edges, or will shave things a more closely than intended; it's where the excess goes from that cutting that often makes a difference for the one paying the price. We're going to provide that price."

As the meeting concluded and Diedrich was leaving the office, Hanns stopped at his executive assistant's desk to ask, "Nikki, will you book the good doctor and me on a flight to Dakar. Let's take LAN Chile leaving Santiago and stopping in Buenos Aires probably before the end of the month. Please make all the arrangements and let us know what you confirm so that I can contact Kinshasa to set up the meetings with the president."

"If we're going to Kinshasa, won't we need a flight from Dakar," asked Diedrich thinking that Hanns overlooked something.

"I think our new DVS plane and crew will be ready to pick us up in Dakar so that we won't need a commercial flight to Kinshasa," Hanns off-handedly announced to his associate.

Of course, Señora Jaipa already knew of the new aircraft, so she likewise enjoyed the subtlety of the conversation between the two Germans.

There appeared to be no question in either of the executive's minds, Hanns wanted to buy a plane and establish a flight crew in Kinshasa that would allow him greater freedom and access to other parts of the continent. However, Diedrich thought that a plane could wait, if other considerations took precedence. Certainly, profits from the many operations of DVS Technologies provided adequate money for Hanns to purchase more than one plane, if he wanted. It appeared that Hanns decided now was the time for a plane in Africa.

Virus Vector

Later that day, as Diedrich returned to his offices in Chile, he thought that he and Hanns completely overlooked the laboratory's work, so much in the forefront of their thinking was the African project: "I wonder what Hanns has in mind for our use of the laboratory's special section and my work?"

"Maybe, we can discuss it in Africa," he contemplated how such a conversation might proceed but accepted that Hanns was often in another space when engaged in a new project.

Soon the month's end arrived and with it their trip to Africa. Diedrich enjoyed the comforts of the first-class section of the aircraft during the long flight from Buenos Aires to Dakar in Senegal while Hanns, rather than relaxing, seemed preoccupied and somewhat anxious during the flight.

"What's the matter, Hanns?" asked Diedrich, noticing his friend's agitation. Are you nervous, or tired? You seem a little on edge."

"Nothing in particular. I just want this flight to be over—we've a lot to do in Zaire," replied Hanns.

"That fellow, Mbandaka, is meeting us in Kinshasa, right?"

Hanns, relaxed a little as he replied, "I think he'll be at the airport, but he may just send a representative and a car."

"I wish we had more decision-making power regarding selecting a manager for the office; I don't like the idea of a government-mandated business manager. I'm not sure how much we trust the information, rely on the business results, or even value the decisions made by the manager," Hanns observed to his traveling companion.

"Do you know much about the manager?" asked Diedrich.

"Only that he's educated in England—Oxford, class of 1972—speaks fluent English and several other languages; plus, the president picked him for the job. I suspect we'll have to be careful about how we discuss the business around him. I think his name is Ian Cedric Cherubin, or something similar."

"Almost angelic, in one sense," Diedrich seemed to add jokingly.

Hanns continued, "We got one concession from the government: they accepted our bid for management of the Lumbashi smelter. It'll be interesting to see how we can make that part of our plan fit together with minerals exploration that the Zairians want us to conduct on the high rift in the southeast of the country."

"Kinshasa didn't specify a manager for the smelter, did they?" asked Diedrich.

"Fortunately not; but, that means we have to select someone we can trust and who will manage the operations the way we want them to go."

As Diedrich reclined comfortably in the plane's oversized first-class seat, he thought, "I guess I'm as much to blame for not bringing up the new vector that we discovered as is Hanns for not asking. First thing to do when I get back is to set up a technician to work on the project. It's too bad we couldn't put the pieces together in the last experiment but that will come."

"Diedrich?" The question brought Diedrich back from his thoughts.

"Sorry, Hanns, I was just thinking."

"I've kept some contacts in Germany, some people that know ore smelting, but I've not talk about them." Hanns explained that his contacts helped him understand the market in Zaire.

"Makes sense, Hanns. Anybody you know that can help us in Lumbashi?"

"Maybe," Hanns's answer sounded distant and thoughtful.

"Perhaps, the manager can be someone living in the area, someone with credentials trusted by my associates," Hanns appeared to feel comfortable with his thought and the conversation died away into personal introspection.

"Strange he should bring the idea of keeping up with contacts in Germany," Diedrich mentioned to himself as he reflected, in silence, on a recent correspondence he received from a friend working in the Marburg research facility in Germany. The essence of the friend's information was that a strange new disease entity appeared recently from Africa, only infecting laboratory workers.

Unfortunately, there did not appear to be a precise etiology; possibly the imported green monkeys carried a virus because only workers who contacted the animals became infected.

The discussion between the two resumed, this time with Diedrich saying, "Hanns, I need to discuss the possibility of a new virus. Maybe—" but his thoughts drifted off as he turned to look out the window, the plane began its descent into Dakar's international airport, *Aéroport International de Dakar Yoff*, and he mumbled under his breath, "Africa? In all the years I've known Hanns, he's never failed to surprise me. Well, here's to another adventure!"

* * *

Despite all the planning and his carefully developed German logic, Diedrich did not anticipate the chance discoveries that awaited him in a humble Catholic mission hospital located in *Yambuku*, an obscure village located in a quietly remote part of the northern Zairian jungle. Belgian nuns, who maintained a medical facility at the nearly inaccessible location, treated the sick, administered to the injured, and consoled the troubled without much fanfare. Nevertheless, the mission hospital received financial and moral support from their headquarters in Kinshasa nine hundred kilometers to the southwest, as well as from sympathetic groups throughout the world, including a religious radio broadcast, which sent from a Lumbashi radio station, nightly wishes for the well-being of their "Sisters in the Congo."

In this remote jungle hospital setting, far removed from the rush of the world and from any influence of the DVS Technologies group of companies, the first recognition of a new and strangely lethal virus chanced to surface in 1976. The virus, as later discovered by Doctor Erhard and others, interfered with the inside coverings of blood vessel walls, that is, the cells of the endothelium, and with proper blood coagulation. The infection caused patients to simply, "bleed themselves into shock and death." The ex-Nazi scientist, *der Wissenschafter*, who had no compunction of conducting experimental tests on war prisoners with untried cancer-causing agents, also discovered that the newly encountered virus spread in a *günstig*, or convenient, fashion from patient to patient via bodily fluids, including tears.

As he later described to Hanns, "This discovery, made quite by chance during his trip upriver from Lumbashi, might prove the agent for which he and Hanns sought to elicit their revenge, an agent to strike down their enemies who caused the collapse of the Third Reich."

DVS Plane (Kinshasa Headquartered)

Hanns appeared to obsess about owning a plane or two, if possible, stationed in at a convenient location in Africa, just as other corporate officials often obsess about club memberships, stock options, expensive offices, and many other trivializations they seek as their minds dwell on self-importance or the self-aggrandizements purchased with an easy access to large amounts of money. More than likely, his experiences as an officer in the failed German bellum-state, his flight from harm's way before the war's conclusion, and his extensive political influences developed while establishing a widely recognized business success, inscribed on his character undesirable traits. He was arrogant, certainly self-centered, and easily distracted when pursuing personal pleasures. Hanns Krieg frequently felt that he arrived in his station in life with its many accompanying comforts, deservedly so because he alone was capable of accomplishing that which he did so well in his own eyes. There were few people, if any, who challenged his self-assessment.

The opposites in personality seen with Diedrich perhaps seemed odd in that both men shared similar backgrounds and successes. Nevertheless, Diedrich accepted life on different terms, did not expect others to recognize his work, and met each day as a new adventure.

Despite what some people might describe Hanns's outward traits as personality negatives, he was inwardly a fierce defender of German superiority, which drove him to limit the search for an aircraft to German production. Later he discovered that the founder of the Dutch aircraft manufacturer, Fokker, was an expatriate German. He found this aircraft much to his liking and suited for the challenges of Africa.

As the international flight from South America touched down in Senegal, an anxious group of executive-looking men compared notes and moved to meet the plane at its arrival gate. Immigration and Customs officers already cleared the DVS executives, without reviewing their documents, and waived procedures to permit this small clutch of European aviation executives to meet Hanns and Diedrich as they departed the plane. The rest of the passengers delayed briefly, until the two men deplaned and were securely with their welcoming party, rushed toward the immigration arrival desks without seeing the small group making formal introductions.

"My name is Hank de Bruyn from Amsterdam," a tall, healthy-looking man with a swirl of blond hair that looked as if it disliked control stepped forward and extended his hand.

Hanns knew the name and appeared to recognize the throaty sounding German spoken by the man. "Yes, Mr. de Bruyn, we spoke on the phone. You have something for us?"

"Please follow me. We'll go directly to the executive section of the airport; we have a car waiting just outside the doors," replied de Bruyn.

The turbo-prop Fokker was impressive at first sight. Sleek white exterior with outwardly non-descript identifying numbers and letters on the tail section.

"I see you followed my instructions regarding the tail numbers," observed Hanns as the car neared the plane. I've always been fond of the number '222' since my youth in Germany," Hanns offered the group. No one seemed to know the significance of the number except Diedrich, who recognized at once the führer's favorite sequence of numbers.

"Let's go onboard and meet your pilot, Mr. Krieg," invited the Dutch Fokker representative. "I'm sure you're going to enjoy the plane."

Once onboard and in the air, Hank de Bruyn transferred an exclusive-appearing leather-bound portfolio to Hanns Krieg. In it, the new owner found the purchasing paperwork, completed and certified earlier, in addition to the title. Hanns decided to purchase rather than the more common practice of leasing the aircraft, thereby satisfying his passion of ownership.

During the flight to Kinshasa, Hanns and Diedrich took turns sitting with the pilot, watching the functioning of the new plane. The pilot in perfect German explained his flight from Amsterdam, following the coastline down Spain, across the Gibraltar Straights, and directly into the Senegal airport. The pilot described the plane's characteristics, including the cabin pressurization that gave it an ability to fly at higher altitudes. Its smaller size, up to eight or nine passengers plus two crewmembers, gave the plane wider flexibility of runways for takeoff and landing. By the time the plane touched down in the *République du Zaïre*, the new owners were seemingly electrified with their new corporate asset.

Ian, the Angel

The new Fokker turbo-prop touched down at the Kinshasa airport and taxied to a separate section of the airfield where three black Mercedes touring cars waited. From one of the plane's portholes, Hanns could see one man standing at the driver's side of each car and another man waiting near the last car of the three. He thought he could just make out the shapes of several other men seated inside two of the cars.

The pilot eased the plane to within a few feet of the parked cars. After closing down the engines, he opened the door and let down the stairs to the tarmac. Hanns, with Diedrich following a few steps behind, descended the stairway and stepped forward to meet their new manager for operations in Zaire.

After leaving the plane, Hanns took a little time to offer instructions to de Bruyn. He had enough time to reserve an appointment the following day to meet with the Dutchman and the pilot for additional debriefing regarding the new plane. Thereafter, neither

Hanns nor Diedrich paid any attention to the departure of the Dutch aircraft officials who, after departing the plane, slipped quietly into the terminal.

"Mister Krieg, Doctor Erhard," a smiling man about thirty-five years old dressed in a taupe-colored hunter's jacket and matching slacks addressed them, "I'm Ian Cherubin. Welcome to Kinshasa." The man's welcome appeared genuine and carried with it the nasally British overtones, which foreign students frequently learn in becoming the *highly educated* while studying at Oxford.

"We'll take you to the hotel and decide our plans for the rest of the week. President Mobutu sends his best and hopes your visit will be successful," offered Cherubin. "Joseph Mbandaka will join us with the president when we meet tomorrow," he added matter-of-factly.

"The president waived all immigration and customs requirements for you, so we can leave as soon as you're ready," Ian Cherubin announced with a smile.

"Please call me Ian," the man's apparent good organization becoming evident as the group entered the cars and sped from the airport.

Hanns noted that one car with three well-built men proceeded the car he, Diedrich, and Ian took while another of the waiting cars followed with another three men. Everything moved so smoothly and quickly that Hanns could not detect if the men carried weapons.

As the motorcade slipped quickly through the wide avenues of modern Kinshasa toward the hotel, Hanns thought that it had been some time since he experienced such a level of security and wondered if the precautions portended difficulty in the future.

CHAPTER SEVEN
Return to Africa

The African Business

Ian Cherubin proved pleasingly well informed about the needs of the DVS Technologies mining company in Zaire; on the other hand, his intelligence gathering lacked considerably concerning the personal aspirations of the company's executives from South America. Had he fully understood their intentions for wealth accumulation, at the expense of the African mining opportunities, he and Joseph Mbandaka might have been more circumspect about their handling of the contracts.

Another change might have affected their contacts in Zaire; Joseph Mbandaka now carried the more prestigious title of minister. He dropped the former responsibilities as director of Internal Resources and now assumed the position of minister of Commerce and Trade. Despite his new role, neither Joseph Mbandaka nor Ian realized that Hanns and Diedrich sought a manager for the smelter operations who "could cut the truth just a little more thinly" than the next person and thereby under-report, misappropriate, or redirect certain processed minerals for the DVS executives.

Nonetheless, meetings with government officials proceeded the day following their arrival in Kinshasa and considered by Hanns to be mercifully uneventful. Hanns anticipated increased and substantial demands from the Zairian president and his ministers; surprisingly, there were no new annoyances placed on his company.

Hanns, when finally alone at the end of the day, breathed a little more easily as he realized the scrutiny he expected was less than severe.

For the present, he and Diedrich felt comfortable with Ian as the DVS African Business Manager. Additionally, nearly all of the needed personnel, office requirements, and official documents were virtually complete and waiting for their approval signatures.

The sole remaining point in concluding the agreement with the government was establishing a management team for the smelter. Ian, sensing some hesitancy in Hanns, offered several suggestions for selecting a manager, finally recommending the current operations chief of the Lumbashi facility. He felt that a meeting with the manger in Lumbashi would convince Hanns of the correctness in his recommendation and suggested that the three men, Hanns, Diedrich, and he, travel south to visit the facilities.

"Certainly, your new plane will make the journey so much easier," he concluded.

The German executives wanted some time to assess the facilities, without government oversight. While not expressing his feelings directly, Hanns preferred making his own decisions regarding management and finally commented, "Ian, I want you to make the needed arrangements for our visit to Lumbashi. Diedrich and I would like to visit the area, alone."

"Perhaps, you feel like being pioneers," Ian joked. "I'm not sure it's safe for you to be alone in that part of the country."

To Hanns, the negative comment concerning their safety seemed contrived, perhaps a little too convenient.

"Then again, Ian, I'm sure you can work some magic for us," replied Hanns who did not flinch at the seemingly manufactured warning of danger.

Finally, Ian's office made the necessary arrangements with government and business officials so that they scheduled a trip, alone, south to the Lumbashi smelter the following week. During the interim few days, Ian became a most knowledgeable tour guide for the two mining executives as they sampled the sights and sounds of Kinshasa. They were fortunate to receive several recommendations for some relaxation; although, some of the ideas required more time than they were willing to commit for sightseeing. For example, when the group met with President Mobutu, he encouraged them to enjoy *Kin la Belle*, or the Beautiful Kinshasa, while they were in the city, and then suggested that they include a river trip up *le Fleuve de Zaïre*, perhaps more widely known as the Congo River or the Zaire River.

"I know you may not have time to visit the interior of our great nation, but if you were to travel upriver, maybe ten or twelve days to Bumba, you would find the small village Lisala. In that village, near where a large libanga tree now grows, is my birthplace," the president told them, obviously proud of his humble birth and heritage.

"I'm not sure," interjected Diedrich, always the curious scientist, "what is a libanga tree?"

The Africans in the room all used a hand to cover their mouths as they smiled at the question; they did not want to embarrass the foreign guests.

"The African tree is quite humorous looking," offered Joseph Mbandaka, as he explained that a libanga tree is a tree that looks as if it is growing upside down, with a very large broad trunk and stringy branches that resemble roots coming from the top of the trunk.

"An upside down tree! Now that would be a sight," commented Diedrich.

Minister Mbandaka suggested that if they had time, that Hanns and Diedrich also include a side trip to his hometown and origin of his family name.

"Travel upriver along the Zaire, or as you may know it, the Congo River; it is adventurous but quite safe," Joseph Mbandaka offered.

"Well, traveling on the Zaire River sounds exciting, and we would like to visit both places, I don't think we have the time to make the trip to Lisala. But how far is it to Mbandaka?" questioned Hanns.

As the minister realized that even in good weather the nearly six hundred-kilometer, one-way river trip would require at least a week, he suggested the trip might be better at another time. Hanns agreed that even a six- to ten-day trip would be too much time taken away from the business necessities and they tabled the thought for another time.

Tory in Lumbashi

After the few days spent as tourists, the impatient Hanns and the always-curious Diedrich were ready to continue their business by getting on to Lumbashi. The flight was particularly satisfying in the new company plane. They were, as they commented, "comfortably alone and to ourselves." While they were aboard the plane, their worries seemed remote that someone might hear their plans, so they spoke freely with one another about future encounters in Lumbashi.

After a few hours in the air, the plane touched down on the paved runway in the former city of Élisabethville, now renamed Lumbashi, in southern Zaire. Unlike their arrival in Kinshasa, no one greeted the plane, no group of black Mercedes cars waited next to the small building that served as an airport office and terminal.

Ian's office made reservations at one of the excellent hotels in the city; the taxi driver found it with no difficulty. The activity of Kinshasa was many-fold greater than here in the, "slumbering part of the mid-continent Africa," as Diedrich observed.

"I wonder if we can get a good cup of *kaffee* here in Lumbashi," Hanns thought aloud.

The hotel concierge recommended, within a short walking distance from the hotel, an espresso bar, which the two executives decided to visit for their afternoon coffee.

Thinking they were somewhat safe by speaking German, they were less cautious, in the espresso bar, than normal while discussing plans for the smelter. As they spoke freely of their plans, a man at the next table apparently listened with a rather acute sense of understanding. Hanns, ever aware of his surroundings, motioned to

Diedrich to stop their conversation and to be mindful that someone listened to them.

The man inched his chair away from the table where he sat and stood to face the two Germans sitting at the next table. They were now fully cognizant that the man overheard them and that they were the subject of the man's attention. He was black, most likely African who dressed in western clothing. He wore a less-than-crisp off-white tropical three-piece suit, white shirt, and dark-colored tie.

Both the Germans recognized that the man was about to speak but the sounds he spoke were unusually familiar to Hanns and Diedrich, yet unique to be hearing in a remote café in the southernmost major city in Zaire.

He carefully pronounced his words, clearly, and in excellent German, "*Herren, ich belauschte Sie, Deutsch sprechend. Sind Sie von Deutschland?*"

"*Ja, Ja, aber wir kennen Sie nicht, und wie Sie kommen, um unsere Sprache zu sprechen!*" Hanns replied curtly and with a former but still powerful military bearing. He questioned the man's presumption that they were German, reiterated that they did not know him, and demanded to know how he presumed speaking to them in German.

With Hanns's reply, the African stepped back slightly and flinched abruptly, but knowingly; he was in the presence of the superior ranking German officer.

"I apologize," he continued in flawless German, "I didn't intend to listen to your conversation, but when I heard you speaking German in this remote African city, I thought I could introduce myself and perhaps be of assistance to two gentlemen in this foreign land."

"My name is Ettore Taharqa, but people call me Tory, as a nickname, it's shorter and easier for some. If you like, you may call me Tory."

Again, Hanns rejoined the strange man, casting aside any excuses for the man's imprudence and incivility. Hanns now captured his full attention:

"How did you come to learn German?"

"Who are you?"

"Why did you interrupt our conversation?"

The questions, delivered with machine-gun rapidity, riveted the attention of the man standing in front of them.

Gathering an unruffled sense of his importance, Tory incorrectly assumed that he was finally welcomed, drew up his chair to the table, and then joined the seated duo without a moment's pause. It seemed so normal for him to address the strangers in his midst as friends or casual business acquaintances. However, on the other side of the table, the Germans immediately appeared to gather within themselves physically and with increased alertness, listened to the strange man.

"First, I learned German while I served with the *Afrikakorps* in the North African campaign against the Allies until May 1943," began Tory with renewed energy.

"The unfortunate surrender of the *Afrikakorps* caused me to resume my former life and the desert absorbed another nomad, as is often said in the Fezzan. Since that time I've enjoyed the many adventures of the ever-changing political landscape in Africa."

Hanns interjected several questions about Rommel in North Africa to see if the man was credible about his report of serving with the German army. Still suspicious, but to some extent satisfied with the answers received, he permitted Tory to continue.

"As I explained, I interrupted your conversation to offer my services and talents. I've many friends in this region, and I know much about the geography between here and the Mediterranean. Perhaps, that's why the German officers trusted my advice; oh, but that's such a long time ago."

Tory began to relax and sat back in the chair he brought with him to the table where the Germans sat. "Let me explain who I am," now resting one elbow on the table.

Tory explained his origins while the two Germans listened, appearing vaguely interested. Neither time nor experience away from *das Vaterland* removed the well-exercised and self-assumed sentiment of German superiority from Hanns and Diedrich.

"You may not have heard of my people. We are the *Imajaghan*, the free people of the Saharan Desert. For centuries, we've roamed the sands of northern Africa, at peace with ourselves and with all who permit us to live free," Tory seemed slightly less extravagant to the two Germans with his descriptions than they would have described themselves in similar circumstances. Nevertheless, they were impressed that he appeared to enjoy speaking rather good German, which he claimed to have learned while serving in Rommel's tank corps.

"We're called the Tuareg," continued Tory, "which comes from a Berber name for the area of our ancestors' home. In reality, the Tuareg people assumed that Berber name for the region; however, the Fezzan or Tuareg ancestral area, much of which now exists in the southwestern part of Libya, once encompassed larger parts of the southern and northern Sahara Desert."

Tory continued, "Many Tuareg resist the constraints of the countries that try to control our freedoms; even as we speak, some Tuareg still fight in the mountains of *Adrar N'fughas* against the new government of Mali. The Tuareg are fierce fighters. Some of us, mostly the *Imajaghan*, joined with the Germans and Italians during the Second World War in fighting against the Allies in the desert," this statement further whetted the interest of both Hanns and Diedrich in this strange man who virtually forced his way on them in the café.

"You have our interest, Tory. Tell us, who are the *Imajaghan* and why they were so anxious to fight against the Allies?" Hanns asked.

"We *Imajaghan* are of the noble class and are from a long heritage of warrior-aristocrats who organize clan defenses, lead raids on other tribes, and supervise many of the longer caravans through the desert. The *Imajaghan* are above the daily rituals performed by others. We do not serve; we are the served. The Third Reich understood the *Imajaghan* and sought our help in the desert. The Allies sought no advice from the Tuareg who know the most about the shifting sands, the dry river valleys, remote oases, and barren mountains of the Fezzan; so we offered no advice."

Hanns began to understand the aristocratic nature of the strange man who sat before them, even as one comparable spirit frequently recognizes another. Not unlike Tory, Hanns felt that many in Berlin did not recognize the value Hanns offered to the Third Reich, which forced him to leave before the war's end and ultimate victory achieved. Nevertheless, he did not know the person before him and experience taught him to distrust the unknown.

The Smelter

"We've not a lot of time," Hanns drew on years of experience handling subordinates and instructed the new, impudent person who sat in front of him in this strange place, "for history lessons."

"No, I suppose you don't. On the other hand, you are interested in the management at the smelter. Am I correct?" countered Tory, also unwilling to assume a subordinate role in the new relationship.

"Tell me what you know of that subject," Hanns demanded, now somewhat concerned that the man may have heard more of their plans than intended. He questioned internally what threat this desert Tuareg posed to their plans.

"Not to worry, my friends," smiled Tory. "A very close friend of mine is a manager at the smelter and I'm sure he will be extremely interested in talking with you."

"We have our introductions!" replied Hanns firmly.

"Yes, I understand—they're likely very formally placed and all from Kinshasa—is that correct? Of course, we all know of the efficiencies of the president's office in Kinshasa—but, my friends, do the introductions also include getting you to the right person who 'can cut the truth just a little more thinly?'" asked Tory, still smiling and full of a self-knowledge sitting at the tip of his tongue, waiting to get out.

"If you like, I'll make the arrangements for you to meet with my friend from the smelter," offered Tory with an understanding nod of his head.

Now, Hanns and Diedrich realized their dilemma, they were not cautious in discussing their business in a public place, especially in a foreign country. A protective shell, perhaps unused for some years, now encased the two executives, as they looked to each other for answers. Almost by instinct, Hanns felt for his revolver, but it was in his baggage at the hotel. Their determination expressed itself on their faces, as they hardened their external appearances.

Tory recognized the signs: he pushed the Germans too fast and presumed too much. His knowledge of their language would not carry him through his mistakes at this initial chance meeting and he needed to fall back to a more neutral line of reasoning.

"My friends, please, understand—I'm just a casual observer of your purposes here in Africa. I happen to understand German, I overheard, quite by accident, your conversation and I presumed too much. Please excuse my clumsiness. I only thought that I could assist you—you appeared to be somewhat worried about the decision you face at the smelter. I have friends and associates in many places and I thought I could be of assistance to you," apologized Tory.

"Tory, you presume too much by trying to understand our needs!" Hanns rejoined in acutely formal German.

"Never presume to know more than your superiors," warned Diedrich. Tory noticed Hanns's nod to affirm his approval of the warning.

"Nevertheless, we might have some interest in meeting your friend," continued Hanns with an apparent distraction that was more feigned than real.

Diedrich added, "But then, how would we know that he could manage a difficult operation such as a smelter? And most importantly, why would we be interested in such a chance encounter?"

"Permit me to arrange a dinner this evening—my friend will join us and explain his experience," Tory offered, "a dinner in a quiet place with no listening ears. Kinshasa has far too many ears in Lumbashi!"

Diedrich and Hanns looked to each other for support. Finally a guarded Diedrich offered, "Nothing ventured—nothing gained."

"Very well—we'll meet you and your friend this evening," agreed Hanns, sensing no real alternative to their dilemma.

"But you realize that we do *not* trust you!" Even the emphasis on the word "not" in another warning from Hanns seemed deflected by a broad smile on the face of Tory.

Tory left the café and the two Germans discussed the strange turn of events. Diedrich was first to offer something positive about the chance encounter.

"Hanns, we know that Kinshasa has many eyes and ears that watch and listen, even here in Lumbashi. Let's meet with these two Africans this evening; it won't be difficult to assess our good luck, or on the other hand, of finding someone in the plant that might create havoc—" Diedrich did not finish his thought as Hanns interjected a possible conclusion.

"Our fallback position is the manager suggested by Ian. The upside outcome of this chance meeting: we find someone to manage the smelter and to follow our directions—well, this will be in our back pocket when we meet at the smelter tomorrow morning."

* * *

Location of dinner was not as Hanns and Diedrich expected but rather in a quaint village some kilometers east of the city. The restaurant, loosely described as such in the mind of Hanns, was in surroundings that were little more than a few tables adjoining an outdoor kitchen, within a simple fenced yard. There was no floor, just hard-packed red dirt worn smooth by many feet that sufficed as a floor surface in the eating area.

As Diedrich and Hanns arrived, the two waiting Africans rose from their evening *kahawa* to greet them. Tory suggested they join them with cups of *kahawa*.

"This is a traditional form of coffee in this part of Africa. For *kahawa*, we boil freshly ground coffee beans in water with whole and ground cardamom seeds and, of course, ground ginger," explained Tory, continuing to speak in German.

"Cardamom is a rather expensive spice, harvested locally from a low-growing plant, and is somewhat similar to ginger spice. It gives our coffee a distinctive taste," Tory explained, carefully not presuming to suggest that the Germans would enjoy the flavor.

"This is my friend from the smelter," explained Tory, beginning his introductions in English. "He's known as George Browne, but his given name is Jorge Hhâlé. Many foreigners find the English version of his name easier so he uses it most of the time."

"The owner of this restaurant is a friend of mine, so I asked him to close for the evening to give us more privacy," Tory explained as he looked around and gestured with a sweeping arm to reassure the Germans of all the empty tables.

Diedrich spoke first for the two visiting Germans and continued in English, as used by Tory.

"We're happy to be here this evening and to meet with you, George. Let's have a seat and you can tell us about yourself. We know little about Tory, other than the extensive history lesson we received about the Tuareg. What's your background, and why are you interested in working with us as manager of the smelter?"

The group sat at a table in the center of the eating area and almost immediately began earnest dialogue.

Options

George Browne was a well-worked man, accustomed to physical labor. He spoke English reasonably well, with a French accent, but his outward appearance betrayed the depth of knowledge he conveyed to the visiting Germans as he spoke during the evening. It was apparent to Hanns and to Diedrich that the man was extremely proficient in his work at the smelter, which became substantially more obvious as he passed all the tests they gave him. It appeared that, quite by chance, they might have found the expert they sought for the smelter.

The issues in staffing the smelter were significant: foremost was obtaining the approvals of Ian Cherubin and the Kinshasa offices of Joseph Mbandaka. While George might well serve the DVS purposes, the hurdles in Kinshasa appeared most challenging.

As large platters of *coupé-coupé* arrived, the group's discussion reached an intense point—intense from the point of circuitously discussing how the new manager might divert trace minerals, such as gold, from the main shipments of copper and cobalt.

Changing the direction of the discussions, Tory suggested, "Let me explain what we have here is the traditional Central African *rôtir au gril* or *faire griller de la viande au barbecue*. In South Africa, they have something similar but here we marinate the meat in a special aroma sauce and cayenne pepper for several hours; then, very slowly cook the meat over an open wood fire or charcoal fire. We call this *coupé-coupé*, which simply means—"

"Isn't that from French meaning to cut?" interjected Diedrich. "But why is the word repeated?"

"We often repeat words or syllables in the languages used here in the countries south of the Sahara Desert," George explained, entering into the discussion.

"No particular reason, I guess, but it just sounds better," added Tory.

The discussion resumed about the smelter as the group began their meal by layering baguettes with the meat and smothering the sandwiches with *pili-pili*, an all-purpose African hot sauce.

George was first to speak about moving the processed ores out of the smelter, "Transportation out of Lumbashi is limited. We generally use the railroad west of the city but parts of that railway are in bad shape."

"The roads outside Lumbashi are virtually non-existent," added Tory. "Most freight and passengers use the rivers or travel by plane."

Diedrich asked, "For higher value-to-weight metals, could we use air transportation or would it make more sense to stay on the ground?"

"Yes, yes, either way, but we need to get the refined metals from here to markets outside of Africa," Hanns's presence now took more control of the situation with a simple statement. "I doubt changes in the present system of transportation seem wise!"

George spent the next half hour explaining how the current system uses the Katanga railway line as far as the Kamina Junction where "we transfer the freight to barges at Ilebo for a river trip to Kinshasa."

"For us, it's no problem," concluded George, as he explained the river barges and the long delays at Kamina because of the very sporadic service schedule. "You see, freight collects at the port until there is enough to fill a barge; only then is the trip to Kinshasa started."

"Too inefficient," interjected Hanns. "We can do better."

"Perhaps," observed George.

George picked up again with his descriptions of the shipping practices with the freight offloaded from the river barges at Kinshasa.

"We can't continue on the river because of the Livingstone Falls so we load the minerals on another railway, the Mitada-Kinshasa Railway, for the final leg to the port at Mitada and shipment to markets aboard ocean-going freighters. The length of time from the smelter to the markets is exceptionally long, but we don't mind the length of time it requires."

"Why not?" asked Hanns.

"The president tells us not to worry about the cost, so we don't. We're helping the country to grow, he says."

Diedrich asked if the smelter seals the cargo containers before they leave Lumbashi and if they remain sealed until they reach Mitada. "It seems too valuable a cargo not to be sealed."

"We try to protect the cargo, bills of lading, weights, measures, and all but there are always adjustments to the paperwork when Kinshasa reviews receipts," replied George. "They expect some slippage in the numbers."

At this time in the conversation, Hanns had enough; he was tired from traveling, eaten sufficient *coupé-coupé*, and found the present company beginning to be slightly tedious. His Germanic disposition, perhaps coupled with years of independence conducting highly stressful mining operations in South America, now left him little patience for what he considered *arbeiten Sie am besten behandelt von Juniorbetriebsleitern*; in other words, it is work best handled by junior managers.

As he listened, his thoughts seemed to displace him, and he missed the first phrases of Diedrich's question.

"—Hanns, Hanns, do you think we can make a decision?"

Still thinking in German, Hanns replied in his native tongue, directly to Diedrich, that he did not hear the question.

George, not understanding any German, wondered silently, as he looked to the other African and appeared to question what happened.

"I asked you if you thought we could make a decision; we still have to meet at the smelter tomorrow and review the qualifications of the current management. What do you think we should do?" asked Diedrich in English of Hanns.

"Let's thank our host and guest for a most pleasant evening," Hanns regrouped and reentered the present. "We've a lot to think about and can better do our work with a good night's rest."

The Germans agreed to contact Tory after their visit with the managers at the smelter; in any event, any decision they made still passed by the offices of the minister of Commerce and Trade in Kinshasa, not necessarily for formal approval but an approval nevertheless.

* * *

The following morning, Hanns and Diedrich began to review the smelter operations with the current management team, as expected and outlined by Kinshasa. The inspection was time-consuming and cumbersome but anticipated to be that way; mining engineers and industry executives revel in details. Nothing during their visit suggested concern with the operations, shipping, or values derived from the smelter. The work appeared on par with smelters processing copper sulfide ores, which ores were similar to those mined in the Katanga region of Zaire.

The inspections required several days of meetings with the smelter officials but during that time, neither Hanns nor Diedrich detected any weak link in the connection with Kinshasa that they could exploit. The managers were completely compliant with the directions given them by ministers of the government-mining operations.

As they brought to a close the inspections in Lumbashi, Hanns and Diedrich sat in the espresso bar they had come to frequent, the one where they first met Tory.

"Hanns," began Diedrich, "this is a big undertaking!"

"About normal," Hanns replied. There was obviousness in Diedrich's lack of experience for these types of situations that seemed apparent to Hanns; Diedrich's expertise lay elsewhere, and with other affairs.

"Where are you in your decision to select a manager for the smelter; perhaps, one that can be controlled a little more directly by our wants rather than by Ian in Kinshasa?" Diedrich continued his thinking aloud.

"I'm not sure but I think we can influence the current management team, maybe a little more in their pay, on the side. Don't the people of Zaire call that *pots-de-vin*, or what we call *schmiergeld*?" suggested Hanns.

"Perhaps—what do you think we should do about George and Tory?"

"I think Tory is simply after *schmiergeld* or any other money he can get. He has one person on his mind—Tory! And as for George, we've not committed ourselves; he'll have to take care of himself with the current management," concluded Hanns.

The two sat for a few moments in silence. Finally, Diedrich began, "You know what I want to do while here in Zaire?"

"Tell me."

"There are a group of missionary nuns; I think part of the Salesian Order, which operates a dispensary and clinic in a remote valley in the north. I heard from one of my associates in Marburg that these medical missionaries inadvertently might have discovered a strange virus."

"Did your contact tell you something new or was this just another imagined finding in the laboratory?"

"Hanns!" Diedrich feigned injury to his scientific reputation.

"I think I would like to visit the clinic and talk with lab personnel, especially the nurses and doctors who are handling the patients infected with this new virus."

"Why?" asked Hanns.

"If the information is accurate, I believe we may have our tool for bringing the Allies, starting with the Americans, the vengeance we've sought for so many years."

"Where is this clinic of yours?"

"It's in a valley along a river; I think it's called the Ebola River. I'm not sure, but I think the mission is about a thousand kilometers from Kinshasa in the Yambuku village. The best way to get there is to fly into Bumba and take a Land Rover about two hundred kilometers north."

"Diedrich, are you crazy?"

"Well—maybe—but we're here—and we have a plane. You can land in Bumba on your way to Kinshasa. I'll find a way to get to the village."

"This is a bad idea, Diedrich. Think about it: traveling uncharted roads in the Congo, even if they now call the country something differently! I don't think you should go to some remote village in the jungle looking for an unknown virus that you heard about from a friend in Germany!" Hanns sounded emphatic in his feelings.

"Well, if we're not going to use Tory for the smelter connection and he's as good with all things Africa as he claims, why not take him with me and let him be my guide?" suggested Diedrich, half justifying his decision, but maybe only in his own mind.

"That's even crazier. We don't know anything about the man—a preternatural *Tuareg* from the desert who claimed to once guide the *Afrikakorps*—that really sounds farfetched," Hanns appeared genuinely concerned for his friend.

Diedrich happened to glance toward the door and caught sight of Tory entering the espresso bar. He turned to Hanns and whispered, "Hanns—look, our new friend just walked in."

Without waiting for an invitation, Tory walked directly to their table and motioned as if to ask if he could join them, then sat down.

"Typical Tory," thought Hanns.

"Well, gentlemen, how have the inspections at the smelter progressed? I heard from George that you've been very thorough."

"I think we're pretty much complete here in Lumbashi," replied Hanns. "We can fly back in the day or two."

With a quick glance toward Hanns, Diedrich asked the African in front of them, "Tell me what you know of the Ebola River valley. Have you been in the area?"

"Well, there's a Catholic mission medical clinic operating in one of the villages that receives evening radio broadcasts from here in Lumbashi. I think some people feel the sisters need encouragement. But, I've never been there," replied Tory. "What's your interest in that part of Zaire?"

"I thought I might like to visit the mission and clinic—I don't think I told you that I'm a pathologist by training and practice," answered Diedrich. "I heard that they may have discovered a new viral agent at the clinic and I would like to see what they have for myself," concluded Diedrich with another quick smile toward Hanns.

Tory looked judiciously at the two Germans.

"People don't just travel around the interior parts of the republic without a guide; at least without someone who can offer some protection, who knows the ways of the people, someone who speaks Bantu, and understands a few of the many, many dialects we have in the country."

He waited for a response that never came.

Finally, Diedrich spoke, "You speak Bantu and know your way around the new republic. At least, that's what you told us. How much money would it take for you to serve as a guide for me in that northern section of Zaire?"

"How would we get there?"

"Did you forget about our plane," observed Hanns. "Diedrich tells me we can land in Bumba and from there you'll need a guide and a car to go cross country to the mission."

"What about the smelter and George?" Tory appeared to falter ever so slightly in his confident demeanor.

"I think it's better that you let us worry about our business," Hanns with his well-practiced curtness instructed the man, further increasing Tory's growing uneasiness. Tory remembered their first encounter in the espresso bar and felt certain that the Germans mistrusted him and his judgment. He wondered if the trip was a ruse to remove him from revealing the DVS plans for the smelter and for diverting some of its unreported production. He did not fear the jungle, the people of Zaire, or even the rebels still fighting in many parts of the country, but he was unsure if he trusted the two Germans that he suspected were war fugitives, even runaway Nazi officers.

"Are you ready for a trip upriver?" pressed Diedrich, bringing Tory out of his thoughts and back to the conversation.

"When?"

"We'll leave in the morning, day after tomorrow. Meet us at the airport after breakfast. The plane can deliver you and Diedrich in Bumba before noon and the two of you can organize the rest of your trip from there," concluded Hanns with a definite finality, a German characteristic around which the Tuareg never felt comfortable, even when serving in the German tank corps. It remained something unique and quite non-African.

With a shrug of his shoulders and a simple nod of his head, Tory rose from his chair and left.

When the enigmatic Tuareg from northern Africa was out of earshot, Diedrich turned to Hanns and asked, "Do you think he'll come to the airport?"

"Your trip to Yambuku might be more than just a little troublesome without him," said Hanns.

"I hope you realize how dangerous your idea sounds to me," Hanns added, expressing a seldom seen emotion. "In the meantime, I want to do some thinking—maybe a drive to look at the border with Zambia—," he did not finish his thought before trailing off. Diedrich recognized the signs; he knew them from earlier experiences. Hanns required time alone and he simply nodded agreement with the suggestion that Hanns take time to be alone for a day—or more. They would have time for talking.

CHAPTER EIGHT
Diedrich's Discovery

The village of Yambuku is in Mongala District of the Republic of Zaire, in the midst of a dense Zairian rain forest, in the tranquil Ebola Valley, approximately eleven hundred kilometers northeast of Kinshasa. The closest city, larger than any of the nearby villages, is Bumba, about hundred and sixty kilometers to the south. Transportation from Bumba into and out of the small Yambuku village generally is overland along frequently impassable roads. The fortunate visitors come by Land Rover or other four-wheel vehicles capable of negotiating the unimproved red-clay tracks that serve as roads into this remote part of Zaire. However, most Africans entering the Ebola Valley walk, ride bicycles, or use flat-bottomed boats to navigate the rivers and waterways that wind throughout the jungle.

At Bumba, the Zaire River widens to its broadest point, nearly twenty kilometers from one bank to the other. Here, also, river hyacinths and small islands disrupt a view of the spectacularly wide expanse of water. Continuing to travel farther on the river towards the western borders of Zaire, about a hundred and twenty kilometers west of Bumba, a traveler arrives in a port at the village of Lisala. It is here that officials in Kinshasa suggested Hanns and Diedrich visit, to observe the commemorative libanga tree, and to explore the "humble" origins of President Joseph Mobutu.

Diedrich's Trip

Several years after the end of the Second World War, Diedrich and Hanns renewed contacts with selected professional associates in

Germany, those who knew of their background and respected their participation in the war. Before making these contacts, both expatriates carefully concealed, from everyone, their full identities, and the more objectionable facets of their military service. For many years after the fall of the Third Reich, they severed all connections that might attract attention to their background and their true purposes in escaping Germany before the collapse of the Reich. Even so, their animosities toward those who brought about the failed Nazi culture continued, intensifying gradually as they perceived growing inability to avenge the injustice dealt them. Therefore, Hanns showed no surprise when Diedrich told him that through his contacts at a German laboratory in Marburg, he thought that he might have found the route for their revenge.

The informant at the Marburg laboratory, which laboratory produced viruses for commercial use, told Diedrich that a few employees accidently contracted a new strain of virus and died after experiencing a most painful series of symptoms. The infected laboratory workers suffered red skin rashes, lost fingernails and toenails, and lost body hair. These symptoms often combined with bleeding from the nose, gums, and bowels together with vomiting blood, confusion, and coma before death.

All laboratory employees who contracted the virus apparently worked with green monkeys from the central African nation of Uganda. The medical professionals at the laboratory were at a loss to explain the etiology of the new disease other than the common thread of working with the monkeys. Doctors treated patients by isolating them and trying to make the patients more comfortable. They described the disease as a viral hemorrhagic fever.

Diedrich's passion for studying viruses that caused disruption of blood clotting mechanisms in the linings of the blood vessels began during his university training in Poland and grew dramatically following his work with war prisoners. The new information whetted Diedrich's pathologist appetites; he felt that if he could obtain samples of the Marburg virus that he could produce a weapon for the revenge he and Hanns long sought. Unfortunately, he had not been able to have samples delivered to his laboratory in Santiago.

It amazed Diedrich that he read of no more outbreaks of the strange hemorrhagic fever; then, several years later, rumors of a comparable disease surfaced. The rumors described similar patient symptoms as were in the Marburg reports but the outbreak was at a clinic in the middle of a remote village in Zaire. Many villagers came to the clinic with symptoms of hemorrhagic fever, more patients than were seen at the laboratory in Germany. The reports described villagers, sick with a completely debilitating disease that appeared to spread rapidly from one person to another, a disease that produced high fevers, bleeding from body pores and openings, and painful death in almost all cases.

When a few nurses at the clinic contracted the sickness, and neither the physicians nor the laboratory technicians could identify the mode of transmission, the Belgian officials threatened the clinic's closure, and, perhaps more significantly, to withdraw all medical personnel.

"They'd seen nothing like it," Diedrich told Hanns as they discussed the reasons for Diedrich's planned trip into the jungle.

"Unfortunately for the Africans, their sickness spreads from person-to-person. Anybody in contact with the bodily fluids of a sick patient is more than likely to contract the disease. Also, it moves very quickly and is almost always fatal." Apparently, Diedrich knew more concerning the virus and its behaviors than Hanns anticipated.

"It appears to me to be the same thing reported in Marburg, but I can't be sure until I see some of the patients and talk with the medical professionals in the clinic. My Marburg contact's descriptions were very specific concerning the disease, what they called hemorrhagic fever. If I can get samples of virus, perhaps from the blood of patients, talk with nurses about sickness, make some comparisons, and work on it at our Santiago laboratory—" Diedrich's voiced trailed off a little but his enthusiasm for the project was nearly palatable as Hanns watched and listened to him describe the project.

"Diedrich, how do you plan to get the samples through customs—here in Africa and in Chile? I don't think the health officials will allow you to carry medical samples in refrigerated containers even with a complete explanation," Hanns sounded particularly knowledgeable with his argument about transporting a virulent agent or even blood samples.

"On one hand, I could simply not reveal what I have," replied Diedrich, firmly convinced that he could smuggle the samples back to his laboratory.

"Maybe you can get through the customs agents without problems, but how do you propose to handle the heat? Don't those things need to be cold?" Hanns asked, sounding somewhat informed concerning one of the essential aspects required in transporting some biological samples.

"Frozen, actually. However, I'm not sure what I'll find. Blood, even plasma, and some live virus are not very transportable without deep refrigeration or freezing. I'll see what facilities the technicians have in the clinic laboratory; perhaps, I can use their equipment to reduce the samples to something manageable. I know the blood samples can be dried on microscope slides; I don't quite know if I can freeze the virus—I'll see what they might have developed at the clinic to study the problem," Diedrich sounded more confident with his answer than Hanns understood when he heard it.

"There's another possibility—" Diedrich paused briefly and then continued, "I found some people in the camps during the war; when I injected them with viruses, they showed no signs for periods longer than I would have anticipated incubation to occur."

Hanns looked at his longtime friend and the scientific officer of his company, trying to decipher the meaning of the explanation.

Somewhat drolly, Diedrich asked, "What do you think, Hanns, of us sponsoring a visitor from Africa?"

"I'm not sure what you mean," replied Hanns.

"Suppose, for the sake of discussion—" Diedrich faltered in voicing his thought but Hanns did not interrupt.

"Let's say that one of our associates from here in Africa wanted to visit the company headquarters or the laboratory in Santiago, how could we negotiate the customs, immigrations, and red-tape to get that person to South America?"

"That has a lot to do with the person going and with the Zairian officials. I suspect that we can get clearance through Joseph Mbandaka, if we really want to get someone back to Buenos Aires, or to Santiago. Immigrations at that end shouldn't be too much trouble, if the person can travel and has the papers," Hanns concluded. "What do you have in mind, *der Wissenschafter*?" With this Hanns smiled at Diedrich, a knowing smile, suspecting that the scientist had devised a method for getting his virus back to his laboratory and now needed answers for a few unknown items related to his plan.

"I don't know if this plan is viable, but if we think we don't need Tory any longer for the work at the smelter—" Diedrich stopped mid-thought as Hanns interrupted.

"We're not far enough along to be completely comfortable with the Lumbashi operations. Maybe we will need him. What's your plan?" Hanns asked Diedrich again.

"Well, I might be able to infect Tory with some of the virus and use him as the transport back to Santiago," Diedrich seemed to think his words rather than vocalize them with fervor. Nevertheless, he felt that he could create a human transport-vector for the new virus. For Diedrich, the African would serve his purposes if he could not find other transporting methods. What happened to Tory after carrying the virus to Chile did not concern Diedrich nor did the suggestion did not seem out of place to Hanns; he maintained much of his characteristic Nazi superiority in spite of the many ensuing years.

"Do you want me to start the negotiations in Kinshasa when I arrive?"

"I guess we'll have to wait; Tory may not show up at the airport," replied Diedrich. Then he continued explaining his expedition plans, switching to less scientific matters and more logistics.

"As long as I'm here in Africa, I think I would like to take one of the boats back to Kinshasa along the river. Didn't Mbandaka tell us travel on the Zaire River was safe and somewhat reliable?"

Hanns disagreed with a river trip, perhaps because of the danger or maybe the time required was too great. It really did not matter; Diedrich could easily take more extended vacation, if he desired. Hanns thought about the concept of handling a strangely new and exotic virus and it worried him. Even if the extraordinarily competent *der Wissenschafter* felt immense self-confidence working with viruses, Hanns felt uneasiness but tried not to show it.

"I think river travel is questionable in spite of what our 'friends' in Kinshasa say," thought Hanns aloud. "And, how long do you plan to be in the jungle?"

"I see the trip taking at least three weeks. After you drop me off in Bumba, it might take a day to outfit the trip, hire a guide and his car. I think the guide can supply me with everything I need for the trip into the interior. At this point, if I'm successful, I see no need for Tory, unless I need him for transporting the virus. The nuns and medical personnel at the clinic are from Belgium—they speak French, and my French is excellent."

Hanns listened as the detailed plans unfolded before him. Yet, some of the questions continued to concern him. He was not sure, if they were just unanswerable or if Diedrich risked too much.

"If Tory does join me, I'll see if his expertise is worth anything. I see his greatest help in locating and dealing with the guide in Bumba. It's possible that he can strike a deal with a more reputable guide than I can, as I would be coming into the city completely unknown."

Diedrich stopped briefly to look intently at Hanns and seeing that Hanns appeared engrossed in explanations of the trip and tried to sort the details in his mind, continued.

"We probably can get to the Yambuku village in another day and I think I'll need three days at the clinic but I'm not sure what to expect. Once I'm at the clinic, I'll have to assess the situation. Some time ago, I tried to contact the clinic through the religious order's offices in Brussels but they haven't returned any information. I thought I might receive something while we were in Lumbashi; there are people here who seem to be some sort of contact point, with the radio broadcasts and all. Nothing yet from the group—so, I'm not sure what to expect. I didn't hear anything in Kinshasa."

"And then how are you planning to get back and what will you doing with Tory?" Hanns posed an interesting question concerning the Tuareg, one that Diedrich still considered. His knowledge of Diedrich's work at the clinic might prove difficult in the future.

"I hadn't considered Tory or the guide, as being problems—let me think about the possibilities, and the information they pick up."

"If you decide to take Tory back with you, telephone me in our offices in Kinshasa, or if I'm back in Argentina, telephone me there. I won't make any arrangements until I hear from you. Dealing with Mbandaka and the Chilean embassy shouldn't be difficult," the instructions were clear enough and delivered so that Diedrich understood the importance Hanns gave the new information.

Diedrich continued explaining his plans. "Getting back to the river at Bumba should take a day; that's about six or seven total days. The unknown is the transportation on the river to the capital. When I get a boat, the trip might take ten days, maybe less. But, the river trip might have to wait. I'll decide when things get sorted, and I know which direction I need to take."

It appeared to Hanns that Diedrich had the trip to Yambuku adequately planned, at least as far as possible.

"Both of us are accustomed to adventures, of a sort, aren't we?" Hanns mused aloud and Diedrich nodded agreement.

"I don't think I have three weeks' of work in Kinshasa, Diedrich. Perhaps, I should return to Mendoza and you can catch up when you're finished," suggested Hanns. "You won't need the plane if you've planned to take the river back to Kinshasa."

"I agree. You complete the things with Ian, and Mbandaka. We've decided to stay with the current management in Lumbashi, right?" a fleeting thought about the management team at the smelter entered his mind.

"Don't worry about my trip, Hanns. If I'm successful getting samples of the virus, I'll go directly to Santiago. It's no problem. But, I'll telephone you, if possible, to let you know about another traveling companion."

"I think you're right about Lumbashi. I don't think making changes will help us that much. A little *schmiergeld* may serve our purposes anyway. I'm comfortable with fewer changes; it's the people we 'manage' through Ian that concern me. Tory and his friend opened up too many questions for me. I don't see a 'George Browne' working into our future. He seems skilled but I don't want him taking over the management of the smelter, especially after meeting with the current management team. Well, we still have to wait to see what Tory's going to do," Hanns anticipated a reply, but Diedrich simply nodded.

It appeared to Hanns that Diedrich already set aside mining and smelting of ores, leaving that end of the business to Hanns; Diedrich now appeared occupied with putting added details to his trip into the unfamiliar and mysterious regions of Zaire. Hanns saw rekindled excitement and energy in his old friend that he missed seeing in the past few years. Diedrich Erhard, *der Wissenschafter*, following in the footsteps of *Herr Doktor Blome und Herr Doktor Mengele* during the war, forced into being uniquely different following exiled years in foreign countries, teaching science topics to university students, and managing a well-recognized medical laboratory in Chile, now took on new animation and vibrancy that seemed distant from his friend Hanns Krieg and their mining opportunities in the Republic of Zaire.

Hanns watched and admired his friend, as he saw the excitement of old begin to burn, waiting for release. Finally, he spoke. "In a couple of days, let's leave here after breakfast," suggested Hanns.

Their glasses of dry sherry now empty, Hanns signaled the waiter for the check and both men rose to leave the hotel lounge. The quiet corner in the somewhat comfortable room, where the air moved gently from the motion of ceiling fans, allowed an undisturbed few minutes to discuss the next leg of their collective and separate trips. Quite unlike their first encounter with Tory in the espresso bar, no one overheard their Germanic voices nor did anyone really care what they said. To others in the lounge, they were just two foreign executives at the end of another day.

Tory's Plane Ride

The DVS plane stood readied for the flight to Kinshasa, with a short layover in Bumba, when Hanns and Diedrich stepped out of the taxi that drove directly onto the tarmac. The pilot and additional crewmember greeted the executives, loaded their luggage into the hold of the plane, and completed final preparations for departure. Despite the mid-morning cooler temperatures, the African sun quickly began to heat the pavement and the plane's exterior. The pilot encouraged the executives to board the plane so that he might start the engines and provide air conditioning.

"Do you have anything else to put on board?" asked the crewmember. "Are we ready to depart?"

Unsure if Tory planned to join them, Hanns nodded assent and began to enter the plane. Diedrich boarded the plane before Hanns so he did not see another taxi drive up to the plane's small steps leading to the entryway. Hanns paused at the top of the stairway to watch the taxi and its passenger.

"Tory—we didn't think you would join us!"

"I'm here, I'm here," shouted Tory as he retrieved his canvas travel bag.

Hanns told the crewmember to stow Tory's bag with the other luggage and the three travelers began to settle in for the trip. The pilot previously filed a domestic flight plan so no customs or immigration officials came on the plane to check documents. The plane moved smoothly to depart the Lumbashi airport.

Once in the air, Hanns returned to the main cabin from sitting in the copilot's seat, something he enjoyed during takeoffs. The additional crewmember took his place in the copilot's seat. When the three passengers were alone, Hanns noticed the pale look on Tory's face.

"Tory, are you sick?"

"I think I'll be fine," replied Tory, "but I've never been in a plane. This is my first flight and I feel a little uncomfortable."

Both Hanns and Diedrich roared with laughter. The seemingly unflappable Ettore Taharqa, the *Imajaghan* who fought alongside Rommel's desert *Afrikakorps* had never been in an airplane! They enjoyed the moment.

"Relax Tory—you'll survive," offered Diedrich, as he tried unsuccessfully to suppress his laughter.

"We'll see—" Tory seemed to gain no comfort from the two laughing Germans.

The DVS plane's interior presented an expensive feel for a first-time visitor, with black leather seats and hand-turned burl wood appointments. The manufacturer did not install individual tables that folded down from the back of seats as seen in commercial airplanes; rather, the interior had one round conference table and one rectangular table that served Hanns as a mobile desk. One seat faced to the rear of the plane, next to the bulkhead separating the main cabin from the cockpit and the table suggesting an office arrangement. One of the other cabin seats swiveled appropriately to allow it to be opposite the mobile desk. The other seats formed a semi-circle nearby the round table. The cabin arrangement allotted adequate room for discussion, writing, and card playing by the passengers.

Despite Tory's uncertainty and nervousness caused by his first airplane flight, he surveyed the accruements with respect, recognizing their expensive features—he slowly and adoringly ran his fingers across the fine leather of the captain's chair where he sat.

"I see you appreciate a fine piece of leather," observed Hanns.

"Quality leatherwork is important! By the way, did you know that we Tuareg are artisans and connoisseurs of fine leather?" Tory eased his grip on the armrest as he answered Hanns.

"No, I didn't know that about the Tuareg, but I'm glad you like it," observed Hanns.

"I see you changed into something easier for travel," Diedrich joined the conversation with Tory. At all earlier encounters with the strange man, he seemed to favor the same wrinkled suit. However, now he wore a tan colored poplin bush shirt, lightweight canvas pants, and laced boots. Gone were the scuffed desert chukka boots that he always wore.

"I've traveled in the jungle; the heat and humidity can become quite unpleasant," Tory emphasized his comment by wiping the back of his hand across his brow as a gesture of being too hot. "We've better clothing in the desert for keeping cool but I don't think it works well in the jungle!"

Tory looked at a similar outfit worn by Diedrich and commented with a slight nod of his head, "I see you also know how to dress for the African jungle heat. You know, of course, poplin has been standard for wear by many African guides and safari travelers for more than a hundred years. The fabric seems to breathe, allows the slightest breeze to cool the skin, and keeps moisture away from the wearer. During the war, I saw that German officers always wore poplin but the enlisted men often suffered in cotton and woolen uniforms,"

Tory now relaxed, settled back into his seat. "The epaulets are excellent to keep binocular straps in place and I especially like the oversized pockets here in front. When the bugs aren't too voracious, I roll up the sleeves and keep them in place with these tabs."

As Tory spoke, he demonstrated the points he described on his shirt. It seemed that Tory might have forgotten about the plane as he expounded the features of his bush shirt. Hanns noticed the relaxed features of Tory and smiled toward Diedrich, as if to show his perception.

Hanns spoke, "Tory, why did you join us on this trip?"

Diedrich listened carefully but said nothing.

"I've come to like you two," Tory smiled.

"Tory, don't give me any of that," Hanns demanded.

"Seriously—you're good people."

Hanns and Diedrich stared at the man before them without speaking, showing no emotion. Neither believed what they heard from Tory.

"But—my friends, I *am* naturally curious and I'm not sure what we'll see in Yambuku," emphasizing his feeling of being curious did not appear to move the Germans.

"Visiting new areas interests me," continued Tory, "and I would like to see the strange sickness, of which I've heard people speak."

"Did you decide how much money you want to serve as a guide?" asked Diedrich, wondering about the safari and the needed guide.

"Please, my friends, let's not talk about those minor things right now—I trust you and whatever you think fair will be good for me."

"Your help in finding the best guide and car in Bumba will help," offered Diedrich.

"I know several Tuaregs living in Bumba who guide into the north. We'll not have any problem finding the best guide for our safari."

"We'll need a guide with a good car to take us to Yambuku, stay there for a few days or more, and return us to the river. The guide needs to provide the equipment we need for the trip. Is that possible?" Diedrich asked.

"Of course," Tory always seemed more positive than believable when answering difficult questions. "There will be no problems."

Hanns and Diedrich looked at each other. Diedrich knew that Tory's answers did not reassure Hanns.

"I suspect that you'll negotiate with the right person, a trustworthy and reliably knowledgeable guide—don't you think rumors of the strange sickness in the village might cause some guides to stay away from the area?" Diedrich seemed to wonder aloud rather than question directly.

"Most guides are fearless! We should have no problems."

Hanns looked out the porthole to his right side and observed, "It looks as if we're just about to come to Bumba. If I'm not mistaken, we're just coming up on the Zaire River. It looks so dark and slow moving from the air. Diedrich, do you know how wide the river is?"

"I read that the river is over twenty kilometers wide through this area. But I didn't realize there would be so many islands—some of them look green and moving."

"Actually, river hyacinths clog much of the water and appear almost to be floating islands," Tory added as he looked carefully out one of the portholes.

Bumba

Tory tightened his grasp on the armrests of his seat as the plane touched down at the airport. The flight took a little over two hours and was remarkably smooth over the many warm updrafts generated by the hot and humid jungle landscape. The Tuareg stepped quickly from the plane, glad for the conclusion of his first flight. When he felt firmly on solid ground, he turned to acknowledge his hosts for the flight.

"*Je n'ai pas hink il serait venu, la terre ferme à la fin*, firm ground at last," Tory seemed to speak a number of things rapidly but these were the first words Diedrich understood. Some of the others utterings from Tory sounded a little like a prayer of thanks, or a vow to never again fly.

"Glad to be down to earth, Tory," commented Diedrich. "You didn't think you would stand on the ground again?"

Both Diedrich and Hanns seemed to get pleasure out of the antics of the African and took up their raucous laughter—Tory tried to smile but thought his plight not as funny as did the Germans. Nevertheless, they arrived in Bumba.

"Hanns, there doesn't appear to be much here at the airport," observed Diedrich. "Are you planning a long stay before taking off for Kinshasa?

"I think we have a few minutes while they top off the fuel tanks but that shouldn't be more than half an hour. Why don't you and Tory see what you can find by way of a guide; I'll take off as soon as we're ready."

"We'll stay here tonight," began Diedrich, "and perhaps head out before sunup tomorrow."

"I'll see you back in Mendoza—be safe," Hanns and Diedrich shook hands. "Telephone or use the radio to tell me if you need my help with immigrations and customs," Hanns told his friend.

"I know you realize that the plane *is* available, if you change your mind about the river," Hanns seemed solicitous. "Telephone the office and we'll send the plane here for you and—" the sentence trailed off with a knowing nod.

The crewmember brought Diedrich's bags into the terminal building, a single room served for passenger staging and ticketing and returned for Tory's bag. There was no need, Tory grabbed his canvas bag from the plane's storage and carried it into the terminal.

Air conditioning in the terminal building was completely inefficient for the humid heat of Bumba and Diedrich felt the heavy air coming off the surface of the Zaire River. He was glad to have the lightweight poplin shirt and trousers, which allowed his skin to breathe. When he moved, the slight breeze through the fabric helped him to feel cooler.

Tory seemed not to bother with the heat and suggested that they find a taxi to take them to a hotel. From there he would leave Diedrich and contact a friend about guiding them into Yambuku. Tory asked Diedrich if he could make the hotel arrangements while Tory was away. If he preferred, Tory would stay with some friends and would not need a room for the evening.

"No, Tory, I think if you stayed here this evening that we might discuss some of our plans for the trip," offered Diedrich.

"As you wish. I think we might rest more comfortably with a good meal here at the hotel. I suspect our guide will want to start before dawn tomorrow. We never know what we'll get into on the roads in this part of Zaire. I'll make sure that our guide has a good car, extra tires, and plenty of petrol for the trip. Is there anything in particular that you want for equipment or do you have everything that you need?"

"I'm not sure but tell the guide to outfit us properly. I don't want an accident to interrupt our trip!"

"Good—then—I'll return with our guide in a few hours—you can meet him. In the meantime, decide if you want anything extra that I might get for you," offered Tory as he left the steps of the hotel.

Diedrich registered at the front desk for two rooms for the evening. Rather than going directly to his room, he sent his bags ahead with the bellhop then walked to the shaded open veranda. As he sat down in one of the padded woven wicker chairs and watched the circling arcs of the ceiling fans move the warm afternoon air, he judged the hotel "adequate." Without meaning to, he closed his eyes and soon dozed in the chair, alone with his thoughts, away from the details of the curiously new virus he sought in a distant Zairian village.

* * *

"Doctor Erhard," he heard his name called and roused from his sleep.

"I must have dozed off," commented Diedrich as he looked up to see two men standing in from of him.

"It's nearly evening, Diedrich. You may have slept all day," commented Tory. Diedrich recognized that indeed the day's heat was less noticeable and the sun looked lower in the sky outside the eaves of the veranda.

"Yes, it's the heat of the jungle—we often rest in the afternoon when the heat is most intense," added Tory.

"Here is my friend who will guide us to Yambuku. He says that the trip is safe and his car will take us there with no problem," Tory turned to the other man standing next to him. "His name is Galvan Geoffran."

"Please, sit down here and tell me about yourself and the trip," offered Diedrich, awake and fully alert.

The three men huddled on the veranda, now a little more pleasant with the day's heat beginning to wane. Galvan explained some of the difficulties of the trip and that he felt it might take the entire day even though the distance to the village was not that great. There were at least three river crossings but at places where the Land Rover would have no difficulty.

"Did the doctor have any special needs, food, clothing—other things?" asked Galvan. "No—good then I need tomorrow to prepare for the journey; we'll leave just at dawn the following day. Please be ready and I'll pick you two up in front of the hotel just before the sun comes up."

Galvan rose to leave. "Before I go, I've reduced my usual expenses because Tory is such a good friend but I need half payment now, the rest when we return."

Diedrich paid the guide with large denomination bills in francs and smiled inwardly when he converted the hundred thousand Zairian francs mentally to a mere sixty thousand Chilean pesos. "A trivial amount," thought Diedrich, "for a guide to the Ebola Valley."

Galvin left with Tory.

Knowing that his planned safari would return to Bumba before the river trip, Diedrich confirmed room reservations, arranged to leave some of his luggage with the concierge, and attempted to reserve space aboard a powered ferry to Kinshasa. The concierge could not guarantee the ferry departure date and time but added him to the list of possible passengers, nothing more than a waiting list for when a ferry departed to the capital.

The polite concierge asked, "You do know the trip down river to Kinshasa will take many days? Do you want me to arrange overnight accommodations and meals while you're traveling? For a single price, all can be included?"

"Make all the necessary arrangements for my trip," instructed Diedrich. "I'll pay the *prix inclus* for all the services when I return from Yambuku."

"If messages come for my attention while I'm away, save them for my return. If they're urgent, you may contact me at the clinic in the village," suggested Diedrich, not expecting anyone to contact him.

Toward Yambuku

Early in the morning the day of their scheduled departure, Diedrich met Tory on the veranda to await the arrival of Galvan. Both skipped a full breakfast for the continental buffet provided by the hotel of coffee and croissants.

Galvan arrived as promised just before sunup in an older Land Rover, at least by Diedrich's standard for cars it appeared well used. As Diedrich surveyed the Rover, he saw plenty of scratches inflicted on the paint. He assumed thorns, or tree limbs caused the scratches while cutting new tracks in the bush. On top of the Rover were two spare tires, mounted to wheels and ready for replacement if needed. On a rack at the rear bumper were petrol cans, each filled with eighteen liters of extra petrol.

Galvan felt the need to explain the dents and scratches in his Rover's paint.

"Often, Zaire is flat, dry, but remarkably full of dips and gullies not perceptible until traveling overland," he began. "In these *petit ravin où coule un ruisseau*, or slight ravines where sometimes water flows along the bottom, we nearly always find thick vegetation, bristling with long sharp thorns that cut through clothing and skin, if a person pushes through them without knowing what the thorns can do. When I have to drive through these thorns, they carve deep scratches and grooves in the paint." Galvan ran his hand over the scratched paint to show Diedrich the result of traveling through the brush.

"I try to go around when I can, but even these bush bumpers," he moved to the front of the Rover, pointing to the heavy black metal tubing that covered the entire front of the car, "just coax the bush to move aside. And, when I'm into the middle of them, the thorny branches snap back against the sides. Does a lot of damage to the paint, don't you think?"

Diedrich nodded and ran his finger along some of the gouges in the paint.

"The thorns must be very sharp and strong," commented Diedrich.

Tory looked at Galvan, motioned to Diedrich to get in the Rover's front seat, and then sat in the second seat behind the driver. With luggage loaded, the three began their trip into the jungle.

"We're off then," shouted Galvan with more British intonation than French and the Rover left the hotel driveway.

"Here's the route we follow—" Galvan recited the roads, bridges, and water crossings they were to encounter with great ease, as if he had made the trip many times, and indeed he had.

"We follow the river on this main road, through Alberta and Yamosumba to Yamalais, where we turn north. That's about sixty kilometers from here, maybe an hour, or so. The road is much the same through Baisa to Modjamboli, where we turn toward Yandongi, maybe another eighty or ninety kilometers."

"We drive parallel to the Vicicongo railway line that connects Bumba port with a few cities in the west. This is a very small railway and trains don't run very often," explained Galvan.

"What do you mean that it's a small railway?" asked Tory.

"Most of our railway lines are about one thousand and sixty millimeters wide, a little more than one meter, but the Vicicongo is much narrower. Most trains can't run on these small rails so it doesn't have much traffic," Galvan sounded disappointed. "The Republic doesn't have very many good railways."

While Diedrich listened to Galvin's description of the "small railway," his scientific mind considered the widths of rails in Germany, where he remembered them to be about one thousand and five hundred millimeters wide. He thought the width of the Vicicongo line about the same as cogwheel tramways in the Harz Mountains, which moved passengers up steep grades and between small villages high in the mountains. He offered a single comment, "Galvin, it doesn't seem that these rails can move much more than a few people!"

With a nod of agreement, Galvan resumed his description of the route to Yambuku, "From Modjamboli, the road is difficult in spots—we'll see if we have problems. At Yandongi, the road we take to Yambuku is to the west and graded in some places—other places we may have to take a track across the grasses. The Rover is fine on these roads, but we must drive a lot more slowly. A short distance from Yandongi, we leave the road entirely onto a track, which is in some spots very rough, that takes us in the village. There are no bridges for the water crossings on this stretch of road into Yambuku. The water is not a problem for the Rover, don't worry."

"How long do you think we'll take getting to Yambuku?" Diedrich asked.

"It's about a hundred and fifty to a hundred and sixty kilometers to Yambuku—difficult to say how long we'll need for driving—it depends on the road and how much rain we've had. In some places past Yandongi, if the water is too high, some of the earth washes away from the road and we may have to make a new track to get around the washed out area. If the rain fills the water crossings above the top of the Rover, we'll have to wait for the water to go down. Can't say for sure how long the trip will take," Galvan's estimate was too ambiguous for Diedrich.

"Well, then, what about an estimate?" Diedrich tried again.

"I think we'll be there before dark. We won't travel on these roads after dark. Don't worry, if we have to camp, I have all the things needed. Besides, we pass several villages on our way that if we need, we can arrange a place to stay for a night, but I doubt that we'll have to stay out tonight," Galvan assured the two travelers.

"We'll stop in Modjamboli for more petrol and for something to eat. Modjamboli is a smaller city, certainly not as large as Bumba but many people live there. I'll check the reports for any problems on the road to Yambuku," Galvan sounded reassuring about the trip into the valley. Indeed, Diedrich relaxed after Galvan's description of the roads they would encounter; as he relaxed, he began to enjoy the sights and the sounds of underdeveloped Zaire. Everything was so different from his experiences in Chile and Germany. As he thought of the development possible in this part of Zaire, he heard his name called.

"Doctor Erhard," asked Galvan. "Do the medical people at the clinic know of your visit?"

"It's hard to say, for sure. I wired several months ago to ask if I might visit but I didn't hear anything from them. I wired again from Kinshasa about two weeks ago to tell them I planned to be at the clinic this week. They may know that I'm coming but I've not heard anything from the clinic or from their headquarters in Brussels."

"I don't think they'll have a problem with your visit," thought Galvan aloud to Diedrich. "They're very friendly people in the village. You know, I have a cousin who works as a nurse's helper at the clinic. She's not a nun, but they employ her for many things. I think she's a big help. It will be good to see her again."

Diedrich thought of his good luck, "At least there'll be a family member in our group arriving in Yambuku; maybe, there'll be fewer problems with the management of the clinic about my visit."

CHAPTER NINE
Transportation

Kinshasa and DVS

The plane dropped down onto the Kinshasa airport tarmac with the ease of a landing bird. As the plane taxied to the terminal and parked, a black Mercedes town car pulled from the side of a building. The car stopped at the plane's stairway, which unfolded outwardly open to allow Hanns to descend from the passenger cabin. Ian Cherubin and the driver stepped from the car to greet the plane; both wore open-necked shirts common to Zairian military and business people. Hanns thought the shirts resembled *guayabera* shirts favored by many men working in Latin America businesses.

"But, these are not the same style," Hanns observed out loud and to no one in particular as he remembered the bush shirts Tory and Diedrich wore on the plane.

He reflected on some of his clothing in Argentina, especially the shirt style worn by many Latin Americans and considered appropriate for more dressy occasions, those *guayabera* shirts with long sleeves and elaborate stitching. However, the shirts worn by Ian and the driver were quite different from the *guayabera* shirt; the Africans wore tan-colored, short-sleeved shirts that had no elaborate stitching, sported multiple flap-pockets for carrying small items, and appeared suited more for military use than for business. Each of the shirts worn by the Zairian men meeting Hanns had epaulet flaps on the shoulders, which reminded Hanns of military styles he saw earlier in Germany.

"Welcome, again, to Kinshasa," Ian Cherubin called up to Hanns, smiling broadly.

The pilot left the cockpit to follow Hanns to the top of stairway in order to receive any last minute instructions. Hanns turned to him and said, "Very smooth flight. Thank you. I won't need the plane for the next few days. I've business to complete here in the capital. I'll phone you when I'm ready to leave."

From the open hatchway, the pilot watched the crewmember retrieve the luggage from the aft storage and carry it toward the waiting car, placing Hanns's bags on the pavement.

"Thank you," replied Hanns as the crewmember set his bags next to the car then turned to receive any instructions. "I told the pilot that I won't need the plane for a few days. I'll phone him."

"Yes sir," the crewmember responded smartly and returned toward the plane.

Hanns enjoyed the attention to detail given him from the professional crew and their decorum, which they afforded him as owner of the plane. He seemed to hover, ever so slightly, admiring the plane and his personal self-worth before Ian spoke.

"Hanns," Ian called to him politely, "shall we leave?"

Ian and Hanns entered the car while the driver placed the bags in the boot then closed the passenger doors, first for Hanns and then for Ian. Ian sat in the front seat next to the driver; Hanns was comfortable in the back seat.

"I reserved two rooms for you and Diedrich at the same hotel," Ian spoke over his shoulder to Hanns. "I expected Diedrich to be with you," the implied question hung in the air.

"Diedrich stopped for a side trip. He wanted to investigate some things at a medical clinic in a village called Yambuku."

"I hope he finds things interesting," replied Ian. The Oxford-trained African wondered what would interest a mining executive from South America in a tiny village in the north of the country. There is nothing of mining importance in that area, all the mines are in the south. He thought of the reports he read concerning rebels in the area and wondered about the safety of the foreign executive. In addition, Ian questioned the wisdom of traveling where rumors of a strange sickness existed at the Belgian clinic operating in the village.

"That's an odd place to visit," he muttered.

Hanns did not hear the comment and sat quietly thinking about his friend traveling into the jungle. "I wonder what he'll see and what stories he'll have when he returns," he reflected.

It was late afternoon when the plane arrived in Kinshasa. The refueling and layover in Bumba was uneventful but Hanns now felt he needed some time alone; so upon arriving at the hotel, he asked Ian to forego dinner with him and to pick him up in the morning for their scheduled meetings at the DVS offices.

* * *

The next morning, Ian arrived at the agreed upon time, with the driver and car, to take Hanns to the offices. The driver drove quickly and directly through the busy Kinshasa streets to the office building wherein the DVS Technologies Africa headquarters were. At the office building, the car went directly into the gated and guarded underground parking.

Hanns commented, perhaps with more than a hint of concern, "I appreciate the care you've taken in selecting a secure building for our African headquarters. Have you had any problems with security?"

"Nothing! I think Joseph Mbandaka is especially watchful to ensure the safety of our foreign executives and their businesses. Did you notice the army across the street as we arrived?"

To be sure, Hanns saw a camouflaged dark green and tan colored *petit camion* parked at the head of the street when they made their turn into the avenue where the office building stood. Two armed men sat on plastic chairs in the small truck's open bed and two more armed men stood next to a wall not far from the office building, smoking and talking. They looked as if they were younger, but dressed in military uniforms, and each carrying automatic weapons, they appeared very seriously older.

"Indeed," replied Hanns. "Do you feel the army is needed here?"

"It's easier to keep the peace and prevent potential *criminels* from taking advantage of a situation. We're also watchful for any rebel activity that might threaten," Ian's French-British accented English sounded a little unusual to Hanns, who simply smiled a response and followed him to their offices in the building.

During the morning, Hanns described his findings to Ian regarding the management team at the smelter. Ian seemed pleased that the current group of managers "passed muster" as Ian described the findings in his more stylized English.

"I think we'll find them most competent managers," suggested Ian, reassuring Hanns of his concurrence in the selection.

"I'm quite concerned," Hanns began on a serious note, "with transportation out of the smelter. The management team in Lumbashi and I reviewed the railways between the Matadi Port and the smelter. What they described was not very encouraging. As I listened to them explain the present system, it's likely that we could lose a lot of time and money waiting for—how did they describe it—'*le prochain bateau pour arriver*'— or something to the effect, which told me that our shipping expediency could wait. How can we run an efficient business if we have to 'wait for the next boat to arrive' before making vital connections? This is not at all acceptable."

"The infrastructure here in Zaire is not fully operational," explained Ian. "We might be able to affect some changes—"

Hanns interrupted the train of thought begun by Ian.

"Why can't DVS operate its own barges on the river, for example, as long as you don't have a fully developed railway or shipping systems in the new Zaire?"

"Possibly, but we have to cross the river someplace between the port and the smelter," Ian tried to explain a few of the difficulties he faced.

"The river is very wide and we still don't have any railway bridges; ferries and barges only. Additionally, after crossing the river or traveling on barges from Ilebo to Kinshasa, we must use the railway to Matadi and the port because of the Livingstone Falls on the river. I know it must sound silly, but the Matadi Railway is a standard rail width but some of the other tracks to Lumbashi are much narrower. We need to consider these differences."

"I think we have to standardize, at least in the size of our shipping containers so that the processed metal is not off-loaded and then re-loaded several times here in Zaire!"

"I'm not sure what can be done to change the transportation system; we're a growing nation and have much to accomplish. There isn't a complete railway from Kinshasa or even Matadi, to Lumbashi; we use what we have."

Ian's comments did not make Hanns feel more comfortable about his mining investments in the country. Before entering into the agreement with Zaire, Hanns calculated the costs associated with extracting the minerals, moving the ore to the smelter, processing it, and transporting the refined metals to profitable world markets. The exploration for new deposits carried expense, but he made allowances for that operation. In addition, there were fees payable to the government for the DVS agreement. His accountants built some slippage into the costs but what at this moment confronted him, the escalating expense of intra-Zairian transportation, caught him somewhat by surprise. Now he wondered and even doubted that siphoning unreported gold would cover expenses. He had hoped for more from the project.

Seeing Hanns deep in thought, Ian hesitated to interrupt but finally said, "Hanns, we have meetings this afternoon with Joseph Mbandaka. I think you should discuss your concerns with him. Perhaps, he has solutions and answers for your questions."

"I need some time alone, to think. Ian, would you mind?"

Ian politely left the office and Hanns was alone with his thoughts about what might be the premature unraveling of his agreement for mining operations in Zaire and his dubious schemes for accumulating wealth at the expense of the unwitting Zairians.

"I'm not sure I want to meet with Mbandaka," he complained under his breath. "It's likely to be just one excuse after another for not getting things done!"

Traveling: Mongala District

Traveling through towns and villages adjacent to the Zaire River reminded Diedrich of the tiny hamlets, or *aldeas*, he visited during his experiences with the Chilean rebels in the Andean backcountry. He remembered the weeks he spent moving from one *aldea* to another. In each small community, he found people inviting and hospitable, willing to share their meager possessions with the rebel group moving toward the freedoms of Argentina.

"There aren't that many differences when life hovers at subsistence, and poverty is the norm," he muttered quietly.

"What is that?" asked Galvan.

"Nothing—just thinking about the people and the villages," replied Diedrich to the question.

"Yes, there is much poverty in Zaire," the guide offered his opinion as he also saw some of the same sights. "Often, we don't pay much attention to the appearance of poverty until someone from outside Africa visits," Galvan concluded.

As the Rover neared Modjamboli, Diedrich felt a need to stretch his legs, perhaps walk a little, and drink something. Even now, with the light breakfast digested, he began to feel hunger.

"I'm ready for something to eat and drink," Diedrich commented as the Rover entered the town center.

When Galvan made his turn onto the main street of Modjamboli, Diedrich noticed that the streets eked out an existence through satisfactorily serving both pedestrians and vehicles: no one street appeared to be a throughway. There were a few automobiles on the road: perhaps a taxi or two, and at least one well-used bus packed with passengers pushed a dusty line through the semi-congestion in Modjamboli. The collection of baggage, boxes, and crates haphazardly carried atop the bus suggested that it was a connector between several villages. However, generally, only the more affluent of society, the safari guides, and the occasional visitors to Zaire used individual cars and taxis; almost everyone else walked or rode bicycles in this part of Zaire.

The buildings in the town were dull by Diedrich's standards: uninspiring in their single-story design, nothing more than simple square boxes, painted various shades of a faded reddish pastel color, and all butted at various angles directly on the streets. The colors looked weatherworn, washed by near constant sun and frequent afternoon rain. These houses and buildings appeared as if they felt the closeness of the equator. Diedrich surmised that the ever-present Zairian red-hued dirt, which settled on everything when the hot African sun dried the dirt to a fine powdery dust, added to the pastel shades of the buildings.

Most doorways in the buildings stood open, allowing easy access and unencumbered views into the living quarters or businesses. Windows without screens or glass coverings frequently had wooden and metal slats pushed up out of the way and opened wide to the interiors of the buildings. These slats closed to protect the interiors when heavy storms drove the rain sideways. The exposed entries allowed breezes to flow through the buildings and cool the interiors.

Close by nearly all the houses, sat or played numerous children, seemingly comfortable with the warmth of the mid-day heat. Diedrich thought it unique that virtually none of these children wore shoes, or maybe they had just simple plastic slippers, loose-fitting tee shirts, and shorts. There appeared to be a "uniform" in which the children dressed.

Some vegetation—mostly vines and stringy-looking short trees—grew in empty lots and beside the buildings. None of the trees was the libanga tree Mobutu told him marked his birthplace; at least, none looked to be growing "upside down," in any event. Diedrich was not sure that these trees and shrubs ever received care from the inhabitants of this small Zairian town, nor was there a need in the equatorial climate.

"We'll stop here for a short rest," offered Galvan as he pulled to a stop in front of an unimpressive general store. "They have sandwiches, beer, soda, and water inside. Get what you want while I get some petrol from the back of the building. The prices here are very reasonable—I know the owner and he'll not overcharge you. He speaks some French but Tory can translate if you have difficulties. There's a restroom to the side of the building—separate entrance from the store. We'll leave in about thirty minutes." He gave the instructions without seeming to take a breath.

Stepping into the general store, or *magasin général*, as Galvan described it, Diedrich found the open doorway elevated about thirty or forty centimeters on roughly finished cement, worn and discolored gray by the foot traffic. A quick survey of the merchandise convinced Diedrich that his choices were limited; the wooden planking satisfied as display shelving, bowed slightly to the middle of each shelf, apparently from the weight of products stored there over time. Diedrich wondered how the few bottles and cans displayed presently on the shelves possessed enough weight as to cause the planks to create a gentle U-shape.

"*Ce qui peut j'arriver pour vous?*"

Diedrich thought the French nuances of the shopkeeper quite good and replied that he would appreciate a croissant with cheese and a cup of coffee. Tory ordered the same.

One small round table stood outside in a shady spot created by a nearby building overhang and a few taller trees. Next to the table were several worn-looking and rusted metal chairs. The two travelers sat at the table to enjoy their snack. As they relaxed in the shade, they watched several small children playing on the narrow street. Diedrich now noticed that along the street, a few palm trees growing rather haphazardly around the buildings swayed gently in a soft breeze.

"Not much traffic in the city," commented Diedrich rather idly.

"No, we won't see too many automobiles the farther we travel into this district. The Mongala District is very underdeveloped; business is one of the many things needed here," Tory sounded knowledgeable about the district but Diedrich wondered how much he really knew.

"This is one of the larger cities?"

"Not really," answered Tory.

After refueling the Rover with a hand pump, from the barrel at the rear of the store building, Galvan cut across the sunny storefront to the shaded table and chairs to join Diedrich and Tory.

"I see you got something from the store," Galvan's voice changed the tone of their idle conversation and brought the two travelers back to the present and to considering the trip awaiting them.

"I filled the Rover with petrol so we can start anytime you're ready, but take what time you want. We've the roughest part of the trip ahead. The roads might get a little uneven, or they might be dry and easy to pass—never know."

"We've finished here. Right, Tory," commented Diedrich rather than questioning if Tory was ready to depart.

"Good, I'll bring the Rover around and we can start. From here, we travel pretty much north until we come to Yandongi, that's a little more than a hundred kilometers. I'm not always sure of the road; we sometimes have a few difficulties. There are a couple of very small villages along the route but very, very small ones." With this brief explanation, Galvan strode off to retrieve the Rover.

When the Rover pulled into the tiny junction village of Yandongi, all three occupants were pleased the road behind them had been clear and the trip uneventful. Galvan began a brief description of the area, in a fashion of guide reciting for a visiting group of tourists.

"The Yandongi village sits at the crossroads of four roads, diverging in each of four directions, and a little more than thirty kilometers from the confluence of the Mbomou and Uele rivers. These rivers combine to form the Ubangi River, which feeds into the Zaire River about a thousand kilometers to the south at Mbandaka."

"Some people estimate that it takes about six months to travel by automobile from one side of Zaire to the other but I've never tried to take the trip. There are very few paved roads in the country; most of the roads are just dirt but a few have crushed rock surfaces.

Storms often wash away the road that's why I prefer this Rover; I can navigate almost any obstruction in my way."

Galvan waited for questions as he pulled the Rover onto the side of the road. Not receiving questions, he continued, "While Yandongi may serve as a junction in the roadways of the district, there is no extensive commercialization of the area—people live here in mainly agrarian lives. We are very close to the Equator here so life is taken very slowly."

They turned west onto another earthen road, not highly maintained but adequate for the Rover. To either side of the road was dense equatorial undergrowth that kept Diedrich from seeing any farther off the road than a few meters, except for a few clearings with mud and thatch huts situated close to the road. Another water crossing came about two kilometers after leaving Yandongi and the Rover eased into the water slowly. When the river water reached midway up the door, Diedrich looked out his window at the water, thinking he was not so happy that the water flowed against his side of the Rover rather than the driver's side.

"Not to worry," declared Galvan. "This is the deepest one we cross today and we can make this one without any problems."

He explained that he retrofitted his Rover with something that allowed him to cross deep water without flooding the engine. Galvan equipped his Rover with the exhaust pipes that left the engine compartment in the front, followed the edge of the windshield, and then vented over the top of the vehicle.

"It keeps water from getting into the crankcase and the carburetor," was the simple explanation.

"By the way, Doctor Erhard, this is the Ebola River. It's not too big or too deep—the river begins a little way north of Yandongi and runs a short distance from here on the north side of Yambuku village—serves as their main source of water, you know, then, it disappears into the floodplains feeding into the Ubangi River about fifty or sixty kilometers farther west," Galvan explained details of the river as he pushed his Rover past the middle of the crossing and up the far bank where they picked up the road again. He showed no concern at the water depth or the rocks that caused the Rover to roll from side-to-side and its frame to creak as they moved through the riverbed.

"Is this part of the Ebola Valley?" asked Diedrich, as he held tightly to the handle attached to the inside roof-body of the Rover just above his head, and tried to stabilize himself through the bumps.

"Right—the valley starts on the other side of Yandongi," Galvan answered, "maybe you saw the beginnings of it in the village when we passed through? The valley is a rather narrow depression in this part of the Uele River drainage. We've been traveling about the last thirty minutes along the sides or in the middle of the valley."

About five kilometers from Yandongi, Galvan eased the Rover to a stop at a field filled with thick grasses and other vegetation. From beneath the ferns, grasses, and short-stemmed undergrowth, there appeared two small red streaks, each about tire width of the Rover, which gave the appearance of a road or track cutting across the field into the trees not far distant. The track struck out in an almost southerly direction.

"Yambuku is down this track about four or five kilometers," Galvan looked into the far group of trees, as if to see the village in the remoteness of jungle. The growth in the field looked at least even with the bottom edge of the windows in the Rover; it could have been taller.

"Ready?"

With no fanfare, the Rover jerked left onto the red-tracked bush land and headed south toward the village of Yambuku, deep in the midst of the Ebola Valley and into a remote part of this northeastern Zairian rainforest.

As Diedrich considered the trip thus far and looked ahead into the thick growth, he wondered if he anticipated such remoteness. When he remembered planning this trip and of hearing the stories of a rare virus reported coming from Yambuku, he decided that his explanation of both to Hanns lacked an indiscernible essence of the actuality being stranger than anything he ever experienced.

"Indeed, this is a bizarre and peculiar part of the world," he muttered in a slightly inaudible voice.

Minister Mbandaka

Joseph Mbandaka entered the DVS office of Hanns Krieg with commanding presence, a presence developed through a self-assurance generated by his position in the government. Ian Cherubin followed a few footsteps behind.

After acknowledging both men, Hanns rose from behind his desk and walked to meet the minister and Ian in the middle of his office. The men shook hands and Hanns invited the visitors to sit in the conference alcove that was part of his office. Mbandaka elected to sit on the divan, as did Ian, while Hanns sat in one of the club chairs opposite the coffee table. Hanns noticed the physical changes in Mbandaka, compared with their first meeting, particularly the minister's increasing size, and thought life in the new government must be comfortable for the man.

The executive secretary Hanns recently employed took orders for coffee and returned shortly after with a refreshment tray, briefly interrupting the discussion to place the coffee servings and a few *biscuits*, or cookies, on the table. When she left, the discussion continued.

"You found the meetings in Lumbashi productive?" questioned Mbandaka declaratively after sipping his coffee. "The manager of the smelter reported positive meetings with you and Doctor Erhard."

"Yes, I believe we'll find their management skills very helpful in producing high quality copper and cobalt," reassured Hanns.

"He indicated that you spent several days and were very thorough in your inspections. I'm glad to hear that you took things so seriously, not that we ever doubted," reassured Mbandaka.

Hanns remembered the warning of Tory when they met in Lumbashi that Kinshasa had many eyes and ears in all parts of Zaire. It was obvious that Mbandaka received reports about his inspection visits at the smelter. His mind raced ahead of the discussion and he asked himself, "What else did the minister hear about the visit? Did George Browne, or someone, report the discussions with reference to diverting unreported minerals?" Hanns studied the men sitting in front of him for an indication of where the discussion might lead and what they knew of his plans. He did not wait long for an answer.

"You enjoyed our *coupé-coupé* while in Lumbashi?" the question again sounded more like a declaration. In fact, nearly all of his questions carried the self-awareness and weight of a declarative style of speaking.

Joseph Mbandaka smiled and looked closely for the reaction he expected. The growing fleshiness of his face gave its eyes a slight squint and an affected shrewd-like appearance.

Hanns, with many years of experience in similar circumstances, returned the smile and said, "Yes. We found the taste quite to our liking. I particularly enjoyed the *pili-pili* sauce on the croissants. The sauce gave the meat a very distinctive flavor that I quite enjoyed."

Nothing more needed saying—both parties understood the unspoken message: operatives of Kinshasa ensure no surprises arise in business dealings with foreign companies.

"Minister Mbandaka," began Hanns, "there is one thing we need to discuss—your country's transportation systems."

"We're quite concerned that the railways are inefficient, perhaps inadequate to transport the refined minerals to the port at Matadi. Moreover, I don't know what to do about the shipping on the Zaire River. How can we work with such hindrances?"

The minister smiled broadly, before he answered, "I'm sure you expected something different, maybe something similar to German efficiencies? We're growing here in this part of the world and our republic is very young. How would you have us change, *Mister Krieg?*"

Hanns felt the criticism intended but continued to express his concern for the inadequate transportation systems and the costly delays they would create when DVS began mining operations. He told Mbandaka that the government should increase oversight of the shipping, at least. There was little profit made while refined minerals sat on the river docks, awaiting "the next boat to arrive."

"Our agreement with DVS allows you *only* to manage the smelter, not to own it. We will be concerned about the 'inefficiencies' as you describe them," the minister smiled again at Hanns, the clever appearance of his eyes as he smiled seemed to accentuate the message.

"Yes, true," replied Hanns, "and our contract payments to you—" Hanns paused briefly to increase emphasis of his statement to follow. "We calculate payments based on refined volumes and delivery to markets throughout the world—" Hanns paused again— "to several of your approved vendors. Aren't you concerned about lost gains or unrealized profits that the DVS management might not bring to the operations?"

"I think you will generate your promised outputs. The returns for the Republic will happen as expected and maybe even a few francs extra for DVS!"

Hanns was unsure of the minister's last remark: did he simply overstate the revenue expected by the Zairian government, or did he mean to say that he knew of plans to syphon unreported gold, even copper and cobalt?

"I've a thought for you and your mining team," Mbandaka began. "Ian is extremely well schooled in operational efficiencies, and he is most interested in protecting your interests, as well as those of the Republic. Perhaps, he will organize a committee to study the problem. Would that help to alleviate your concerns?"

"An excellent idea," answered Hanns, realizing that he would get no further than an agreement on a committee and if the committee extended its study of the problem, he would have sufficient leeway to take necessary steps, at least somewhere in the system to ensure his profits.

"Adequate," he thought. "Just adequate."

For another hour, the three discussed the other details of the contract, exploration plans, and management of the smelter. The contract between DVS and Zaire might benefit both parties; however, both parties felt the agreement favored their individual positions. As such, the contract underwent no amendments. The meeting with Mbandaka reinforced for Hanns what he repeatedly learned through contractual negotiations with governments; it is not obvious, but there is always a winner and too often a loser. The challenge for Hanns was ensuring that he won—always.

As Mbandaka rose to leave, he posed another question to Hanns and spoke as if it were an aside comment to Ian, "Tell me, *Mister Krieg*, why did Doctor Erhard rent a car and hire a guide in Bumba? What does he expect to find in Yambuku?" Hanns caught what appeared to be a concerned look on Ian's face. The minister had a unique manner for pronouncing the title word, "Mister," and his name.

"Doctor Diedrich Erhard is always an explorer of new things. I suppose he thought he would like to see some of the interior of the country before returning to Chile," replied Hanns. "I don't think he felt he could add much to our mining discussions here in Kinshasa."

"May I offer a suggestion: before you two executives decide another trip into the interior, please obtain clearance from me. There are diseases and other dreadful things, unsuspecting things, you pick up in the jungle," suggested Mbandaka. However, Hanns heard more than a suggestion; the instructions and warnings were apparent.

"As you may know, *Mister Krieg*, there are rebels fighting with the new republic and they kidnap foreigners to hold for ransom. I'm not sure how long the Belgian nuns will be safe in the country, even if they're part of a religious order that provides medical care to villagers."

Ian smiled at Hanns and followed Mbandaka from the office.

When finally sitting at his desk, Hanns thought of the warnings and the veiled threats he received over the last three hours. Joseph Mbandaka, the minister of Commerce and Trade in Zaire, had connections in all parts of the country and Ian was his right-hand man in making sure DVS stays within proscribed limits. Diedrich was right, "we do need more caution while working in Africa."

"These operations are going to be challenging," he thought. "Very challenging!"

His pensive attitude then turned to his friend and he wondered how Diedrich fared, or where he was now on his "safari."

MEINE RACHE

Yambuku Clinic

The Rover moved much more slowly on the red track earth through the field than when on earthen roads; it seemed as if Galvan took extra caution as he drove. Perhaps, five hundred meters from the earthen road and along the red track was a clearing in the brush to the east of the pathway. Three small metal houses, not much larger than huts stood in the center of the clearing. As the Rover approached, several people from the houses came out to see who was on the road.

"These people are farmers and cattlemen," explained Galvan, "although, they are not too prosperous. These small houses are common in this area. Nothing more than salvaged, corrugated iron sheets, I'm afraid, and in most cases, the poorer people build their houses with simply mud-and-grass thatch," he explained further.

There was no need to stop, but Tory waved a brief greeting to the villagers as they drove past in the Rover.

"We'll see several more clearings and houses before we enter the main village," Gavan continued. "The houses get closer together along this road until we reach the first of the two main streets in Yambuku. I call them streets but nothing is paved, everything is red dirt. The center of the village crowds around the football field, a clinic operated by the sisters, and the Catholic-sponsored school."

Traveling the red-dirt track was uneventful but slow, but the Rover covered the short few kilometers in about fifteen minutes. As they entered the village of Yambuku, Diedrich saw maybe twenty or thirty small, corrugated iron houses scattered along the one of two dirt streets that made up the entrance to the village, just as the guide described.

Galvan drove the Rover slowly along what was the main road of Yambuku and directly to a walled compound-like football area at the south end of the village. Another road paralleled the compound to the south and a single road crossed both a short way farther. The road into the village on which they arrived, the two roads in the main section of the village, and a third road that crossed east of these two, comprised Yambuku village.

As the Rover pulled to a stop at a cement-block building at the far end of the walled compound/football area in the center of the village, Diedrich noticed that a covered passageway joined this building and another smaller building to the southwest.

"Well, gentlemen, we're here," declared Galvan.

The arrival of a car in the village caused a stir and several people gathered around. As the visitors stepped out of the Rover, one man, who had been standing on the porch of the main building watching their arrival, approached them. He wore a knee-length, crisp appearing white lab coat.

"Doctor Erhard?" the man asked Diedrich and stretched out a hand in welcome. "We received your messages. Thank you for visiting us. Did you receive our replies to your cables?"

"I'm afraid that I didn't, and I wondered about just showing up here at the clinic," Diedrich extend his hand in return. "I didn't get a name of the physician-in-charge or the head administrator of the clinic here, so you have the advantage."

"My name is Doctor Clément Tuatara, but most people just call me Doctor Clément. I travel here from Bumba several times a month to oversee the clinic. In reality, the nurses manage the patients and other things around here."

"We're happy to have you visit, Doctor Erhard. If you and your friends don't mind a hospital bed, you may stay as long as you wish. We have several beds in a separate wing that you and your friends may use. Do you have an idea as to how long you plan to stay?"

"Thank you," replied Diedrich. "I think we planned at least a week, maybe more to see what kind of work you're doing and perhaps to discuss some of your findings regarding the new virus I heard you discovered. I don't think I've read anything given formally in a paper, unless I missed something?"

"No, no, you're quite right—nothing written but we have what looks like a full-scale contagion developing—" Doctor Clément looked a little uneasy and paused before continuing, "But I don't understand how you would have heard about these cases. I've conferred with very few here in Zaire about this problem. Well, let's talk about it later; I must see several more patients before we close the clinic for the evening. Before I go, would you introduce me to your friends?"

Diedrich explained his relationship to the two traveling companions. As he turned to the guide, Galvan suggested that he would like to see his cousin and would likely stay with her family rather than at the clinic.

"Who's your cousin," asked Doctor Clément.

"You likely know her, Angela? I believe she serves as a nurse's aide here in the clinic."

"Of course," the doctor's eyes seemed to light up when speaking of the young woman. "Everyone here loves Angela. She's helping the sisters in Ward B this afternoon, but you can wait for her at the desk inside. They'll let Angela know that you're here. It's probably not wise for you to disturb her right now."

"I really must leave you now," offered the doctor. "I'll see you later at our evening meal. Auguste here—" he pointed to a youthful looking boy as he gave instructions—to the barefooted-young man, dressed in white pants and shirt, he said, "will you help get these visitors settled?" With these final few instructions, the doctor turned and left the group in the courtyard of the clinic.

The young man who served as an aide, named Auguste, invited the men to follow him into an unoccupied wing of the clinic; Galvan, waiting to visit his cousin, remained at the nurse's desk.

"Evening devotional begins at 1730 hours in the small chapel to the right of the main entrance. Nearly everyone attends, but if you—" the aide suggested with his actions that the visitors might be too tired to attend, "—we eat in the dining room at 2000 hours."

"Well, Tory, what do you think?" Diedrich looked at his traveling companion, who had been unusually quiet for the last few hours.

"I would've expected it," commented Tory. "You seem to know about a lot things even in this village, which is one of the most isolated places that I think I've visited. Where do we go from here?" Tory appeared impressed if not surprised.

"Tonight we'll rest and I'll schedule some time with the doctor and the people in the clinic. I think I'll need to be here about two or three weeks. You and Galvan can occupy yourselves, can't you, while I'm busy?"

CHAPTER TEN
Fragile Cargo

Effects of the Virus

Diedrich and Tory awoke before dawn to singing emanating from the small chapel, which was close to the wing where they slept. The humidity and heat captured in the cement walls during the day, dissipated insignificantly throughout the night, leaving them without complete rest, uncomfortable, and slightly irritable. They stepped out of the clinic onto a partial veranda, which was simply no more than a covered cement porch that faced toward the grassy compound. As the newly arrived visitors discovered, morning in Yambuku village began unhurriedly. Cooler evening temperatures gave way, almost begrudgingly, until the sun began its daily equatorial baking of the Ebola Valley; then, as if switched on by a central thermostat, there was humid heat, instantaneously hot searing heat.

From the porch, Diedrich could see people in the village beginning to emerge from their more substantially built houses than he saw on the road to the village and he smelt the unique aromas of their lives announcing a start to daily activities.

"Tory," he turned to the Tuareg, "what plans do you have today?"

"There's not much in the village, but Galvan suggested that we might take the Rover to visit areas along the road from Yandongi toward the Ubangi River. I assume you don't have need of us today?"

"I think I'll spend the day in the clinic. I've some things I want to discuss with Doctor Clément before he returns to Bumba. I won't need either you or Galvan today," Diedrich thought the plans of the two Tuaregs from the Sudan fit nicely into his.

Looking east from the porch, Diedrich spotted Galvan's Rover moving hurriedly along the red dirt road on the north side of the compound.

"Looks as if your ride arrived," Diedrich head bobbed in the general direction of the arriving car and about the same time, Tory noticed the approaching Rover.

Galvan pulled the Rover to the side of the building and turned off the engine—unusual, thought Tory, if they were planning to leave for the day. Galvan looked anxious as he approached the two standing on the porch.

"I need to speak with Doctor Clément or one of the sisters," he explained as he passed them and walked into the clinic. Tory followed him and Diedrich remained on the porch, enjoying being outside the building in the slightly cooler temperatures of the morning.

Diedrich thought that he sensed more than a gradual increase in the activity level of people in the village. Indeed, he could see more people queue at the patient entrance to the clinic.

"Nothing unusual," he commented quietly and to no one in particular, "with all the patients coming to the clinic."

Some people looked as if they traveled longer distances to be at the clinic early this morning. Diedrich noticed what he thought might be more dust on some of their feet and the bottom hems of their skirts. Virtually all the people in the queue were women and children. The children played somewhat without noise at their mother's feet while the women stood patiently or squatted on the ground, chatting with others waiting in the queue. There appeared camaraderie, of sorts, and none looked as if they begrudged the trek or the wait. Rather, it seemed expected. However, Diedrich may have assumed their feelings because he understood little of their spoken Bantu language. He was, however, a careful and perceptive observer of people.

The colorful dresses worn by some of the women, including those dresses with bold designs common in Zaire, impressed the visiting German scientist. Although not all women dressed similarly, those with colored dresses seemed to favor rich hues of yellow with bold floral and geometric designs in earthy brown shades. Diedrich noticed that all the dresses or skirts were ankle length and all women wore headscarves tied tightly at the base of the head. A few women wore leather slippers, most were barefooted.

Diedrich thought of the people he saw in the larger cities in Zaire, they nearly all wore shoes of some fashion or another but here in this village, virtually no one wore shoes of any kind.

The children wore a similar "uniform" to the children he saw the day before; women carried smaller children, mostly infants, either in a wrap tied around their shoulders and backs or simply carried perched on their hips.

As he turned to enter the building, Galvan and Tory met him as they left hurriedly. Galvan looked apprehensive; Tory turned to Diedrich, offering a quick comment.

"We need to bring Galvan's cousin to the clinic—she's been sick, high fever, terrible skin rash—head sister wants to see her here, quickly."

Diedrich watched the pair leave the village in the Rover before continuing into the building to find Doctor Clément. A short distance down the main hall, he met the doctor who invited him to discuss the activities of the day.

"How was your sleep," asked the doctor, exhibiting the normal Zairian custom of showing concern, and asking about a person's welfare when meeting for the first time in the day.

"Thank you, Doctor," replied Diedrich, "I slept well but the singing early this morning woke me. Do people here at the clinic start every day with singing?"

"And prayer," added Doctor Clément. "Let's go to my office for coffee and then we may talk some about why you came to our clinic. You've traveled such a long distance to see our part of the world," he suggested as he led the way to his small and rather humble office.

"I understand that you are trained in pathology?" asked Doctor Clément. "Where did you study?"

Diedrich explained some of his professional background, excluding his former Nazi prisoner camp experiences. He included his training at the University of Poznan, Diedrich carefully used the Polish name of the university rather than the German name, and in the then developing field of virology. Diedrich expressed interest in the new virus he thought the Yambuku clinic might have discovered. Particularly, he felt his sense of responsibility intensify at being in Yambuku because so many medical institutions throughout South America recognized his pathology laboratory for its leading studies in virology. He was very interested in observing Doctor Clément's work, "first-hand and with my own eyes."

Doctor Clément thought to himself that the visiting scientist had an extraordinarily high self-worth; but he thanked Diedrich for his interest as the visiting pathologist acknowledged the work of the clinic from such a distance, as was Santiago, Chile. He then returned to a gentle scrutiny of his visitor, "Thank you, yes our work is challenging here in the middle of the Zairian jungle. At the same time, you've been active in your published work. I think I've read several of your papers. And your colleague, what was her name?"

"I think you refer to Doctor Anita Muñoz González, right?"

"Yes, if I'm not mistaken, she has an insight in developing phylogenetic trees of various disease entities and of the newly described field of immunological mapping, did I understand the work correctly?'

"Doctor Muñoz is one of the best! Her expertise really lies with diagnostics and explaining how viral infections spread. That's where the tree-concept appears to help explain the spread of a disease or infectious compound but developing the statistical confidence of the branches is a challenge. Nevertheless, I'm very impressed with her knowledge."

"Ah, here's the coffee," the young aide to Doctor Clément, Auguste, brought a tray with an insulated pitcher of coffee and a few somewhat stale appearing *biscuits* on a plate. The clinic had few visitors and these *élite* treats, usually reserved for singular occasions, now carefully exited a special cupboard in the kitchen.

"Thank you, Auguste."

"Have you tried our *kahawa* style coffee?"

"I first had some in Lumbashi—has quite a distinctive flavor," replied Diedrich. He was polite, although he really missed the strong black coffee of Chile and wished the doctor had offered that instead. "I think the cardamom and cinnamon give it a unique flavoring."

The two professionals exchanged ideas and discussed credentials of their respective staffs during the next hour, although each in a divergent direction. Doctor Clément continued to ask questions about the pathology work of the laboratory in Chile while Diedrich showed more interest in effects of the new virus discovered at the clinic.

"You say infected patients exhibit symptoms similar to hemorrhagic fever," Diedrich posed the pointed question to the clinic doctor and continued. "Do you think it is similar to Crimean hemorrhagic fever? As I recall, the Russians and Germans had monstrous problems with an infection caused by ticks, in their troops about 1943 or 1944. I worked at the pathology laboratory in Poznan during the war and I believe we concluded that the ticks carried *Nairovirus* in the *Bunyaviridae* family. Have you ruled out a tick-borne infection?"

"Interesting question, Doctor," the clinician answered. "We thought the symptoms were similar to those caused by the tick-borne virus that we found in 1969 here in the Congo. Those symptoms and virus structure appeared virtually identical to the Crimean virus so that now, I believe many virologists now refer to the infection as Crimean-Congo hemorrhagic fever."

The doctor is current, thought Diedrich, and asked, after a moment's pause, "Are the symptoms of the new viral infection similar, maybe the same?"

"You're right, of course, but only to an extent. Patients here in our clinic present with sudden onset of signs and symptoms, including headache, high fever, joint pain, rash, severe bleeding, and vomiting. These symptoms are similar to the Crimean tick fever but the more severely infected of our patients usually don't survive two or three days after infection. Initially, we thought the symptoms resembled malaria and treated them with quinine. We very soon found these patients were entirely different from those with a malarial infection."

"Did you say that the mortality of this infection is virtually a hundred percent?" asked Diedrich.

"Well, not quite," replied the doctor. "We're seeing an extremely aggressive progression of the viral infection in some patients with case-fatality approaching ninety percent."

"I've never heard of such morality rates with any of the viruses I know. How accurate are your records, I mean, when did you first see this virus?" Diedrich was astounded with the information and hardly believed its validity. If accurate, the virus was the most lethal virus ever described in medicine.

As they spoke, Auguste entered the room with a message for the doctor, which he whispered in his ear. Both the doctor and the young boy looked anxious. Doctor Clément then looked to Diedrich and offered an invitation. "It appears we may have another patient with the infection. Would you like to follow us as we examine her?"

"Most definitely," replied Diedrich as he followed the two from the office.

The Death Ward

The ward to which Doctor Clément led Diedrich was far more than a few steps along a narrow passage heading away from the office where they discussed the effects of the virus. The hall led to an isolated section of the clinic, near the outer wall of the west side of the building. Before entering the ward, clinic procedures required all who visited to cover their street clothing with protective robes, caps, facemasks, and gloves; in addition, the clinic required wearing covers for their shoes. Admission rules of the ward allowed no other patients than those infected with the new virus.

Diedrich's interest, piqued by the earlier discussion and by the chance to witness firsthand the effects in a patient possibly infected, now felt challenged by his lack of control in the situation. He simply observed and followed clinic procedure when told he was to put on protective gowning. Diedrich hesitated briefly when told that the clothing barrier might protect him from infection; however, the clinic personnel helping him were not certain.

"Did he wish to continue?" asked one of the nurses. The nurses spoke to him in French, explaining that the patient's fluids might be infectious and he was not to touch anything in the ward.

Diedrich listened intently as the head nurse explained details of the new patient's symptoms to Doctor Clément. Then he discovered that the patient was a worker, an aide in the clinic whose name was Angela. There appeared more than casual concern in the voices of the attending staff; they knew this patient personally and to see her in this condition concerned them. Diedrich thought he understood that the new patient just arrived, brought to the clinic from her home by her cousin, a guide who also just arrived in the village yesterday with two other visitors.

Doctor Clément turned to Diedrich and asked with a voice muffled through the surgical mask he wore, "Have you been to this woman's house since you arrived?"

"No, I stayed here at the clinic since yesterday. What's the problem?"

The clinic doctor asked one of the nurses to escort Diedrich back to his office to wait for him but before he left said, "Diedrich, I'll be a few minutes with this patient. Perhaps you would wait for me in my office or, if you prefer, on the veranda?"

Diedrich realized that the doctor wanted some time to direct the care of the patient and that he felt better to be alone with the patient-colleague who just came to the clinic. Diedrich supposed that the patient, who may have contracted the fatal infection, might be Galvan's cousin.

There were no questions from Diedrich; he followed the nurse to a scrub room, washed and cleaned appropriately, deposited the used protective clothing in a bin, and resealed it before he left the anteroom.

He decided to wait outside despite the heat of the midday. On the veranda, sitting on wicker chairs in the shade, he met Galvan and Tory. Diedrich joined the two and sat in an empty chair nearest the edge of the porch; although, he would have much preferred one of the chairs closer to the building and farther away from the sunlight.

Tory spoke first, "We just brought Angela to the clinic. Galvan fears she may have developed the fever and infection from the patients."

Diedrich now realized that the patient to whom Doctor Clément gave so much attention just a few minutes ago must be Galvan's cousin. If she contracted the virus through her work with the patients, concern for the clinic's staff would certainly escalate in intensity. It also raised new questions for Diedrich regarding transmission of the virus, could he obtain a sample of live virus, and the most difficult to answer, how might he get the sample back to Chile. He turned to Galvan and asked when his cousin began to feel ill.

"When we arrived yesterday, I went to her house but she said that she felt sick. As we had supper with the family, she complained of having fever and stomach ache. She went to lie down and the rest of us continued talking and eating. This morning, her husband came to me and asked that I go to the clinic to get help. He said he couldn't wake her and she was groaning. You saw me come in earlier and when I spoke with the head sister, she told me to bring her immediately."

"How long do you think your cousin was sick before you brought her to the clinic," asked Diedrich. In his mind, Diedrich started to add times together to see if he might figure the incubation time for Angela's illness but he did not know when she might have contacted the virus and if the contact was from a patient in the clinic.

"Maybe she felt sick for two or three days, maybe longer, before we arrived," answered Galvan.

Transmission and Incubation

The three sat in silence for a few minutes, each preoccupied with personal thoughts. Perhaps fifteen minutes passed before Doctor Clément came onto the veranda looking for Diedrich.

"There you are," the doctor smiled at Diedrich. "The patient is resting now so we can continue our talk."

Galvan rose to ask about Angela.

"The nurses are caring for her but she can't have visitors," the doctor explained to Galvan. Perhaps he could return later to check on his cousin, suggested the doctor. Then both medical professionals turned to enter the clinic and to the doctor's office.

The two Tuaregs from the Sudan, still standing where they once sat in the shade, left the small veranda, and walked, perhaps with no forethought on the part of either man as to their direction. They walked slowly side-by-side, in silence from the clinic, and wandered in a direction toward the football field, where they found a large tree to the far side of the compound, and sat on the grass in the shade. After they seemed somewhat comfortable, Tory asked Galvan what he thought caused Angela's illness, but Galvan did not respond immediately. Then, with a shrug of his shoulders, he hinted indirectly that he thought his cousin picked up a virus from the patients in the clinic or maybe she suffered a relapse of malaria.

"But," began Galvan, "you know she bled so much when she was in the Rover. That's not something that happens with malaria. You and I—both of us have had malaria and I don't remember it ever causing me to bleed. Do you?"

"It's strange—but she looked so different," Galvan completed his thought before Tory had a chance to respond.

"No," said Tory, "I've never seen bleeding with malaria—plenty of aches and pains—fever even, but no bleeding."

"Maybe while we wait," suggested Tory, "we should try to clean inside the Rover. Might take your mind off things. What do you say?"

Both men walked back across the compound/football field toward the Rover parked at the front entrance to the clinic, climbed in the car, and drove it toward the public well, which was on the north side of the school. The blood remaining on the rear seat and floor of the Rover concerned neither man who used what was available, mostly a small rag or two, to clean the soiled areas. They rinsed the rags in a pool of standing water at the well and returned several times to wipe the seat and floor of the vehicle. Their hands turned red from the blood and fluids as they worked to clean the areas. When they finally completed cleaning, both rinsed their hands in the water at the well. They parked the Rover a short distance from where it had been by the clinic, more to the sheltered side of the building, and returned to the shady spot in the compound.

* * *

Diedrich and the clinic doctor returned to the office for another cup of coffee. Doctor Clément suggested that he still had misgivings about the illness.

"I heard that a clinic in the Sudan had an outbreak last month—the symptoms were very similar to the few patients we've seen here," he explained. "The Sudanese thought the patients contracted something from bat guano because the first patients worked in a cotton processing plant where there were lots of bats using a warehouse as a dark place to sleep during the day. The medicos thought the men inhaled something from the droppings, maybe an animal virus, or something that infects *Chiroptera*. They didn't find any dead or sick bats in the warehouse but when two or three more men presented at the hospital with similar findings—but these men worked in the mines around Nzara—," the doctor paused, "therefore, the medicos thought bats were the natural reservoir for the virus or the infectious agent, whatever it is."

Diedrich thought for a few moments before he spoke. "Doctor Clément, I don't think from my experience that I could support an air-borne infectious agent; it just doesn't sound right. My colleagues in Marburg told me that the laboratory workers who contracted the virus did so through contact with the infectious agent or agents while harvesting monkey kidney cells for production of a polio vaccine. The pathologists determined that the agent was a *filovirus*."

"You may be correct; none of our patients here at the clinic report contact with bat guano. However, we have some people who include bush meats in their diets but so far, none of the patients with the illness admits to eating monkey or chimpanzee. So we might exclude that as a source of the virus," observed Doctor Clément.

"I remember that the infected patients in Marburg initially presented with high fever, vomiting, and diarrhea, which might suggest malaria. However, as the patient infections progressed, they experienced hemorrhaging from nose, gums, stomach, and bowels. I believe the hospitals reported nearly seventy-five percent fatality rate in these patients," Diedrich tried to sound as if he brought the information from the recesses of his memory. In fact, he had followed closely the reports from Germany. Through his professional contacts, he was acquainted with the reports almost as if he was present during the outbreak.

"Initially, we thought the patients, especially those with just high fever, aches, and pains were suffering a relapse of previous malarial infections. We treated them with quinine and kept them hydrated. But, when we found one or two of them began bleeding and vomiting blood, we decided malaria wasn't at work."

Diedrich asked more pointedly if the doctor excluded the effects of malaria, eating bush meats, and handling or breathing bat guano dust as avenues of infection or transmission of the virus. Doctor Clément was certain that the patients were not suffering a malarial infection but whether eating bush meats or breathing dust from dried bat guano caused the infections, the doctor was unsure. He expressed deep concern at the increasing numbers of new patient infections, more almost daily arriving at the clinic.

Diedrich's more than obvious apprehension stemmed from his trying to identify the virus, which his pathology experience told him that Doctor Clément did not know because of the manner in which he spoke of possible effects and symptoms. Diedrich was certain the medical professionals in the clinic still had not properly identified the agent with which they dealt. He knew that during the war, his experimentation would have given him the answers much sooner than these clinicians seemed to be achieving. Diedrich needed to get his hands on samples of an infected patient's blood to test in his laboratory.

"Doctor Clément," began Diedrich, "I would like to stay here a while longer to see if I might be of some help to you. May I work with your laboratory people to look at samples of patient blood?"

"Of course; you have a bed and we've plenty to eat, stay as long as you need, but remember, we start each day in the same manner, singing, and prayer. Do you think you can handle our music?"

Both men chuckled at the obvious humor to Diedrich's complaint about the early morning singing in the chapel.

"Come with me and I'll introduce you to our laboratory staff," suggested Doctor Clément. "They may not be as fluent in modern techniques as you but I think they're pretty good."

The doctor and the pathologist walked down the corridor to the laboratory. Doctor Clément described more of the operations of the clinic and it surprised Diedrich to discover that this small clinic, situated in an unquestionably very remote area of Zaire, provided basic healthcare for nearly fifty thousand people living in the surrounding area. While traveling to Yambuku, Diedrich saw no major concentration of people that would account for such large numbers coming to the clinic.

"But, Doctor Clément," asked Diedrich, "where do all those vast numbers of people live? I didn't see anything that would approach those numbers while traveling from Bumba—and—how do they get to this remote medical clinic?"

"You've so many questions; where do I begin? It is a little deceiving," replied the doctor, thinking ahead of the answers to Diedrich's questions. "I suppose it's easiest to simply tell you that there are many, many people living in extraordinary primitive settings in the surrounding jungle. We don't see most of them very often; many prefer their local witch doctors for diseases, aches, and ailments.

But our mission here is to bring better healthcare to the Zairian people—"

"Doctor Clément," a voice called out from a distance down the hall, "we need you here in the ward to look at Angela. Can you come now?"

With the call, the doctor excused himself, leaving Diedrich at the door to the pathology laboratory. As he looked inside, Diedrich found familiar instruments and one person dressed in a lab coat peering through the lens of a rather modern-looking microscope.

"Hello, may I disturb you for a moment?" Diedrich stepped into the laboratory and the technician turned to greet him. "I'm Doctor Erhard, visiting here for a few days."

"Yes," replied the technician, "I heard that you were here and that you are a respected pathologist visiting from Chile. Please come in."

"I came to see firsthand what the strange new virus is. What can you tell me?"

"I'm sure we have a virus, but I've not been able to determine the family. It does appear to be more complex than anything I've seen before," replied the technician.

Diedrich asked a few more questions and discovered that the technician was certain that infected patients seem to be infecting others, including family members, and with the illness of Angela and other nurses, maybe even medical personnel. Diedrich thought he heard concern in the voice of the technician.

"This is not the first infection in clinic personnel, is it?" asked Diedrich.

"No—there have been one or two others; I believe we've had nearly fifty infected villagers in the last several months—and I believe they all died," the technician's voice betrayed a sense of exasperation, as well as concern.

"Did you send samples to one of the major laboratories in Kinshasa?" Diedrich continued to question.

"I packaged several samples of blood from infected patients and sent them by courier to the *Laboratoires Centraux*," replied the technician. "We've not heard of any results—but I think the government is very concerned about an outbreak or epidemic of a strange illness that is so lethal."

"Did you send the blood in ice, or do you have capacity for deep freezing?" Diedrich questioned, thinking that he might find an answer to transporting samples back to Chile.

"Unfortunately, we packed the samples in an insulated carrier filled with ice from the kitchen. I don't know how well they traveled in the heat."

"Probably not well at all," commented Diedrich. "Have you experimented with spotting the blood samples on filter paper?"

The technician paused for a moment, thinking of what the visiting pathologist just asked. "No, but that might work for transporting the blood sample, even in this heat. Do you think the virus would be viable for study, if we tried that?"

"I used the filter paper approach during the war in Germany—"

The technician interrupted Diedrich briefly with a comment not discerning any German accent to his French, assuming what he detected in the pronunciation was a hint of Spanish. He seemed to ask, nonverbally, for whom he served during the war in Germany. Diedrich thanked him for his compliment regarding his ability to speak French and continued.

"Never mind about that. For now, let's take a few samples of infected patients' blood and try spotting some paper. Do you have fresh samples to use? Don't treat the samples differently when spotting the paper; let the filter paper samples air-dry. Use a laminar-flow hood as the work area. I'll stop back later to see what you have. Agreed?"

"I've plenty of time to start right now," replied the technician. "In fact, I just received samples of the blood drawn from Angela a few minutes ago. I'll use that sample to see how it works."

Diedrich excused himself and went outside on the veranda. Inside the clinic, ceiling fans kept the building temperatures moderate, but outside the heat of mid-day was noticeably warmer and uncomfortable. The technician's questions raised thoughts of Germany, memories of the war camps, and discoveries of the strange new viruses. These thoughts flooded the mind of Diedrich and occupied him while he sat in a chair on the veranda. He looked out over the village and noticed that the general activity of the people he saw earlier in the morning, now was missing. The heat and humidity tended to slow nearly everything in the village to a virtual standstill. In the distance, sitting in the shade on a grassy turf under a tree, were Tory and Galvan. Only for a moment did his thoughts wander to wonder what Galvan and Tory discussed. Then, his thoughts returned to his problem, obtaining a reproducible sample of the new virus and transporting it in a viable state to the laboratory in Santiago.

As he mused about his problem with his eyes closed, Tory and Galvan made their way across the compound to the veranda toward Diedrich and upon reaching the steps of the porch, climbed them to stand in front of him.

Tory spoke to Diedrich, asking him if he finished his work in the clinic. He explained that Galvan was quite concerned for his cousin and asked if Diedrich heard anything about her from the doctor. Diedrich knew nothing more to add about Angela's condition. As Galvan entered the clinic to find one of the sisters, seeking information about his cousin, Tory sat in a chair beside Diedrich.

"I'm concerned for Galvan," Tory announced. "Besides being worried about his cousin, he said he felt as if he had a fever."

"It's the heat and humidity of the jungle," replied Diedrich, not really giving much attention to the Tuareg, with whom, until recently, he had neither known nor developed much of a caring relationship. He looked at the man with evaluating eyes since the discussion with Hanns about using the strange man from the Sudan as a human carrier for the lethal virus back to Chile. He reviewed the possibilities and weighed the ramifications as he sat in a chair in the remotest part of the world that he had ever visited.

Galvan and Tory

Later, a little before the evening meal and after the chapel service the nuns conducted at the end of each day, Galvan returned to the clinic from his cousin's house, where he visited after discovering that Angela died of the virus during the afternoon. She was the third of the medical personnel to contract the new illness and the forty-sixth patient to die at the clinic, of the approximately fifty admitted to the clinic in the last three months. Galvan found a somber mood among the sisters in the clinic; they all loved Angela and hated to see her death. In a small show of mutual respect, they dedicated the chapel service to Angela's memory.

As he spoke about Angela with a small gathering of sisters in the chapel, he slumped forward in his chair and crumpled on the floor. The nurses quickly attended him, while feeling for a pulse, discovered the man feverish and conscious, but complaining of joint pain, generally feeling achy all over his body. They called for help to move Galvan into a ward bed where they could comfort him and check him more thoroughly. Doctor Clément arrived, checked with the sisters, spoke with Galvan while observing him carefully, and instructed that they move Galvan into the isolation ward in the west wing of the clinic. Apparently, the new virus infected another patient.

Galvan's symptoms worsened the next day; struggling painfully during the afternoon and evening, his strength was not sufficient to fight the infection of the strangely lethal virus. He died during the night, a little more than three days after he arrived in the small village of Yambuku.

As Tory and Diedrich came to the breakfast room the next morning, the head sister told them of Galvan's death during the night. She confirmed that they suspected Galvin contracted the new virus but were uncertain as to how.

"Perhaps, it was his close association with the cousin's family," the sister hypothesized.

It surprised Tory how quickly Galvin succumbed to the infection because he seemed to feel fine just a few days earlier. Diedrich, of course, observed the progression of the infection and death of the guide from a clinical viewpoint, desiring to obtain a sample of the virus to take with him to Santiago. Neither seemed concerned for their own safety, assuming the virus would have no effect on them.

Later in the day, Tory was sure that he felt his body temperature rising and that an abnormal general malaise, including joint and muscle ache, seemed to overtake him. By evening prayers, he felt so intensely ill that the sisters admitted him for observation in one of the general clinic wards.

When Diedrich heard of the illness, he asked Doctor Clément to review the case as soon as possible to determine if Tory, similarly to Galvin, in some way, contracted the new virus. The primary concern for Diedrich was to determine the method, or vector, of infection for these two Tuaregs from the Sudan. It seemed strange and a bit odd that they should contract the illness just days after arriving in the village. "The number one issue for us to determine," suggested Diedrich, "is how the virus spreads. Is it airborne, or does it require contact? Maybe, you're correct in assuming contact with an infected person disperses the virus. I've never seen anything like this for lethality and infectiousness."

The following morning, the doctor confirmed for Diedrich that the initial tests suggested Troy's infection with the virus; although, his symptoms appeared severe, Tory seemed to be staying ahead of the normal progression seen in some patients.

"Tory may be one of the few survivors of this virus," the doctor said, sounding hopeful. "We moved him into the isolation ward during the night and we'll watch his progress throughout the day."

"I think I'll stay a few more days, if you don't mind?" asked Diedrich. "I'd like to see the outcome with Tory."

"Then you're not concerned about your own safety?" asked Doctor Clément.

Diedrich showed little personal concern regarding the possibility of contracting the virus and followed up the doctor's question with simply, "No, but I would like to see if I can find a safe and effective way to transport some samples back to Chile."

"I've had a warning come from Kinshasa. They want to study the effects of the virus here in the village. I think that simply means they want to keep it here. I don't know if the authorities would allow me to export samples out of the country. I'm sure you understand, Doctor Erhard."

However, the discussion regarding the transportability and viability of any samples leaving the village continued for some time. At last, Doctor Clément became adamant about not letting samples of a live virus leave the clinic.

The doctor was unaware that Diedrich already collected several samples by spotting filter paper with patient's blood, placing them in labeled vials, and sealing the vials for discrete concealment if he needed to transport the samples without approval. Diedrich, however, wanted the doctor's approval, which he felt would permit him to carry live virus samples out of the country.

After leaving the doctor's office, Diedrich continued an internal debate with himself about the feasibility of using Tory as a human virus transporter. He walked into the mid-day heat of the village compound and toward the shaded area at the far end of the football field.

"How convenient, that he should come down with the infection," muttered Diedrich, "and at this time. But would he survive the trip to Chile?"

Convinced that moving Tory back to Chile, in his present, incapacitated condition would prove impossible, Diedrich decided to bide his time for another week to observe the prognosis of Tory's infection. He thought that if Tory died in the next day or two, Diedrich could make necessary arrangements to return without difficulty. The added time would allow him to work with the laboratory perfecting the blotting of blood samples.

"Odd," he thought, "I don't know what communications are here in the clinic; I wonder if I can get an overseas telephone call to Hanns?"

As he seemed caught up in his thoughts and discussing the options with himself, the doctor's aide crossed the compound and asked if he would join the doctor in his office. It appeared as if there was something new regarding Tory's condition.

Doctor Clément explained to Diedrich that Tory's condition remained serious but the symptoms appeared to ameliorate slightly.

The doctor wanted to know Diedrich's plans; apparently, instructions to invite Diedrich to come to Kinshasa came via telephone. It appeared that the minister of the Zairian Department of Health would like to speak with him before he left the country.

"Well, I had planned to stay a few more days," replied Diedrich. "In fact, I planned to take a boat down river to Kinshasa. However, if you'll let me use your telephone connections, I'll make a few calls to re-arrange my schedule. Is there an international operator I can reach from here?"

"Of course, I'll ask Auguste to help you place your call."

The first call was to Hanns in Mendoza. He spoke in German to prevent those who listened to his call from understanding. He explained that he needed to leave as soon as possible, and that he wanted the company plane to pick him up in Bumba. He also explained that he felt it wise to fly directly to Dakar to catch a flight to Santiago.

Hanns heard the anxiety in his friend's voice and told him to be in Bumba, perhaps within the next three days for the flight. Hanns would make all necessary arrangements and keep the plane ready for Diedrich at least until he heard that he did not need it.

Diedrich decided not make a second call to anyone in Kinshasa, but arranged with Doctor Clément for a driver to take him to Bumba so that he could travel to Kinshasa. Doctor Clément assumed Diedrich might use a commercial plane traveling to the capital; however, Diedrich did not dissuade the doctor's assumption or explain his plans to fly out of the country from Bumba via the DVS company plane. He resolved not to stop and not to meet with officials in the capitol.

CHAPTER ELEVEN
Die Herausforderungen, **(The Challenges)**

Hanns sensed from the unique nature of the telephone call that his business associate and friend faced danger in the remote jungles of Zaire. Diedrich spoke in the German dialect both understood as a language between themselves and which they infrequently used, except when they felt the need to disguise their conversation; Hanns was uncertain if the danger came from the deadly virus Diedrich sought or if the danger originated with government officials in Kinshasa. Regardless, Hanns acted quickly, arranging for his pilots to fly to Bumba in the company plane and then directly to Dakar to meet an international flight to Santiago. They were to file incomplete, or at the very least, inaccurate flight plans with the authorities in Kinshasa and if questioned later, explain the plane needed spare parts only available in Dakar. They were not to include Diedrich's passage or their stop at Bumba. Rather, if questioned they were to indicate in a routine flight, mechanical problems arose requiring a landing at Bumba and that the needed parts only were available in Senegal; thus, the subsequent flight to Dakar.

Quite by accident, perhaps fortuitously, Diedrich discovered that a clinic employee traveled for supplies and made a round-trip from Yambuku to Bumba once or twice a month in a well-worn Rover. Through Doctor Clément, Diedrich arranged to travel with the employee under a pretext of then traveling on to Kinshasa and meeting with authorities in the capitol city. The driver planned leaving in two days: Diedrich would have time to gather his belongings in Bumba, cancel the river trip, and meet the DVS pilots on the third or fourth day.

The clinic employee, who made the supply trip seemingly with considerable angst, spoke to himself and sometimes in an aside manner to Diedrich, throughout the entire trip. Cursing in French, which Diedrich understood, often stringing a long group of sounds in his native Bantu tongue, which Diedrich did not understand, he alternatively cursed the conditions of the roads, the length of time required for the trip, and nearly everything in between. The employee did not share a tourist guide's mentality and cared little for the jostling of Diedrich or his belongs, both of which seemed to rattle carelessly in the rear seat compartment of the Rover.

The driver traveled the distance to *la grande ville*, the big city of Bumba, as he muttered frequently and which words Diedrich thought he understood over noise of the Rover and chatter of the driver, in a fraction of the time Galvin spent driving Tory and Diedrich to Yambuku. It was of little consequence to the clinic employee what Diedrich did once both arrived at the hotel and Diedrich stepped out of the Rover, collected his bags from the rear seat area, and moved quickly away from the Rover allowing the driver to speed away, cursing in an ever louder voice.

Diedrich stayed that night and the next in a hotel in Bumba, the same hotel he shared with Tory a few weeks earlier. His sleep was fitful and he welcomed the early morning hours that provided some relief from the angst he felt since leaving the remote jungles of Zaire. He cancelled the river trip to Kinshasa without difficulty, a task he disliked after planning the Congo River adventure for several years. He telephoned Hanns in Mendoza to confirm the flight arrangements and learned that the pilots awaited his arrival at the airport. A short taxi ride brought him to the Bumba airport early on the morning of the third day.

The DVS pilots met Diedrich and without any fanfare or extraordinary attention given to the departing scientist, the company plane with three men and the fragile cargo carried by Diedrich, left for Dakar. Hanns reserved first-class space for Diedrich aboard the

Aerolíneas Argentina late-night flight out of Dakar. Diedrich arrived via the overnight flight to Chile in Santiago, about twenty-four hours after he left Bumba.

Hanns was explicit with his instructions to "his DVS" pilots. They were to exhibit no anxiety if asked to explain after they returned to their base in Kinshasa; they would honor their commitment to Hanns without explanations to authorities.

Diedrich's Work

Diedrich extracted all of the valued blood samples from the Yambuku clinic by carrying them in a hard-sided business briefcase to the Santiago laboratory of *DVS Laboratorios*; each sample desiccated on small semi-squared pieces of ordinary laboratory-grade sterile filter paper, retained the telltale, slightly brown-red color of dried blood. Of particular value was one sample a nurse in the clinic's isolation ward drew from Tory, as he lay semiconscious in his hospital bed in the clinic. The Sudanese Tuareg knew nothing of the blood removed and of the blotting made by Diedrich.

Additionally, Diedrich slipped vials of samples from other patients into his briefcase before leaving the clinic; he wished that he could have frozen samples of the patients' blood but felt pleased with himself that he managed to collect and dry samples from five separate, infected patients. He knew that four of the five died of the virus infection; he still did not know the status of Tory, who remained semicomatose and nonresponsive to his surroundings when Diedrich left the village.

Diedrich now wondered if he could reconstitute and harvest the live virus, capable of infecting another person from the samples. He felt certain that he could reconstitute the samples to determine standard blood work; he did that sort of laboratory work from similar samples while still in Germany. Harvesting a virus might be more difficult. Nevertheless, he immediately met with the laboratory manager, Anita Muñoz González, to discuss the work.

"Doctor Muñoz, I brought several blotted paper samples from Africa. The samples are from five patients infected with a new virus. It's a very lethal virus—almost none of the infected patients survive—I want to see if we can obtain a viable virus from the samples. You'll need to exercise the utmost caution in handling these samples."

"If the virus is so lethal," asked the laboratory manager, "why do you want it here in the laboratory?"

"I think if we're lucky, we can develop a panel to study; maybe, our work will assist others to identify the source of the virus—maybe even a cure or some preventative measure. I don't know what to expect but I think if you take the right precautions, it's safe to have in the laboratory. Consider it infectious! Take precautions to protect yourself and the equipment. Maybe, we should dedicate a space, isolated space, in the laboratory. Work under a laminar-flow hood. Do we have some space you can use?"

"Of course," replied Doctor Muñoz, slipping on a pair of sterile vinyl gloves to accept the samples from Diedrich.

Diedrich did not give Doctor Muñoz the real reason for bringing the deadly virus to Santiago: he planned to develop a weapon he could use in avenging his long-seated animosities toward those who assisted the Allies during the war. He felt, rather, that she would do as he told her and without too many questions.

Following his instructions to the laboratory manager, Diedrich went to his office and placed a telephone call to Hanns.

"I'm glad all the plane connections went without problems," commented Hanns after Diedrich explained some of the anxiety he felt in Zaire.

"Tell me," continued Hanns, "what was the emergency that caused you to cancel your long-anticipated river trip?"

"Hanns, remember how you felt just before you left Germany?"

"Unfortunately, I think about that time nearly every day—the anxiety I felt may be a little less now but it's still present. Is that similar to the feelings you had?"

"I don't want to be maudlin, but I had the same feelings when I felt things closing in on me at Posen. Perhaps, the big difference in Zaire was that nobody blamed me for the outbreak of strange infections, a fire in the laboratory, or for the fantasy of some sort of failure on my part."

It was evident to Hanns that Diedrich retained bitter memories of the harsh words and actions of his Nazi superiors, things that were now over thirty years in the past. Nevertheless, he sympathized with his friend to ease the mounting tensions. "Unfortunately, the führer tended to keep everyone responsible for the slightest deviation from his plan, didn't he?" commented Hanns.

"The infections in Yambuku—the people coming to the clinic, rather, just kept increasing and no one knew what to do about the problem," complained Diedrich. "Even my guide and Tory became infected within a day of each other! Now that I think about it, somehow, they probably were exposed at the same time and same place."

"Do you have a plan?" asked Hanns.

"I collected a few samples and discussed the clinic's results with Doctor Clément before I left. Shortly after I asked to take samples with me, the officials in Kinshasa invited me to meet them. I'm convinced he reported my interest and observations to them and they didn't want to let me out of the country with samples of a live virus."

Hanns interjected his growing frustration with the operations in Zaire, "It's hard to be—well, work without any loyal backup—someone to really depend on—in that foreign country. Do you suspect that Kinshasa wanted to prevent you from studying the virus?"

"Right," agreed Diedrich, "and I didn't want to chance losing my independence to some bureaucrat! Especially, to someone without a sense of what I'm doing. I'm convinced they wouldn't have let me out of the country with the samples."

"Tell me again, what's so unique about this virus of yours?" asked Hanns with true curiosity and showing no hint of condemnation nor demeaning his associate's work.

"This is the most deadly virus and with the quickest onset of infectious symptoms that I've ever encountered. If I can harvest and control the virus, we might very well have our weapon for revenge on the former Allies."

There was silence on the phone line for a few seconds. Hanns then asked, "It's been such a long time, Diedrich. Don't you think we've been through enough that the old issues are better forgotten?"

Diedrich's vocal chords tightened, just as they often did when he stressed through fear, anger, or frustration. He felt the sharp emotional pain some people often feel when new roadblocks spring up in the path toward a long-awaited objective, not really a pain but some churning sensation deep inside. His thoughts raced; was Hanns ready to give up on their collective goal when it seemed closer to achieving than any time since leaving Germany?

"I've kept one thought paramount since 1944, Hanns, that is extracting my revenge for the humilities heaped on me by the losses we faced as a great nation at the hands of people who were not worthy to lick my boots."

"Maybe," Hanns spoke then paused. He felt the powerful attraction of financial gain that often infects the truly successful, blinding them to all other facets of life. He did not see signs in himself, just as is common in similar men of prominent financial stature. Family, friends, and members of immediate society often recognize the symptoms of self-aggrandizing wealth accumulation before the individual sees changes in his personal behavior.

Rather than challenging Diedrich and his strong feelings, Hanns simply replied, "Diedrich, please let me know what you find out with your work on the virus. In the meantime, when are you planning a trip to Mendoza?"

"Hanns, I'm forgetting the work we're doing in the mining venture with the Africans—I apologize. Let me see what I can do here in the laboratory and I'll schedule a trip as soon as possible."

These men frequently had personal agenda, which they pursued with enthusiasm. Both respected the other man as highly skilled in those agenda yet both genuinely found personal interest within the other's plans and activities. They enjoyed an unspoken kinship developed through years of mutual respect and collaboration. Now was not the time to interrupt that camaraderie.

The challenge for Hanns, however, was to ensure that he always won. Diedrich did not share the same passion for winning all of his personal battles. Nevertheless, Diedrich possessed a consuming passion for equalizing the injustices he felt other people brought upon him; he often confided to Hanns that he felt little responsibility for his present circumstance and that he would have received numerous awards, honors, and positions if he stayed in Germany, in the Third Reich.

DVS Mining in Africa

Hanns hung up the phone and his attention immediately shifted to the communique, which arrived via the main corporate telex earlier from the headquarter offices of DVS Technologies Africa in Kinshasa.

> *Hanns*
> *We must talk—manager in Lumbashi reports major setback in operations—might be mechanical but I suspect sabotage—please phone at your earliest*
> *Ian*

Hanns lifted the paper and blankly studied the words, which he had already read so many times that he memorized them sometime earlier. "'Sabotage,' what does he mean?" thought Hanns. "How can we have sabotage in the plant, and for what purpose would someone want to sabotage one of the primary employers in the city?"

He checked the time and commented to himself, "No sense telephoning now," he realized that it was after six thirty in the evening in Mendoza and with the four-hour time difference, the Kinshasa offices closed earlier. "Too bad—I'll miss Ian this evening—I'll try early tomorrow—I wish he had a telephone at home so that I could reach him at a more convenient time for me—I must make another change in the operations."

* * *

Following instruction in his note left on her desk, the executive secretary for Hanns arranged the conference call with Ian Cherubin in Kinshasa before Hanns arrived at the office the next morning.

"Señor Cherubin is ready to speak with you when you are ready," she suggested when he arrived at his office.

"Thank you, let's connect immediately," replied Hanns, eager to resolve the issues with mining operations in Zaire and to learn what Ian's concern was. Hanns rehearsed in his mind all the possible scenarios during his semi-sleepless night caused by the message from his operations headquarters in Kinshasa.

Initially, Hanns wondered if Ian realized that there were always variations in major production at smelters similar to one in Lumbashi. That smelter was antiquated and produced variable amounts of copper and cobalt, frequently depending on personnel issues—the degree to which management got the most out of an inefficient labor force, which in the opinion of Hanns, frequently worked at such a slow pace that he referred to the workers as *faul*, or simply lazy. He knew Ian would disagree if Hanns suggested the cause of the problems rested in the management of the smelter.

Another possibility Hanns considered regarded Jorge Hhâlé, the floor manager at the smelter whom Diedrich and Hanns interviewed while in Lumbashi. Was he the source of trouble? He told the two Germans when they interviewed with him that they needed him to carry out their plans and without him, they would not succeed—a threat that Hanns now considered a possibility. What could the rejected floor manager accomplish that might be considered sabotage by officials in Kinshasa?

In addition, there was always threat from the surrounding countries pilfering or outright thievery. The threat came from government-sponsored incursions and from individuals seeking some of the wealth of the rich mining areas in the southern sections of Zaire. More than likely, a combination of the two was happening.

Hanns recognized the competitive challenge facing the smelter because it processed cobalt into broken cathodes of approximately ninety-nine-point-eight per cent purity, which was exactly the same processing output as that of the large Zambian smelter a few kilometers across the border. There was a possibility that workers in the Lumbashi smelter pilfered cases of cathodes, then smuggled them into Zambia where the Zambian smelter included the pilfered cathodes with their product to increase its output figures. The financial gains could be substantial.

Finally, Hanns considered the wretched conditions on the transportation connections from Lumbashi to the Matadi port. It was entirely possible that the Zairian government was now realizing losses occurring along the route, which he anticipated and explained when he spoke with Joseph Mbandaka.

It was with these thoughts in mind that Hanns answered the ringing telephone and the conference call with Ian in Kinshasa.

"Good morning, Hanns," the familiar voice greeted. The Oxford-trained country manager always seemed polite and pleasant.

"Ian, I received your telex last night. What seems to be the problem?" Hanns controlled an urge to criticize before he heard what appeared to be wrong with the operations.

"I mentioned in the telex that we're having some difficulties with the smelter. Let me explain what's happening, maybe you can help." Ian described the situation reported from Lumbashi and from which he accounted for noticeable missing production.

As Ian described his dilemma, it was apparent to Hanns that a normal maintenance issue could have caused an occasional cooling of the smelters, which slowed production, resulting in a drop in ore smelted. The manager of the smelter should have easily recognized the problem and made corrections. Hanns was irritated with the incompetence of Ian and his reply was curt.

"Ian, the problem is common to all smelters—in fact, I suspect the manager in Lumbashi told you as much?"

"Well, yes, but I thought there was more to the problem that you should know," countered Ian, sounding somewhat contrite.

"Yes, smelter personnel completed all necessary thermo-coupling maintenance, and in a timely fashion each time it happened, but I think the slowdown in production doesn't account for the drop in cobalt output. I think some of the workers may be pilfering during the cool-down periods; slipping about ten shipping cases of cathodes out of the country."

"Tell me, Ian, what do you mean 'each time it happens?'" questioned Hanns. "Are you seeing more than expected failure of the couplers?"

"Historical reports from the smelter show routine maintenance for coupler replacement occur once every three to four months, but we're seeing the frequency jump to more than once a month."

"I don't think that's acceptable," commented Hanns. "But why do you think the pilfering has anything to do with the maintenance issues? What are you seeing that leads you to that conclusion? We expect some pilfering, but how many of the ninety-kilo-shipping cases seem to be moving out the back door? Does the timing of the shortfall correspond with the maintenance?"

Ian explained that the investigation showed that inventory of the empty shipping cases at the smelter remained within normal limits, the count of filled cases did not vary from production records, but when personnel loaded the cases filled with cobalt cathodes in rail cars for the shipment north, clerks often found discrepancies in bill of lading amounts. No one could explain why fewer cases came to be in the railcars than left the doors of the smelter, a few meters distant; loaded cases left the smelter for a fenced holding area until sufficient copper and cobalt stored completed the capacity for a cargo train toward the Matadi port in the north. No other rail freight accompanied mineral shipments from the smelter. The volume of cobalt lost averaged less than one metric tonne per month.

Hanns asked if they discovered copper missing, in addition to cobalt. Ian reported that accounting could not justify production reports for a few ninety-five-kilo ingots missing each month. He also discovered a few ingots of processed gold missing from the shipments.

The experienced German offered three immediate suggestions to his country manager: First, investigate the personnel at the plant for connection with the Zambian government; Second, carefully examine the floor supervisors and their access to the maintenance of the couplers; and Third, increase the security at the holding areas for finished product. With each of these suggestions, Hanns told Ian what to expect and how he should handle the result.

"Then, again," Hanns continued, "we may have a supplier for the maintenance parts that's giving us faulty parts. Check them out! However, it sounds as if we might have several employees collaborating to slow production, thereby creating a holiday for most of the smelter employees. During the holiday, the collaborators bring around a lorry to the holding yard to pick up finished product. I'm sure that the lorry is small and that at least one security guard is part of the ring. They don't steal much at one time, so that there's no attention drawn to missing items waiting for shipment. From Lumbashi, the lorry makes a quick trip to Zambia for sale of our metals to corrupt outlets. In any event, you need to go to the smelter and investigate personally!"

"Hanns, I think that makes sense but there is so much crime in that area that for me to stop a gang operating in the smelter might be very difficult—and dangerous. If I try to stop it, I may wear a noose to bed one night!" Ian referred to a favored method of execution for eliminating those who interfered with the operations of a gang. He feared for his safety in that southern city of Zaire.

"Well, you have the ear of the minister—talk to him and see if he can give you protection. Certainly, the army will take orders to protect the resources and operations of the government?" Hanns continued to chide Ian for his temerity, finally telling him to call Mbandaka for protection, if he felt he needed it, but correct the underlying cause of the problems he reported, or DVS Africa would need a new country manager!

"Ian, I expect losses of this nature and volume. We're producing millions of tonnes per year and to be exercised over a few kilos lost somewhere in the system is futile. Before you bring Mbandaka or others into the problem, think about the bigger picture and work to compensate for the missing tonnage somewhere in the production schemes." Hanns bid Ian luck and hung up the telephone.

The next detail Hanns took care of personally. Despite his feigned inability to operate the telex or to place international calls, both his executive secretary and he knew of his prowess with international communication devices. He thoughtfully walked to a small closeted space, near his office, wherein was a telex machine and from which he personally sent and received messages. He sat at the keyboard, typed a few words, pushed the send button, and watched as the telex tape exited the left side of the machine's housing, feeding directly into the decoder/printer located on a separate table to the left. A single paper copy of the following message exited the printer.

Les bureaux de Hhâlé et les Associés
Troisième étage, Kin Bâtiment de Bureau
Lumbashi, Zaire Zone 9

GB
Kin la Belle likely sending army—consolidate and secure connections to Nkana—same for all material pointing to DVS—if questioned, disavow all connections with Mendoza—no further communications on this matter possible until further notice—secure your safety
HK

Hanns re-read the message. Satisfied with its content, he typed a second message; he addressed this telex to a confidential contact in Zambia.

Offices of KitweMining
Livingstone Street West
Nkana, Zambia

Mctribuy
Kinshasa may pursue Au, Co, and Cu shortage—take precautions—they may direct investigation toward Zambia
Hanns

Hanns closed the telex connections, not requesting nor expecting replies to either message. He placed the printed copies and tapes of the messages in the crosscut shredder located in the corner of his private communications center. He turned, shut off the lights, left the telex machine on silent standby, and locked the door as he departed the closeted area. Hanns seemed pleased as he thought how useful the small room had served for several years. Only his executive secretary knew of its existence, and she had no reason to betray the confidence Hanns placed in her.

"Now, let's see if my man in Lumbashi can follow orders," Hanns spoke quietly and with some hopefulness. "The operations are beginning to pay some dividends," still speaking softly to himself, "I hope he can think for himself and not let his bureaucratic bosses dictate to him."

He was sure Diedrich would be pleased that the DVS group now saw the rewards of investing in the contract with the government of Zaire; although, Hanns felt no urgency in sharing the information about the money generated by the clandestine operations in Zambia. That information could come later, when Diedrich and Hanns could speak privately. Perhaps, a leisurely dinner, at their favorite restaurant, looking out onto the foothills surrounding Mendoza, would be a good time to explain how well their private secondary market for Zairian metals progressed.

While he thought about the circumstance of setting up the connections, it surprised him how easily he established a promisingly lucrative black market trade with a Zambian "personal friend" suggested by Tory. Initially, Hanns doubted the value of the contact, because to the two German executives, Tory seemed so obnoxious and brazen. However, it appeared that Tory was correct and that retrospective accounting so far demonstrated a value readily available for Hanns and Diedrich.

Just before leaving Lumbashi, Hanns made a few telephone calls, met with Tory and his friend, a Zambian with only one name, Mctribuy. He gambled on a possibly profitable venture by setting up an unwritten, tentative, very guarded, and extremely secretive agreement with Mctribuy for diverted metals out of the Lumbashi smelter.

It surprised Hanns how willingly was George Browne to set in place the smelter slowdown actions, and the transportation to the border of several tonnes of cobalt and copper. Gold ingots were more difficult to syphon off, but the plan devised generally netted the covert operations about three to ten kilograms of the precious gold bricks every other month. George seemed impressed with the third-floor, one-room office space Hanns leased, which he equipped with a telex machine and telephone. George Browne was to use "GB" only in his communications; Hanns assumed the simple initials of "HK." Instructions to check for messages, at least once a week, seemed easy for GB to follow.

Spurious connections were never so easy to complete. In the ever-scheming mind of Hanns Krieg, losses to the mining and smelting contract with the Republic of Zaire should have been as miniscule as to be unnoticed; however, the commotion now made by Ian Cherubin confused and concerned the German-Argentine mining executive. He needed to get a simple solution to cover his actions; maybe, a little *schmiergeld* would suffice Ian, at the appropriate time.

Hanns felt secure that payments to an offshore merchant account in Belize provided distance and confidentiality for money received from his Zambian operations. He considered one or two of the banks in Berne for the transfer payments but excluded them because of the added security measures the banks required in establishing merchant accounts and the increased fees the Swiss banks charged. On the other hand, Belize banks were very relaxed and required almost no information, considerably less in fees, all of which Hanns preferred.

CHAPTER TWELVE
Reflections

The Scientist

Diedrich sat in his office at the laboratory, his desk's cluttered appearance represented current work, including a review of the latest reports from Doctor Muñoz; she continued to experience significant difficulty obtaining any virus structures from the samples Diedrich returned on blotted filter paper. She understood the care he took in collecting the blood samples but after rehydrating, the samples seemed to lose viability, at least in her work to date. Diedrich thought about the results and knew that he expressed disappointment to Doctor Muñoz; on the other hand, they failed in their collective efforts to "harvest" any virus to replicate but he took no responsibility for their failures.

He heard the customary double knock followed by the office door open. "Doctor Erhard," announced the secretary as she entered the office, "you have an international call on line three. I believe it's Doctor Clément telephoning from Zaire."

"Thank you," Diedrich replied as the secretary left the office and closed the door; such action was polite conduct in professional offices in Santiago.

The voice on the telephone line was decidedly French speaking that reflected the unique combination of tones and rhythms of French spoken in Zaire. Diedrich recognized, almost immediately, the voice of Doctor Clément from the Yambuku village. Just as quickly, his mind automatically reverted to French from his daily Spanish, as the two medical professionals continued speaking.

"Doctor Erhard," began the Zairian, "I trust you've been well?"

"Perfectly well, thank you. How are things in Yambuku?"

"No, I really need to know! How you are feeling?" Doctor Clément continued in more serious-sounding tone than before. "Have you experienced any fever, joint pains, or rashes since you left us?"

"Did you think I contracted your new virus during my visit?" Diedrich sounded a little flippant but understood the question. He really was in danger at the clinic when the new virus just began to spread. In his mind, Diedrich recalled, instantly, all the possible sources of exposure he faced, including shaking hands with Tory and Galvan, visiting the isolation ward with the nurses, even eating at the dining room with the clinic personnel. He was certain that the virus did not spread through airborne vectors, such as the Sudanese medical researchers assumed occurred among laborers in the warehouses storing sacks of cotton and with miners exposed to dust from dry bat guano.

Doctor Clément continued, "I'm glad you're fine and haven't experienced any of the symptoms of the fever. You left the country so quickly that I thought, perhaps, you might be ill. I imagined that you were to stop at the Ministry of Health in Kinshasa—but they reported not seeing you—"

Diedrich interrupted, "Just a change of plans. There were no problems."

"Good to hear you're well. Have you developed any more thoughts on the virus? We're still uncertain of how it moves through the community; although, we're certain that bodily fluids of an infected patient can infect another person."

"I've thought a lot about possible virus vectors and the natural reservoir but I've not made any conclusions," reply Diedrich.

"Our laboratory technician in Yambuku told me that you showed her how to blot samples from patient blood so that we can transfer the work to other laboratories. I assume you took some samples with you when you left Zaire?"

Diedrich doubted whether to reply. While he debated with the possible answer, Doctor Clément continued.

"In the last six or eight weeks, the Belgian sisters left the clinic. I think they all moved to other clinics in Kinshasa. Their Order in Brussels did not want to subject them to further danger by working in remote areas."

"Why were they concerned?" asked Diedrich, although he already guessed that being in close contact with infected patients presented significant potential for infection.

"You know that Angela died?"

"Yes, unfortunate," remarked Diedrich.

"She was only an aide and came in close contact with sick patients. Nevertheless, within a few weeks of her death, nine of the nurses contracted the infection and died."

"That is significant and adds further strength to our argument that contact with bodily fluids of infected patients spreads the virus!" Diedrich seemed to have no doubt on this point.

"I don't think the Order wanted to risk any more of the sisters. Diedrich, if you have any information that would help us, we would appreciate you sharing what information you have." The doctor sounded almost pleading as he reported the deaths of the nuns and the need for information.

"No, I don't have anything yet. We're working to identify the virus properties and structure but there's nothing of value. I'm afraid the information I have would be nothing more than you've developed already." Diedrich was perhaps less than truthful with his reply; Doctor Muñoz reported some minor successes in her research, but he was not ready to release premature data.

"What have you discovered in your work at the clinic, and I assume, at the central laboratories in Kinshasa?" Diedrich now sought information from the doctor in Zaire for his own research.

"Not much, I'm afraid," the doctor reiterated the lack of success they experienced in attempts to find the source of the virus.

"I spend more time at the clinic and less time in Bumba—because—well, because I believe I can make a difference with the people. Maybe you haven't heard but the death count is in excess of two hundred patients in Yambuku, with new infections arriving almost daily. We don't have enough people to help with the work in spite of the health minister sending workers—we're really overloaded—are you sure you can't help us with some information about your work with the virus?"

"Have other locations reported incidents of the infection?" asked Diedrich, remembering that the Sudanese medicos reported a few cases.

"Unfortunately, we heard of one or two cases in another remote village not far from Yambuku. We don't have anything to confirm about those case reports, however. By the way," began Doctor Clément anew, "your friend, Tory, didn't survive the infection—he suffered tremendously. I'm sorry."

The news of Tory's death confirmed that Diedrich had been right in not trying to take Tory with him when he left Yambuku and that he correctly assessed the weakened condition of those who contracted the hemorrhagic fever after infection with the virus. It also suggested to him that the virus was far more dangerous than he originally supposed and many more times as lethal as the tick-borne fever discovered among soldiers in the Crimea.

"I'm sorry to hear that he didn't survive," Diedrich's mind focused more on the anecdotal data about the lethality of the virus than on the death of Tory.

"Well, Doctor Clément," Diedrich spoke sounding rather pensive, perhaps thoughtfully, "I suspect the Centers for Disease Control in Atlanta will be most interested in reviewing your files and patient records. Have you contacted them?"

"Yes, the minister of health alerted them to our contagion and a research team arrived here in the village last week. I suspect they'll finish their work shortly."

"In my experience, they seem to work quickly but efficiently," commented Diedrich.

Doctor Clément continued, "The head of the team told us that they would try to transport blood samples to the Rockefeller Yellow

Fever Research Institute at Entebbe, to study and to analyze the virus structures in patient blood. They brought with the research team a portable carbon dioxide freezer but I don't know how successful they'll be."

"Anything might be better than packing the samples in ice from the kitchen," the half-serious, more humorously intended comment by Diedrich caused both men to remember earlier that the Yambuku laboratory sent samples to the *Laboratoires Centraux* in Kinshasa using an insulated container filled with ice.

"I guess that's why I thought your work with the blotted filter paper might be valuable, comparatively," added Doctor Clement, understanding the humor but deflecting it by renewing his request. "Are you sure there's nothing you can add to the study?"

Diedrich realized that the investigations by the CDC would highlight and bring media attention to the virus; he was certain that he did not want to entertain bureaucratic poking around in his work.

"Sorry, but there's nothing I can add at the present. Please let me know what happens."

As the two professionals concluded their telephone exchange, Diedrich realized that with the involvement of the CDC, one of the world's most thorough research laboratories, he needed to hasten his activities toward perfecting the studies begun while he was in the Yambuku village. The element of surprise for which he long wished in his virus-weapon could easily slip out of his hands if the world discovered a treatment, or preventative measure for the new virus.

The Virus

Diedrich's efforts to speed the research resulted in achieving nothing toward his "virus-weapon." His laboratory, however, achieved an important milestone in the study by successfully photographing the virus structure using some highly sophisticated equipment that he convinced Hanns he needed. These micrographs (photographs) showed the thread-like structure, with spikes extending from the surface, which convinced him that the virus was indeed of the *filovirus* family.

Doctor Muñoz worked to isolate the virus from the desiccated blood cells on the blotted samples. She realized that viruses could only replicate by entering a cell of the infected person and then use the metabolism of that person to grow and divide. Nevertheless, subsequent animal trials proved that the virus she harvested retained none of the infectious qualities of the original virus. Obviously, the air-drying of the blood on filter paper and transporting the vials in a hot, humid briefcase significantly attenuated the virus. She convinced Diedrich that heat killed any possible infectivity of the virus she had in the laboratory.

Despite the setbacks, Diedrich continued research in his laboratory. He never was able to obtain a live virus to study, because the consensus of epidemiologists and other medical professionals worldwide concluded to allow only the CDC research with live virus.

Additional outbreaks of the virus in Zaire and other African countries claimed additional lives, as the infection spread quickly, especially attacking close-knit groups. Within small villages, when the virus struck, the governments were unable to change the primitive customs and historically long-accepted practices of handling the bodies of loved ones. People continued to keep the bodies of the deceased close to their immediate families at home, frequently hugging them and kissing them as they bade them farewell. In these conditions, the virus quickly spread after once beginning, until it ran its course and the last infections in patients appeared to end, nearly as quickly as they began.

Diedrich reasoned that the natural reservoir for the virus was not in humans, and that the lethality of the infections, killing an infected person in a matter of days, prevented humans from carrying the virus naturally. Still, no one announced research where to find the virus naturally and then how to eliminate the natural reservoir. Laboratory research developed no cure, no prevention. Once the virus began in a population, isolation of the infected patients appeared to be the only prevention of added infections.

Undaunted by the failing research regarding the new virus, Diedrich continued to seek the ultimate weapon for his revenge. His laboratory business in Chile thrived, as did the mining ventures of DVS Technologies. Hanns did not interfere with Diedrich's work or question him much concerning his successes; perhaps, as Hanns thought Diedrich reached a plateau in his efforts in the laboratory.

The Mining Executive

Hanns sat in his office chair, admiring the details of the fine leather on the armrests. The luxuries of his office he afforded himself with no regrets or thoughts of the expense.

"After all," speaking to no one in particular and as if to justify the extravagance, "I built this company from scratch. It's mine to enjoy the fruits! Many thousands of employees get their living from the revenue the company generates."

He felt congratulatory of his accomplishments since leaving the small village of Plauen in the German Saxony region.

He permitted his mind to drift to earlier times when he and Diedrich frequented, in pre-war Dresden, their favorite coffee house, *die Kakao-Bohne*, or as they called it, *das Bohnechen*. Fondly, he remembered the greasy tablecloths, the straight-backed metal chairs, and the smoke-filled room jammed with students busily discussing events in the world. He wondered if the little business on the corner of a small street in the inner city, not far from the University of Technology, existed. However, he recalled that the multiple Allied carpet-bombings, using incendiary devices, destroyed the *alte Stadt* that Hanns enjoyed as a college student. Those times seemed so distant now that he viewed the current luxuries of his office in Mendoza, Argentina.

As he contemplated many things that transpired during the intervening years, his mind seemed to focus on numerous incidents affecting him, personally. Those events forced on the people of Germany, and the long-lost dreams of *lebensraum, raum, um frei zu leben,* were secondary in his mind!

He saw no contradiction in accepting Argentina's vast space where he lived as free a life as he wished, and the earlier visions of the führer's *lebensraum*. Indeed, his company provided virtually unlimited wealth to use as he enjoyed, including that spatial freedom of the foothills below the Andean Mountains.

His military role in the Third Reich gave him tremendous status with his small clutch of friends, in his immediate family, and among the general society of German military hierarchy, but he enjoyed more far-reaching influence as chief executive officer of the worldwide DVS Technologies mining operations than he ever hoped to enjoy as *gauleiter* for the führer in the *Sachsengau*.

"How," he muttered, as he thought about his earlier experiences. "How did they all lead to this?"

He knew that he could never alter the events, which propelled him from the end of the war in Germany to his present status as a multimillionaire executive whose company he personally founded and established its offices on several continents. Furthermore, he now realized that to regain the former glory of the Third Reich was nothing more than a futile dream. However, he questioned certain things so profoundly within himself that their possible answers haunted him. For example, Hanns could not answer why so great a nation as was pre-war Germany, in the end, voluntarily submitted to a cabal of nations hardly able to defend themselves.

A comment made by Diedrich entered his reflections with sudden impact. The comment Hanns dismissed when he heard it spoken. He tried to reconstruct the comment in his mind. What did Diedrich say, "I've kept one thought paramount since 1944—that is extracting my revenge for the humilities heaped on me by the losses we faced as a great nation at the hands of people who were not worthy to lick my boots."

As frequently occurs in some highly successful people, the exaggerated self-value Hanns placed in front of him, as it were, a mirror to view and to delight in the reflected image, the pseudo-image he enjoyed changed him philosophically. That he never married gave him no concern; a wife, a family, to impede his personal achievements was never his plan. Now, he thought of himself differently than during his wartime undertakings in Germany. He struggled with the feelings he knew existed earlier, including his aggressive tendencies that accompanied his desire for vengeance. Although, he now seemed to be less desirous of extracting revenge on the former Allies than was Diedrich, he wondered why the zeal for that revenge now seemed nearly absent in his makeup.

While he deliberated in this state of mind, he considered the intervening three-plus years since he and Diedrich met with the government leaders in Zaire to establish mining contracts for DVS Technologies. Significant accomplishments of that venture proved their worth many times. The company enjoyed tremendous financial gains in copper, cobalt, and some other traces of mineral by-products from their operations in southern Zaire. Even the early skirmishes with losses, or as Ian thought he discovered, sabotage, proved easily discounted.

George Browne carefully re-apportioned the smelter cooldowns, spacing them to occur less frequently, and modified inventory paperwork that effectively eliminated missing product. George appeared to know what to do to prevent further investigations. Hanns did not need the details; he required only that the strict oversight of Ian eased, moving to virtually non-existent. There were occasional "dust-ups" for the sake of appearances, but nothing rose to the level of concern first expressed by Ian during the early months of operations. Browne never mentioned money used to pay for Ian's silence, or was there any evidence that smelter operations were less than acceptable.

Although the Zairian government received all requisite, payments for ore mined and smelted, minerals shipped and sold, Hanns perceived that officials in Kinshasa never completely believed the information provided by DVS Technologies Africa. The minister of Commerce and Trade, Joseph Mbandaka, remained questioning, almost indifferent in meetings and during conversations that he conducted with the Mendoza DVS executives.

Hanns noticed that Mbandaka seemed to delight in the aggravation he caused Hanns Krieg by not acting upon Ian's committee recommendations to improve transportation infrastructure from Lumbashi to Matadi, a non-action Hanns felt reflected the minister's distrust.

The Mctribuy connections in Zambia continued without major problems; nevertheless, Hanns did not want to entangle the company in further arrangements with the Zambian government. He learned through sources outside that country that the government knew of the arrangement with the Lumbashi smelter, by way of DVS operatives, but kept a distance from actual involvement. Rather, the Zambian police, border inspectors, and customs officials approved the occasional "Browne lorry" crossings from Zaire with no interference; there were no traceable indications of money changing hands, or required for the clearance and ease given by officials in the border crossings.

Payments into the Belize account continued, Mctribuy communicated infrequently and regularly deposited the appropriate amounts in the merchant account, so that Hanns considered the connections running without significant glitches. As planned, Hanns and Diedrich discussed the merchant account in Belize, what to expect from payments by the Zambians, as well as the risks of the venture. It satisfied Diedrich that Hanns, who set up the account allowing Diedrich access to the money, conducted the management of the covert operations and that he did not involve him in the decision-making.

Hanns conducted regular trips to the office in Kinshasa, ensuring that the operations ran smoothly and that his key personnel maintained a proper sense of efficiency for the mining and exploration aspects of the contract. He found the company plane extremely useful on these trips, arriving by an intercontinental commercial flight from Buenos Aires into Dakar, arranging for the pilots to meet him, and flying from Senegal into Kinshasa. The required traveling time was substantially less than if he used all commercial flights. He arranged with an aeronautics management firm to manage use of the company plane when he was not in Africa. The management company, based in Senegal, leased the plane to a cartography company for occasional flights, mapping areas for government agencies. Hanns felt certain that the maintenance arrangement provided kept his plane up-to-date with the latest improvements and safety equipment.

Hanns reclined farther in his leather chair, placing his hands behind his neck with fingers interlaced; he reflected a picture of the well-satisfied business executive.

He knew he was overweight and that the physicians recommended more exercise for a developing atherosclerosis risk, but he felt comfortable with his station in life. At sixty-nine years old, when many men consider that they could leave the rigors of daily business to younger men, he thought little of retiring. He visualized expanding his mining business into other areas, perhaps other countries in Africa. Several Tanzanian companies offered joint ventures in exploiting the copper, gold, and cobalt reserves in that area of Africa. It seemed logical: the rich ore-bearing geological uplift running through the Katanga region of Zaire and the Zambian Nkana region extended in a northerly direction through Tanzania. He thought that taking over a small company with less than two hundred employees might be ideal for the concepts he envisioned in Tanzania. However, the company must have mineral rights secured with the government and transportation to the smelters already in place. No longer would he deal with a rail system and shipping infrastructure as inadequate as that of Zaire.

"Yes," he uttered somewhat more aloud, than he thought, "there are possibilities that need my consideration."

If his words sounded self-serving, even self-aggrandizing, Hanns gave the criticism no thought. He genuinely felt that way regarding the future and his influence. He felt neither threat to his business empire nor to himself. Such thinking was fundamental to his personal philosophy, which impelled him to look forward, into the future, rather than to the past.

In the quasi-reverie state that Hanns Krieg found himself, he practically forgot the pledge that he made with Diedrich, to seek revenge for the losses they felt resulted from the war. Contemplating his present wealth and the pledge of revenge, he tended to favor his wealth. It was ubiquitous in his daily life; he could not complain about the status that he delighted in after moving to Argentina. Overall, he enjoyed an unnatural sense of virtual immortality.

His mind drifted toward Diedrich's work with the new virus, reports of semi-success developing a weapon for settling of scores, and he found it difficult to focus on the issues that seemed so important to his friend.

The Restaurant

"You realize," began Hanns, "that a German geologist was the first European to climb our mountain?"

"Which mountain is that?" replied Diedrich as the two sat comfortably at their favorite table in *El Restaurante Alemán*. The expansive floor-to-ceiling window allowed them an unobstructed view to the west and of the Andes Mountains. In the distance was a group of peaks to which Hanns now pointed, specifically the highest. Despite the nearly one hundred and ten kilometers distance, Diedrich could just see the peaks and their jagged outline.

"The Aconcagua, of course, which is the highest peak in South America. It stands just about seven thousand meters." Hanns continued to talk about a few of the features of the mountain that he was sure Diedrich once knew but now forgot.

"He made the climb in 1883, but he had to bribe local natives to go with him to help carry the equipment." The idle conversation in progress now appeared to take on a life of its own as Hanns continued.

"Paul Güssfeldt told the natives that there was gold and treasure on the mountain so that they would make the climb. There's no record of the natives from either side of the mountain climbing it before Güssfeldt."

The two Germans and business associates came to the restaurant for their usual monthly meeting but more specifically to relax; they enjoyed the high mountain air and the vast stretches of scenery that reminded them of the Harz Mountains in Bavaria.

Hanns continued, "You know, Diedrich, it's remained the same, for years and years—people need an incentive to extend themselves. Few men will ever leave the comforts of their hearth to slay and conquer the dragons in life!"

"That sounds a bit cynical, maybe even narcissistic, doesn't it, Hanns? Do you believe that people only think of themselves and their personal comfort in life?"

"Well, consider the people in Lumbashi, Kinshasa, and Nkana. The only way we got more out of the operation in Zaire was to use a little *schmiergeld*. Now things move along without too much effort, don't you see?"

"All right, but what's your point?" Diedrich showed no criticism of his friend with this question. He knew Hanns often seemed pretentious, or at the least freely gave his opinion on many things affecting him. Therefore, he showed no anxiety when Hanns continued to expand his thought.

"You've been working for nearly four years since returning from Zaire, trying to develop a new virus and a weapon for revenge. I haven't suggested much to you about the laboratory, but I wonder if you're giving the people enough incentive. It seems as if you're still in the foothills when the peak is a long way ahead. Don't you think it's about time to change direction?"

"Hanns, we've made a significant breakthrough, but I've waited to tell you until I was somewhat certain; our efforts to capture the virus and infect animals didn't amount to much until we experimented with a small population of monkeys that we imported from Uganda. In the first results, and they're still early, it appears that we might have found where the virus thrives without killing our experimental animals. It looks as if we might have a natural reservoir for the virus."

"Diedrich, you'll have to explain to me why these results might be important. I simply don't understand these things; certainly you see that spending good money to infect monkeys with a strange virus seems to be a little wasteful!"

"If we're successful in our work, we can obtain a live Ebola virus, and the next step is to determine the best manner to get it into the population, to create a weapon using the virus. Up to this point, we couldn't obtain sufficient virus for any kind of biological warfare," explained Diedrich as simply as he could.

"You mean that you've finally obtained your virus?"

"It looks as if we did, but we need to determine if the virus has the same characteristics after infection that I saw in the Yambuku village. Do you remember me telling you that almost all patients die after becoming infected with Ebola?"

"Right, where do you think you are now?" Hanns showed a surge of enthusiasm. "Can you use the virus as a weapon?"

"We're not quite there yet—I think we have much more to do to try stabilizing the virus before I'd feel safe handling it, even if we could put into some kind of explosive device, or— Hanns, I've worked all these years assuming that at the right time, I could develop something creative and lethal but now that it might be here, I don't think I know how to create a weapon using the virus!"

"It's for certain that you can't spray it from an airplane or tank as we did in Russia—so *what* do you think we can do?" the special emphasis asking "what" seemed to catch Diedrich midstride. He realized that he could not give Hanns a reasonable approach to handling the virus as a weapon for revenge.

"I'm not even certain," began Diedrich, "that I can make a suspension or a powder using the virus—there's so much more work needed."

Hanns chuckled in a good-natured manner with his friend and both looked out the window at the mountains in the west. After a few moments of silence, Hanns spoke using a feigned professorial voice that needled Diedrich, as Hanns thought it would.

"Well, my friend, it looks to me as if you're a little higher up on the shoulder of the mountain but to reach the summit you have, still, a long way to climb!"

Despite the slightly irritating comment and the tone of voice used by Hanns, Diedrich joined with him in a good laugh, raised his half-empty *bierkrüge* in a toast, drank the last of the warm beer in the stein, and looked again at the menu for dinner. Hanns was correct, of course, there was a long way to climb before they could again approach the Allies in a form of battle.

CHAPTER THIRTEEN
Victoria Ultimo Sumptu (Victory at all Costs)

Diedrich returned to his laboratory feeling energized following the dinner meeting with Hanns. He felt Hanns supported his efforts to perfect the virus-weapon so that they might use it to wreak havoc on their former foes of the Second World War. However, against these persistent self-styled ambitions of the two former Nazis, it seemed unfortunate only to Diedrich that so many people forgot the messages of the Third Reich; even among the German population, whose country now disconnected by artificial borders, appeared to demonstrate little enthusiasm for vengeance. The ravages of two wars recently fought on their homeland sapped much of the eagerness to bring added burdens to their intentionally weakened national wealth and resources.

He thought aloud and while speaking softly to himself in disbelief, muttered, "Even Russia now dominates a collective of pre-war countries that once held socialist ideals paramount."

As he continued his deliberation, he shook his head in a form of disgust and said, "And what is this group the Russians formed: the Union of Soviet Socialist Republics? They're nothing more than communists!"

Despite a less hot-blooded comportment Diedrich demonstrated to many of his associates, his abhorrence of select groups of people changed little over the intervening years since the war; "*Nein, es war meine Krieg,*" no, it was his war, as he liked to think of it. Moreover, he was not through fighting it!

In the Laboratory

Commercial work of the DVS laboratory, such as reporting chemistry panels and other analyses back to medical facilities, continued in Santiago. While Diedrich was President, Doctor Muñoz managed the routine work of *DVS Laboratorios*. Its research laboratory and testing center were dominant among independent Chilean medical laboratories. Investments in the *análisis automatic*, or automated analysis, a highly productive system that the laboratory acquired several years earlier along with other pre-programmed technical equipment supported the work of the laboratory. Reportedly, much of the medical and scientific world in South America thought the *DVS Laboratorios* "state of the art" in its applications with advancements of automated technology.

Diedrich encouraged his technical people to publish their research findings, but instructed them to exclude his name as co-author, which was often a common practice to acknowledge the senior medical person to give greater credibility to the research. He remained active in the functioning and basic research of the laboratory; however, few entered or discussed the private section he reserved for his work. Entering the highly secretive portion of the building, required admission by an electronic combination lock, to which Diedrich frequently changed the code.

As part of the expanding functions of scientific research, Diedrich invested in a separate facility that maintained several types of test animals, including expressly bred rats and mice, both derived from rodents common to Europe and bred explicitly for research. In addition, the animal facility maintained another section, confined to specialized mammalians, primarily monkeys imported from several African countries. It was in this portion of the facilities that Diedrich carried on experiments with the Ebola virus and monkeys. However, he restricted admittance to the *affen*, as Diedrich described them, or simply *monos*, as the assistants and Doctor Muñoz called them, to Doctor Muñoz, two assistants, and of course to him.

Diedrich preferred one of the assistants, Hector, to the other and gave him substantial responsibility for the projects working with the *affen*. They often joked together about the young man's name, and Diedrich referred to him as his Trojan horse, because research with the new virus was as the ancient Greek mythological gift to the people of Troy; only a few knew of the danger the horse posed to the city. Diedrich often reminded Hector that only a few in the scientific and medical worlds knew of the potential lethality of the virus. Diedrich warned Hector to keep silent about his findings, only reporting them to Doctor Muñoz or to him.

"But, Doctor Erhard," observed Hector with a smile, "if I'm as one of Homer's Nine Worthies, you don't think I'll be killed in one of the battles and the kingdom fail, do you?"

Both scientific men, one considerably more experienced and older than the other, laughed at the humor but only Diedrich seemed to realize the significant potential for disaster should the virus escape the laboratory confines, or even the specialized procedures used to contain it while handling the virus. If Hector haphazardly or mistakenly infected himself with the virus, he would suffer a similar fate, and perish, as did the mythological Hector. Diedrich saw the effects of the virus in patients while at the jungle clinic in Zaire; he desired not to repeat the experience within his laboratory in Chile.

* * *

Diedrich left the *affen* section of the animal farm of the laboratories to return to his office in the main building of the DVS scientific campus. He looked around at the buildings, the space they occupied, and the landscaping that beautified this major scientific center in Santiago. In his mind, he could still see 1933 and a similar group of buildings, although much larger in scope, as he walked onto the campus of the University of Poznan in Poland. His memories forced him to think of many things that changed in the interim, yet he reflected that so much remained the same.

At his desk, Diedrich read the requests for simian test animals from research centers in North America. These requests surprised him; aware of his reputation in South America, he did not realize that his reputation for providing pre-screened animals reached beyond South American research facilities. However, there seemed to be a growing demand for animals that tested negative for numerous simian diseases. They were desirable for research to avoid contaminated results.

He found an animal brokerage in Recife, Brazil reliable for virtually all of his needs, and depended on the broker to provide the right kind of simian test animals from any place in the world. The broker seemed to obtain even the most unobtainable animals, for a price, and always could issue the informational and genetic forms to suit any client's need.

Perhaps he should consider North America. He thought of the ramifications: the licenses, the permits, and the things required seemed unending, but he had staff that handled the need for documentation.

"Easily done," he thought. "But for now—"he set the requests aside with a note to Doctor Muñoz to process necessary documentation to certify the *DVS Laboratorios* for the North American market; nevertheless, he remained unsure of the success of opening those new markets.

He picked up another report from Doctor Muñoz. Scanning the contents he decided that a face-to-face meeting with her might help him understand the findings more clearly.

"Anita," he spoke into the telephone, "can we schedule some time to discuss the virus work and results included in your report?"

"Certainly, I'll come right over."

His laboratory manager was extraordinarily confident in her results, thought Diedrich. When she arrived, they discussed the findings and he asked her why she felt so strongly about the results reported.

"We've seen a lot of failures with this project," she said, confident that he understood the meaning of the words without asking her to explain. "But, as I looked at this recent set of tests, it became evident that we've isolated the virus and stabilized it in a commercial preparation of human normal serum albumin. I'm confident that the virus is viable in this state and remains stable in the solution, but I haven't tested it in our new *monos*. That's next—I've already scheduled Hector to begin work on the simian model."

Diedrich studied the paper in front of him as he spoke, "Do you suppose, once you inject the *affen*, that you'll be able to re-harvest the virus, demonstrate that it's viable outside the host, and then re-stabilize it for the future?"

"I'm convinced that the study will succeed."

"I guess the next step is to begin with the *affen*," suggested Diedrich. "Which group of animals do you think will be best for this study?"

"We just received a shipment from Recife, of a Philippine species of *crab-eating macaques*, or the *Macaca fascicularis*. I thought we would use them for the trials—we've not had any experience with this particular animal, so I think it will be useful to explore their resistance to the virus and our work. I've asked Hector to begin injecting the virus solution in the new batch of test animals. We'll observe them for effects of the virus. You remember, we used a similar virus solution in several of the other animals but they didn't survive the subsequent infections."

"That's a good approach," offered Diedrich. "While you're here," he continued, "what do you think of entering the North American market for test animals?"

"There are certainly many suppliers, already. Why do you think we have a good chance of succeeding?"

"I've several requests for pre-tested simian research animals. I guess our reputation for these types of animals here in South America expanded to the north!"

Both laughed a little at the moderate compliment they felt that came from the success they had with specialty research animals.

"Well, give it some thought," suggested Diedrich. "If we go into that market, there will be a lot more work for the animal farm, the brokerage here in Santiago, and the importer in Recife. I can see some success, if we play the market correctly."

On to Tanzania

In a routine management telephone conference between Mendoza and Santiago, Hanns asked Diedrich for some time to discuss an idea, privately. After the other managers signed off the line, Hanns asked Diedrich if he would like to return to Africa.

"Diedrich," began Hanns, "I've an idea about expansion into Tanzania, but I don't want our DVS senior group to know about it before I'm completely certain. The group doesn't know much of what we do but it's always good to let them know when we make major changes in the operations." Diedrich realized that Hanns referred to the small group of German expatriates, former members of the Nazi party that maintained an advisory role to Hanns in Argentina, rather than to those of the management group who were recently in the telephone conference. Although Hanns mentioned the "silent board of directors" infrequently, Diedrich knew most of the men and their support of the company.

"I would like to fly to Dar es Salam, meet with a few people in that city, and then look at some of the mining areas. I'd like you to go with me," continued Hanns. "I think we'll include some of the sights of that area of Africa, perhaps a flight around Mount Kilimanjaro, we might include a flyover of Victoria Falls in Zambia."

An excited Diedrich replied, "When did you want to leave?"

They jointly decided to leave the following month and include on the trip, a scheduled stop at their Kinshasa headquarters, meetings with the staff, and possibly a meeting with the minister of Commerce and Trade.

Diedrich had not returned to Zaire since his experiences in the Yambuku area and reminded Hanns of the missed meetings with the Zairian Health Department.

"I don't suppose they'll even remember that you didn't consult with them when you were there," assured Hanns. "So much has transpired in the last four years that the same people may not be at the department. Let's not worry about that before we go. It will be a good trip."

* * *

The commercial flight to Dakar taken by Hanns and Diedrich was uneventful; their company plane awaited them for the trip to Kinshasa. Hanns organized the plans for the entire trip, most of which would be in their company plane. The pilots pre-filed all flight plans and confirmed them with Hanns during the flight to the Kinshasa airport.

Ian was at the airport, waiting for the pair as the plane touched down. He reserved rooms at the usual hotel Hanns preferred in Kinshasa. While en route to the hotel, Ian leaned over the back of the front seat to hand a leather folder containing the agenda for meetings with the staff at the headquarters, a few business papers that required a signature, an outline of topics to discuss during meetings with Joseph Mbandaka, and some suggestions for touring while in Zaire.

"Thank you, Ian," commented Hanns. "As usual, you're very efficient. I'll review these items tonight. What time do we meet in the morning?" Hanns preferred a specific nuance in his schedule when in Kinshasa. He preferred being alone the evening he arrived, a private and quiet meal, and as much sleep as he could get to alleviate "jet lag" that might prevent him from fully functioning during his business meetings.

"I'll pick you up at nine in the morning. Do you want me to join you for breakfast? We have Mbandaka scheduled at three in the afternoon. Does that sound about right with your plans?"

Hanns seldom ate breakfast so Ian felt comfortable that he would skip it that morning, but Ian always acted politely.

"I'll see you at nine—no breakfast," replied Hanns as he already began to read the papers in the folder. "Doctor Erhard will join us for all the meetings tomorrow."

Meetings at the headquarters were perfunctory and concluded with no major business decisions needed. The operations appeared to be functioning as expected. In a private session between Hanns and Ian, there was no discussion of the "extraneous" activities at the smelter. They never discussed these items, even away from the formal settings in the office, and both men knew of the consequences of failure in the smelter. They wisely kept the discussions of possible theft at the smelter to a minimum, and privately involved as few people as was possible, in whatever activity they maintained, which they might consider questionable.

It was not the anniversary of the mining contract with the government so there were no negotiations of volumes, pricing, and other commercial points included in the contract.

"Well, *Mister Krieg*," the manner in which Mbandaka said his name still bothered Hanns. "Your mining and smelting operations are very profitable, right?"

"I think both the government and the DVS group are happy with the continuing successes. Thank you!"

Hanns remained dissatisfied, however, with the response of the government to his requests for improved transportation from the smelter to the port of Matadi. Much remained to complete of the promises for an improved transportation infrastructure.

The minister of Commerce and Trade was amiable with the DVS executives in his office, although he did excuse the transportation issues when Hanns brought them up for discussion. The curt dismissal infuriated Hanns, who felt he deserved better, especially when Mbandaka questioned Diedrich about his research involving the new virus.

"I believe we controlled the contagion," the minister suggested.

Diedrich thought about his reply, and that he knew of a second outbreak of the Ebola virus in Zaire, which killed several hundred people in a small village some distance from Yambuku.

"Let's hope that the virus is contained and that we don't have any additional outbreaks. It's a very bad agent," Diedrich decided to comment.

After returning to the DVS offices, Hanns and Ian spent a few hours to review issues of increased volumes from the mines, and to discuss competition from several other mining firms. At the conclusion, Hanns thanked Ian for his efforts and work. He encouraged him to obtain commitments from the government for financial assistance because of the poor transportation. Hanns agreed to stop in Kinshasa for additional meetings on the return leg of his "business trip" to the eastern part of Africa.

* * *

The next morning, Hanns and Diedrich arrived at the airport, both dressed in casual travel wear and anxiously prepared for their flight to Tanzania. The pilot described the flight plan over Zaire and into Tanzania. He included descriptions of the sights they might see during the flight, spending more time than normally might be sufficient with the rivers that cut through the jungle below; although, the clouds somewhat obscured their vision.

"Hanns," said Diedrich about two or three hours into the flight, "I think we're just about where the Yambuku village is but it's so small that I doubt that we can see it from this altitude." Hanns and Diedrich both scanned the green floor below for signs of the village.

"It's hard to tell," replied Hanns. "Are you glad you visited that remote area when you were here last?"

"I think the experience was very challenging and I'm not sure that I want to repeat it," concluded Diedrich. "I can't describe the oppressive heat and humidity and unless you've experienced it, you can't imagine the pressure on your skin. It's as if you're wearing a weighted suit. There seems to be no relief, night or day."

"What about the virus you found?"

"I've never seen anything like it, ever! People get a whiff of the virus and cough up their insides, bleeding from every opening. It's an awful thing to contemplate."

"And now you think you've captured it in your laboratory? It sounds, to me, as if it would be something that I would not want handle casually!"

"We're close, Hanns, so close to seeing our dreams become reality. Before I left, we received a new group of test animals from the Philippines that look as if they can handle the virus injections we give them—first ones to do that." Diedrich spoke with a conviction that seemed lost in the past, as his experiments failed.

"How do you plan to get the virus—make a weapon to use—and who do you plan to infect?" Hanns asked, perhaps with a little in disbelief.

"Well, you know our laboratory is performing very well—we branched out into supplying test animals to research centers in South America. We test the animals for a number of agents that might interfere with results; it's straightforward, really. There aren't too many things that we screen the animals for and only ship the ones that pass the tests."

"But," thought Hanns as he heard the description of screening and supplying research animals, "how does this work bring you closer to creating the weapon?"

"We spoke about the difficulties getting the virus into a place such as the United States; I just don't see us flying a plane overhead spraying the inhabitants, or even releasing something into the water supply. However, if we can infect the research animals that nearly every medical school and some research hospitals use, we might be able to import the virus in the animals. So far, the only success we've had is with the *affen*, and only a few of them seem to survive the infection."

"So far, I follow your thinking," commented Hanns. "But, explain how you plan to get into the research animal market of North America with infected *affen*!"

"That's a problem our reputation solved for us. Before I left Santiago, I reviewed several requests for animals from reputable research centers in the United States. We'll build up the market for the "clean animals," and then begin shipping infected ones. Before they discover the source, I expect the infection to spread from the research centers and the hospitals to people associated with them."

"Therefore, you expect to infect the Allies through infected *affen*," Hanns began to snicker at the simplicity of the plan; Diedrich joined him in the humor and both men laughed aloud. "The plan might work."

Nevertheless, even if it failed, nothing they tried over these many years worked. This plan seemed to be as simple and devious as all those they contemplated.

The plane landed at Dar es Salam where Hanns conducted meetings with several joint venture companies, which sought the support of the DVS Technologies group of companies and offered in return mining rights to copper and cobalt deposits. Unfortunately, none of the groups provided access to smelting operations in the country. Nor could they assure Hanns that they had or could obtain the necessary licenses from the government.

* * *

After three days of meetings in the city, Hanns concluded that the work in the country needed much more research and information. He and Diedrich decided to begin their small sightseeing trip of eastern Africa before returning to Kinshasa. Their pilot suggested a flight to see the Kilimanjaro Mountain Preserve from the air. He felt that they needed most of a day for the trip and that they could circle over Victoria Falls on the return leg to Kinshasa after first returning to Dar es Salam for refueling. They hired an added cabin assistant for the day's flight so that they would have someone to handle their needs. Indeed, it was to be an exciting adventure.

The plane taxied along the runway in Tanzania, lifting off without the least degree of effort; it was a beautiful morning for flying. The pilot headed northeasterly from the airport and caught sight of the mountain in about an hour. Its snow-capped peak showed clearly in the distance and as the pilot explained some of its features, Hanns thought of the Brocken in the Harz Mountains of Bavaria. He loved seeing the mountains and he asked to change places with the copilot so that he had a better view of the distant mountain.

When the plane reached the southern tip of the mountain, the pilot banked easily to the east and north. He eased the nose of the plane slightly downward and leveled out along the shoulder of the mountain so that they might get a closer view of Mount Kilimanjaro's magnitude. The plane followed a long climbing and prominent canyon after turning east to the north side; the canyon looked deep and filled with dense forested growth.

Hanns noticed an unusual tenseness in the pilot, as he appeared to struggle, tightening his grip on the flight controls. Hanns thought he saw the tenseness move up the pilot's arms and that his muscles moved rather stiffly. Gone was the earlier smooth fluidity that Hanns appreciated in the pilot's actions.

"Problems?" asked Hanns.

"We're into some very difficult updrafts along this escarpment and the plane feels sluggish. Maybe you should change places—the cabin—ask—the copilot to come up here. Everybody should tighten their seat belts."

Hanns could see that there was an ensuing fight between the machine and the man; it looked as if the machine, presently, had an upper hand.

Back in the cabin, Hanns and Diedrich felt the stuttering movements of the plane as it fought to regain control of the air.

"What's the problem?" asked Diedrich.

Before Hanns could finish an answer, the starboard wing of the plane clipped the side of the canyon wall. The pilot struggled vainly, fought for more altitude, and sought to escape out of the heavy suction of the canyon's air currents. The plane cartwheeled two or three times before sliding to a stop near a slight rise in the canyon, just about three-quarters from the summit on the northeast side of the mountain.

After the deafening noise of the crash, an unnatural quiet rested on the plane and in the cabin. Hanns first stirred by slightly lifting his head to survey the damage. What he saw stunned him.

Diedrich appeared dead, as did the three crewmembers.

Hanns felt wetness on his left side: a deep gash ran lengthwise down his side, caused by a cabin brace, which sliced easily through the seats and snagged him as he tumbled in the crash. He felt blood emptying from the wound and filling the space around him. His eyes searched the immediate area for something to staunch the flow; a cabin blanket lay just beyond his outstretched arm. Painfully, he reached for it, pulled it to his side, and used it to apply pressure to the wound.

Diedrich moved slightly. He was alive and as Hanns noticed the movement, he called out. Diedrich was too dazed to respond. Hanns could see the cuts on Diedrich's face; they appeared deep and menacing. A noise drew his attention to a deep chest wound coming from Diedrich's right side chest. He was losing air from his lungs. Earlier military training returned instinctively to Hanns as he scratched around for a piece of plastic or another blanket. Finding both, he tied them as well as he could over the open wound to stop the rush of air and blood coming from Diedrich.

The helplessness of the situation caught up with Hanns as he realized that the plane's exterior skin, much of the supporting structure, and the interior façades now lay together without semblance of their original shapes. He tried to move farther to find the cockpit radio; it was missing. Likely lost as the plane's nosecone crushed during the cartwheeling of the crash, he assumed. He wondered if the homing beacon signal automatically started, which the aeronautics management company insisted on installing. He had no idea where it was in the plane.

He tried to move more, even to stand, but discovered that the thighbones of both his legs broke during the crash.

The intense pain of his injuries affected his thinking and he shook his head trying to maintain clarity. Finally, his injuries and pain took control of his mind and body, shut them down to save energy, and allow him freedom from the penetrating pain. He closed his eyes and faded into unconsciousness.

* * *

The rescuers from the Tanzanian Emergency Rescue Team reached the crash site about forty-eight hours later. They discovered two passengers living and three passengers dead. The team extracted the living men and sent them directly to the trauma center in Dar es Salam.

At the hospital, emergency teams worked to restore the vital fluids of the two men, to stabilize them, while they tried to treat their injuries. Both men were grave, with life-threatening injuries. Cases such as these were not common at the trauma center but they managed the patients with skill, efficiency, and compassion.

Information retrieved at the crash site identified the victims of the crash. Neither Hanns nor Diedrich carried more than DVS identification papers and their passports. The plane's registration was in Zaire, owned by DVS Technologies. It appeared the pilots and other crewmember worked for DVS but operated through a management company headquartered in Dakar, Senegal. The hospital notified DVS headquarters in Kinshasa that the wreckage found on the mountain was that of the company's plane and that the two men found alive in the plane were in the trauma center. Hospital personnel believed that the men were the missing executives from their company.

Because of the infrequent event of a plane crashing on Mount Kilimanjaro and in the area of a national forest preserve, the Tanzanian press requested information and details from the spokesperson for the Tanzanian Emergency Rescue Team. Once the press learned that two patients remaining alive from the crash were Hanns Krieg and Diedrich Erhard of the mining giant in South America, their published reports became important for the international media.

Death Reported

Four days after the accident, Ian received a telephone call from the administrator of the trauma center and hospital in Dar es Salam informing him that both Hanns Krieg and Diedrich Erhard died from the injuries they sustained in the plane crash on Kilimanjaro Mountain. The administrator explained that the trauma center tried, in vain, to resuscitate the two executives. He explained that the two men "fought valiantly" to overcome their injuries but the crushing wounds they sustained and the subsequent massive blood loss simply overwhelmed them.

"Yes, they were given blood replacement transfusions," answered the administrator to a question asked by Ian.

"Yes, the blood was supplied from the local Red Crescent blood bank," replied the administrator to another question about where the blood originated and if the blood bank completed all the proper screening.

"But, did you also screen for that new virus," Ian asked further. He was not certain that the administrator knew what he meant by asking about a new virus. Ian was anxious about the possible transmission of the Ebola virus to the men, although he was uncertain that the virus spread through blood transfusions. His knowledge of the virus came from discussions with national health department officials in Kinshasa. Following the earlier visit by Diedrich Erhard to the Yambuku village, the contagion he discovered while there was still a topic of conversation in some circles in the Zairian capitol. Ian knew that the new virus struck several times in Zaire, each time with catastrophic results, but he was unaware of any screening test for the presence of the virus.

"I'm certain the blood bank used all the procedures available to them to ensure the safety of the blood they provided," replied the administrator. He thought Ian was easily mollified with his answer.

Not anxious to pursue a more extended discussion about the testing of blood supplies, Ian concluded the telephone call by asking the hospital to care for the bodies until he could send a plane to return them to Kinshasa.

"Yes, the hospital will certainly care for the bodies, properly, until your plane arrives," assured the administrator.

As reports of the death of Hanns Krieg began filtering throughout the DVS Technologies headquarters in Kinshasa, Ian dismissed the office employees for the day and telephoned Joseph Mbandaka. The minister's secretary answered the phone and then announced Ian Cherubin waiting on the telephone line.

"Hello, Ian," said Joseph Mbandaka. "I read about the DVS plane crash in Tanzania. What have you heard about Krieg and Erhard?"

"I just finished speaking with the trauma center administrator in Dar es Salam. They both expired. I told the office employees a short while ago and let them take the remainder of the day off."

Ian continued, "I plan to take a flight to Tanzania and return the bodies back to Kinshasa. We need to make the arrangements to ship them back to Mendoza."

"I think my office can help with the arrangements," offered Mbandaka. "Tell me, what is the mood of the employees at the office?"

"Hard to say—the news comes as a shock to most of the office staff. I'm not sure what the Lumbashi employees know or what influence the death of Hanns makes to them."

"It's not likely to create much of a disruption in the operations— Do you think we'll need to find another company to manage the contract?"

In his mind, Ian contemplated the substantial money that he acquired since the Argentines assumed the contract for copper and cobalt mining. In addition, he relied on the extra *pots-de-vin* that he collected for his silence. He received money paid for his assistance at the smelter, for looking the other way as George Browne shaved reports about the number of smelted mineral ingots, and for the quiet cooperation with the Zambians. If he suggested changes to the minister, would all the money disappear that he enjoyed so much? As he considered his potential losses, the voice on the telephone brought him back to the present.

"You best schedule a trip to the smelter—make arrangements to change the management, if necessary," suggested Mbandaka.

"I agree, but do you think we need to make changes to the DVS contract?"

"For now," answered Mbandaka, "let's leave the agreement with the Argentines, but I think we should ask our government auditors to conduct a thorough review. Let's ask them to review everything for the last five years, complete top-to-the-bottom audit. I'm sure you'll want that being the country manager for DVS—let's not make a change if we don't need to but—" He never finished his sentence.

Ian now wondered if he fell under suspicion. The uncertainty bothered him and in spite of his distrust of the DVS executives, he was part of the greater conspiracy to divert wealth from the mines in Zaire, from the government, and into his private accounts. He thought of how he could continue to facilitate the "backdoor operations" at the smelter. He needed more time to think. He decided to leave a parting thought with the minister.

"If you agree, perhaps we can consider the management of the mining, smelting, and selling the minerals as a Zairian company. I'm sure we can manage it."

"You might be on to something," thought the minister aloud. "Let's give the idea to a committee for study; that's something you can do easily, and without involving the DVS executives."

At the other end of the telephone, as he hung up the receiver, Joseph Mbandaka thought he recognized the signs of greed and corruption in Ian Cherubin. He recognized the signs because he was not free of them. He was not quite certain how much Ian altered the records that he produced. He liked Ian but he had fallen into the trap laid by the Argentines, and reports of Ian's sizable Swiss bank account concerned him. With all that money set aside, he might not be able to control Ian in the future.

"Perhaps it is in our best interest," he thought, "that Hanns Krieg and his chief scientist met an appropriate end and are no longer with us! We'll do better without them. Yes, maybe Cherubin is correct, Zaire can manage their mineral reserves without help from foreigners."

Mountain Burial

Approximately ten days after the death of the two DVS executives in Tanzania, their bodies arrived in Mendoza, Argentina, the coffins containing the men flown there via special airfreight arrangements with an Argentine commercial carrier and accompanied by Ian Cherubin from Kinshasa.

Within the grounds surrounding the executive headquarters of DVS Technologies, Hanns had reserved a special place for his burial and that of his friend, Diedrich. Hanns made the directive several years prior to his death, leaving explicit instructions as to the manner of his burial and the perpetual care he wished for the location. He established a fund for the continuation of his wishes.

Ian attended the internment services and was surprised to see a small group of older men, one, or two in a car, arrive in chauffeur-driven black Mercedes executive sedans. As each car reached the site and unloaded its passengers, he noticed that nearly all the men wore similar styled loden-green alpine hats, with adornments that suggested their Bavarian origin. He thought that these men all must be former friends and business associates of the two executives; no one explained to him that they were the secretive and silent board of directors. These men helped financially and in other ways to ensure the successes of the company. Hanns preferred to call them, *die Verschwörer*.

Each man paused as he passed by the coffins set over the graves. Speaking to no one, each seemed caught in his own thoughts. As they stood individually beside the coffins, each momentarily raised his right arm nearly shoulder height, slightly bent at the elbow, extended his hand fully with the palm facing the ground. After the brief salute, each man lowered his arm, returned to his car, and left the mountainside.

An Order and the Victory

Doctor Muñoz read again the telex she received from the officials in Tanzania, informing her of the death of Diedrich Erhard, President of *DVS Laboratorios*. It was hard for her to comprehend that he died so tragically in a plane accident on a mountain in Tanzania. She thought of the telephone call from the DVS headquarters in Mendoza explaining the timing and place of the burial services. She wished that she could attend but that was not possible.

Turning her attention to the business at the laboratory, she thought of the next steps she needed to do, now that Diedrich's death placed her temporarily in control of the operations. Her mind worked scientifically: first, she identified the essential actions: then, her mind worked to prioritize them; and finally, she identified the personnel required for each action. As she thought of the course necessary for the laboratory organization, Hector, one of the two trusted technicians whom Diedrich allowed access to the *affen*, entered her small office.

"We've some bad news, Hector," began Doctor Muñoz. "I received word that Doctor Erhard died in a hospital in Dar es Salam."

Both were silent as they contemplated the gravity of the situation. Finally Hector replied, "We'll miss him, but I believe he'd want us to continue the work."

"Yes, many people depend on the functions of the laboratory," offered Doctor Muñoz. She continued, "What's pending from the work Doctor Erhard left?"

"Well, I've that order for the specialized *monos*, the ones we brought in from the animal broker in Recife. They met all the needed parameters for the order in the north. I confirmed that after he received the *monos* from the Philippines, that the broker quarantined the animals, as required, and then sent them on to us."

Doctor Muñoz thought before replying, "Were these the last of the test animals that Doctor Erhard wanted for testing his virus preparation?"

"That's right. We received them several months ago, completed much of the virus testing before he went to Africa with Señor Krieg. The subjects appear healthy after the tests, and after the injections with the virus solution. You remember we discussed the results with Doctor Erhard before he left?"

"The animals show no effects of a virus infection, after the injection?"

"None so far that we've seen, and it's been more than a month since we gave them the solution," replied Hector.

"You say we have an order for the specialty *macaques* that we have? The research center requested the *macaques*, and not another type?"

"That's right. It's from a testing laboratory in the United States, somewhere in Virginia, I believe. Doctor Erhard worked with an animal broker to obtain the highly desirable order in this prestigious laboratory near the capitol of the United States. I know he wanted it to be successful—should we ship the animals?"

Doctor Muñoz looked at the telex telling her of the death of Diedrich and Hanns, as if to obtain permission from the deceased. After a moment's silence, she decided, and announced her decision.

"Hector, let's honor his name, and fill the order to place these animals in the laboratory in the United States. It's one of the last things we can do to fulfill his desire for this, his final accomplishment."

EPILOGUE

Although this story is completely imaginative, should any devious person succeed at developing a "blood coagulation interrupter" weapon as devised by the fictional character, Diedrich Erhard, the consequences could prove considerable and disastrous for society. Fortunately, no one has developed anything as sinister, or as lethal.

However, infection with the Ebola virus remains without a cure. For the hemorrhagic fever resulting from exposure, prevention requires interruption of the vector or pathway of infection—precluding initial exposure. When the virus infects the human cell, it is capable of mutating into alternative identities and causing cells to produce massive amounts of cytokines. Too much cytokine, an important protein needed for cells to communicate with one another, creates an overload interrupting normal immune functions of the body. The infected patient may survive only a few days but with an immune system so compromised as to ensure successive failure of the organs and death.

Since early outbreaks of the viral infections described in this story, hemorrhagic fever caused by the Ebola virus continues without a cure or prevention; there have been at least six reported outbreaks of the virus, the two most recent in June and July 2012 in remote Uganda.

During 2010, officials of the Centers for Disease Control opened a new research institute at the Uganda Virus Research Institute, or the URVI, (formerly, the Rockefeller Yellow Fever Research Institute) to study Ebola, Marburg, and other viruses causing hemorrhagic fevers. Researchers in a highly secure section at the facilities now attempt to discover a cure and prevention for these highly lethal viruses. Currently, science identified five species that characterize the genus of *Ebolavirus*: *Zaire ebolavirus* (initially described 1976), *Sudan ebolavirus* (also initially described 1976), *Reston ebolavirus* (described 1989), *Côte d' Ivoire ebolavirus* (described 1994), and *Bundibugyo ebolavirus* (described 2007). Each species differs slightly from the next, and all have significantly different mortality rates in the infected patient. The *Zaire ebolavirus* remains the most lethal, killing nine out of ten infected patients.

One method, which proves reasonably successful for studying the possible virus vectors, includes collecting live bats from potential hot zones for the virus, euthanizing them, harvesting their organs, and desiccating the samples for study at UVRI. The rehydrated samples contain sufficient live virus for research. This is somewhat similar to the methodology employed by the fictionalized Diedrich Erhard to smuggle samples of patient blood and virus out of Zaire.

Medical mistakes at jungle clinics still include misdiagnosis of infected patients as having malaria, and symptomatically treating patients for a malarial infection. These diagnostic errors provide infectious patients increased opportunity to spread the virus to family members and clinic personnel, similarly as described happening in the story with Angela, Galvin, and others.

With the discovery that infectious bodily fluids infect others who contact these fluids, officials attempt to alter cultural practice relating to handling the dead when an outbreak occurs, but more education is essential to alter long-standing traditions. Despite this knowledge, cultural behaviors regarding the handling of the bodies of loved ones (i.e., kissing, hugging, and other forms of "saying good-bye") remain acceptable in some rural African societies.

Not until 2002 did science settle on a unified taxonomy for the *Ebola virus* and the *Marburg virus*, including both as *filoviridae* (rather than *filovirus*), with two separate and specific genera: *Ebolavirus* and *Marburgvirus*.

Given all that medical researchers discover about the various strains of the virus family called *filoviridae*, including use of the most recent technology and computer-generated tools, research continues with, at best, limited funding. Few government agencies and yet fewer commercial companies express willingness to invest in significant research to discover a cure and prevention of a lethal virus, generally isolated to remote areas of the earth, from which less than eleven hundred people have died from since its first description approximately thirty or forty years ago. Until research describes adequately the virus reservoir, how the virus moves from that reservoir to humans, preventing the virus movement to humans, and developing a cure, the potential for work by unscrupulous people similar to the characters in this story remains.

Made in the USA
San Bernardino, CA
07 June 2013